gift

gift

andrea j. buchanan

OPEN ROAD

INTEGRATED MEDIA

NEW YORK

Gift

www.facebook.com/OpenYourGift

Copyright © 2012 by Andrea J. Buchanan, www.andibuchanan.com

Illustrations copyright © 2012 by Alexis Seabrook, www.alexisseabrook.com

Musical interludes by Fredrik Larsson, www.freddegredde.com

"Is It All Right?" copyright © Andrea J. Buchanan
Music and lyrics by Andrea J. Buchanan
Arranged and performed by Fredrik Larsson

"Don't Look Back" copyright © Fredrik Larsson
Music written and performed by Fredrik Larsson
Lyrics by Andrea J. Buchanan

Cover design by Andrea C. Uva

ISBN: 978-1-4532-2023-8

Published in 2012 by Open Road Integrated Media
180 Varick Street
New York, NY 10014
www.openroadmedia.com

gift

part one

one

I found her in the bathroom of the 300 building. Slumped in the corner, pressed up against her own reflection in the mirrored wall, she could have been crying, or sleeping, or ignoring me. But I knew as soon as I saw her that something was seriously wrong.

"Vivi?" I knelt down next to her. I wanted to be reassuring or helpful but, truth be told, I didn't know her all that well. I didn't know why Mr. Terry had asked me to go find her. We didn't even sit next to each other in class, let alone hang out together. I could tell he'd been able to read the confusion on my face when he asked me to check up on her and find out what was taking so long. He'd handed me the long wooden block, smoothed and shaped and branded with the words HALL PASS by some other student years ago, back when the school still had a shop and woodworking course, and said, "Just go check it out. You're the only one I trust to actually come back to class." With a smile, as though we had some sort of understanding.

I understood nothing about Vivi, only that she sat in English class furiously drawing in a notebook and occasionally talking to herself. But she's the kind of girl that nobody notices unless they actually look at her closely, so her strangeness was unremarkable. She was simply lost among all the personalities in the room. Cheerleaders, student government leaders, goths, mathletes. And the other people, like me, who didn't seem to fit into any category. I suppose in this sense Mr. Terry was right; Vivi and I were of a sort, and maybe we *should* be friends. But she was intense. From the first day of my first year at Castle Creek High this past fall, I had been a little wary of her.

I'd checked the bathroom nearest English, but it was empty. In the 200 block, it was the smoky den of black-eyelinered, green-haired ditchers, seniors who laughed at my prissy sophomore cough upon entering, and at my hasty retreat.

I was going to go all the way up to the main buildings, where the faculty bathrooms are, but I decided to check into 300 before I went that far.

And there she was, on the floor. As oblivious to me as she was to everyone in class, where she would sit, head down, pen moving, until the bell rang.

"Vivi? Are you all right? Mr. Terry sent me to get you."

She raised her head and it lolled back as though she were drunk, or a baby. Her eyes, when she opened them, were frighteningly blank-looking and filled with tears.

"He's not here," she whispered.

"No—Mr. Terry isn't—"

"He's gone," she said, and broke into a sob. Her right hand unclenched and a bottle of Advil PM rolled onto the floor. It sounded empty.

"Vivi, oh my God—" I grabbed her shoulders, shaking her a little as her eyes closed and her head rolled from side to side. I felt my own eyes flood, and my body prickled with adrenaline, the rush of not knowing what to do but having to do it anyway. "How many of these did you take?"

"You don't understand," she sobbed. "It's the only way we can be together. I just have to sleep, and then—"

She stopped suddenly, focusing her heavy-lidded eyes on a space above my head.

"Patrick. You came back."

A smile briefly transformed her face as she closed her eyes and slumped to the floor.

two

I met a traveller from an antique land
Who said: "Two vast and trunkless legs of stone
Stand in the desert. Near them on the sand,
Half sunk, a shatter'd visage lies, whose frown
And wrinkled lip and sneer of cold command
Tell that its sculptor well those passions read
Which yet survive, stamp'd on these lifeless things,
The hand that mock'd them and the heart that fed.
And on the pedestal these words appear:
'My name is Ozymandias, king of kings:
Look on my works, ye Mighty, and despair!'
Nothing beside remains. Round the decay
Of that colossal wreck, boundless and bare,
The lone and level sands stretch far away."

We sat in English class, everyone trying to ignore the poem Mr. Terry had up on the board.

"So, 'Ozymandias.' Crumbled statue in the desert. Anyone care to interpret this for me? Explain it to me like I'm five? Don't all jump in at once," Mr. Terry said to the utterly silent class.

There were no takers.

"Scott? Angela? Daisy?" Mr. Terry tried to make eye contact with me, but I pretended not to notice, suddenly very interested in the blank piece of paper on my desk. I had come to learn, after a few cluelessly enthusiastic responses in class, that answering Mr. Terry's questions impressed him but did nothing to increase my popularity among my classmates. I tried to sink lower into my desk, willing myself to be absorbed into the plastic, and turn completely invisible. I looked across the room where Vivi sat, as usual, her head down, her hand moving as her pen flew across the page, writing something unknowable.

"Vivi Reyes," Mr. Terry said, like a command. "We haven't heard from you in a while."

The tension in the room spiked. Everyone could feel how audacious this was, to call on the girl who had tried to kill herself.

It was two weeks to the day since Mr. Terry had sent me to find her. Two weeks since I'd struggled with her and the empty pill bottle and the smooth wooden hall pass to get her to the nurse's office, and sat with her while she slept. The nurse had let me stay for a little while, but then she'd said I should go back to class, because she was having Vivi taken to the ER just to be on the safe side, because who knew how many pills Vivi had actually taken. I'd told her what Vivi had said, that she'd just wanted to sleep, but the nurse said better safe than sorry, and I knew it was going to be bad, because Vivi would have to have her stomach pumped. I squeezed her hand before I left. It was cold and limp. She didn't squeeze me back.

That day, after being ejected by the nurse, and realizing I'd missed all of History, I'd made my way to Chemistry, where Mrs. Crohn gave me a sour face and a late mark despite the note from the nurse explaining my tardiness.

The other kids in Chem who had observed the whole thing unfolding in English eyed me as though they were seeing me for the first time. *What's up? Where's Vivi? Is it true she tried to kill herself?* I thought about Vivi waking up in the hospital. Would she remember that I'd found her? Would she remember what she'd said to me? I felt oddly protective of her and whatever she was experiencing, and the sudden curiosity from my classmates felt opportunistic and wrong. I shook my head in the general direction of all the whispers as Mrs. Crohn ahem-ed everyone into silence and announced, "Electron configurations, people!"

As I opened my book to the right section, a note slid onto my desk, pushing into my elbow from the desk behind me. The note had been folded our special way, so I knew it was from Danielle. I opened it up as stealthily as I could under Mrs. Crohn's all-seeing gaze and saw that it contained only two words: *What,* in block letters with 3D shading, and *happened,* in floating bubbles. I thought about how Vivi had looked up above me before she closed her eyes, as though she were willing herself to float away. I wrote back "Tell you later" in my regular old handwriting and folded the paper in half, not even fancy note-passing style, pushing it back to Danielle's desk while Mrs. Crohn faced the board.

"I'm just saying," Danielle said at lunch that day after I'd finished recounting what happened, "it doesn't surprise me. I mean, it surprises me, but it doesn't *surprise* surprise me. I mean, she's kind of . . . intense, right?"

"Yeah," I'd said. I'd been trying to remember what I'd noticed about Vivi in class before our episode in the bathroom. "And really good at drawing and stuff. And scary smart."

"Well, duh, she's in all the honors classes," Danielle said. "But . . . wow. I didn't even realize she had a boyfriend, let alone a whole dramatic breakup storyline going on. That's wild. But I still have one question."

"What?" I'd asked, hoping Danielle had some insight. I'd been turning the event over and over in my mind, trying to figure it out. When I'd returned the hall pass after Chemistry, Mr. Terry had joked, *I gave you a hall pass, not a get-your-friends-out-of-school pass* before turning solemn and saying, *I appreciate your helping Vivi today. I hadn't realized the situation was quite so serious.* I didn't know how to talk to Mr. Terry when he wasn't joking, and my stomach felt suddenly twisted up inside, so I'd just nodded and then left before he could say anything else. But I couldn't stop wondering:

Why had Mr. Terry sent me, of all people, to go after Vivi? Why had Vivi allowed me, of all people, to see even the tiniest piece of her sad story?

Did they both somehow know?

About me?

Danielle laughed. "Who is this Patrick dude? I mean, seriously, he has got to be pret-ty hot to make a girl want to kill herself. And I haven't seen *anyone* that hot around here." When Danielle laughs, her whole body laughs. She's tall, and her blond curls frizz out around her, and her arms and legs are long and awkward, and when she laughs they move around as though she has no control over them.

"Ha ha, very funny," I'd said, but she was already scanning the lunchroom, looking for potential suicide-inducing hot guys, and I was pretty sure she wasn't listening.

When Vivi returned to school the Monday after I'd found her in the bathroom, I'd sought her out by the lockers before first period. She seemed suddenly fragile to me, and I resisted the impulse to stand in front of her like a human shield against the loud and indifferent locker traffic.

But before I could even ask how she was, she looked me straight in the eye, her face tense, her own almond-shaped eyes focused with an eerie intensity, and said, "Let's not talk about it, okay?"

"I just wanted to make sure you were all right."

"I am." As breakable as she seemed, in some ways she struck me as being so much more mature than the rest of us. She dressed like she was going to a job interview, or had recently escaped from Catholic school, with carefully pleated skirts and crisp shirts that had buttons instead of cartoons or semi-ironic pop-culture references like the rest of us. Her dark-brown hair was always shiny, her skin unblemished; she had a purposeful gravity when she walked that seemed unnatural for someone who wasn't yet a grown-up. She seemed like the kind of person Mr. Terry called *an old soul*. Even though I was shorter than her, I felt lumbering and awkward in her presence. Fundamentally not cool.

"Okay," I'd said.

"Okay," she'd replied. And then she'd closed her locker and turned away, leaving for class without waiting for me.

I'd stood there for a few moments, buffeted by the waves of students heading to class, when suddenly she whirled around to face me again, her brown eyes trained on me with their vulnerable kind of intensity.

"We do have a connection, you know." People streamed around her, but she was oblivious. I felt uncomfortable for her all of a sudden, so intense and so sure of herself that she didn't notice or adhere to regular-life rules about fashion or blurting out weird things like that. And yet I also felt envious: She was so directed, so focused, none of the stupid high-school stuff seemed to matter. She just stood there, in the middle of the hallway, looking calm, if slightly crazy, while everyone edged around her, backpacks nicking her as they pushed past.

"We do?"

"We are supposed to be connected in this life. But I don't know when and I don't know why, and Patrick said it's not quite time. So let's not make it complicated."

"Um . . . 'Patrick said?'" I'd asked. "Who's Patrick?"

"Yes," she'd said, ignoring my question and cocking her head as if she were listening to something over the PA system. Then she looked at me again. "So. Thank you for the other day. But let's not talk about it until it's time."

And then she'd walked away, without me.

And she hadn't talked to me since.

She walked past me in the halls like I was a stranger—like all of us were strangers. And even though the rumors about what had happened had already begun to spread, giving her a kind of perverse celebrity, she didn't seem to notice. Not like she was ignoring us, or like she was the queen of everything, but as if we literally weren't there. *As if she could see right through us.* She smiled as though she had a secret the rest of us didn't, something that made her calm, able to ignore the whispers and speculation swirling around her as she walked the school halls.

Danielle couldn't understand why it bothered me. "Let it go," she'd said. "So what? A weird thing happened and she doesn't want to talk about it. I probably wouldn't want to, either. What's the big deal? I know you're, like, *special* and all, but are you also now her guardian for life or something?"

I couldn't explain it to Danielle, or even to myself, really, but it just felt important. Something had happened when I'd found Vivi, and like it or not, we were, as she said, connected.

"Vivian?" Mr. Terry repeated, pulling me out of my reverie.

I felt connected to her now, as all eyes in the room looked to her, waiting to hear what the girl who had tried to kill herself might have to say.

She looked the way she always did: ethereal, fragile, haunted. I realized as I felt the suspense build that I didn't know if she could answer, if she could take the stress of answering. I almost butted in to save her, but she suddenly looked at me—almost as if she understood my impulse—and then she spoke.

"It's like the poem is about the remnants of something that used to be," she said.

Mr. Terry nodded. "Go on?"

"It's like," she paused. "Sometimes something monumental happens and it feels monumental to everyone. But sometimes a monumental thing only feels that big to the people experiencing it."

As she spoke, I heard her voice crack with emotion. My heart started to race as I worried for her. Even from my seat I could see her eyes shining bright with tears she struggled to keep from spilling down her face. I had a feeling she wasn't just talking about the poem. She was talking about what had happened to her. About Patrick.

"And then it's nothing, it's just wreckage, just a broken statue in the desert."

She looked angry now, and her face was flushed, like she was trying very hard to do something. Everyone seemed surprised by her sudden passion. Had she ever spoken this much in class before, about anything? I shivered; suddenly I was very cold, the air-conditioning in the room raising goose bumps on my forearms.

"But when it's all you have, does it matter?" she continued, agitated, her hands moving as she talked. "Does it matter that it's just a shell of its former glory? At least it's something, it's a message, it's a fragment, but it's real, it really *was* something, even if it isn't anymore."

Mr. Terry walked toward her and put his hand on her desk, effectively ending her soliloquy.

"An impassioned reading. Now, everyone: Write about it. Write an essay about the poem, a poem about the poem—write about what Vivi just said about the poem. I want *your* interpretation of what this all means. Twenty minutes. Go."

I sat blankly at my desk, watching Vivi try to compose herself. She looked as though she might pass out. Mr. Terry came by and gently knocked on my head. "You too, Daisy. Just because I know it's all in here doesn't mean I don't need it on the page."

I turned away from Vivi, who sat at her desk with her eyes closed, and I began to write.

When the twenty minutes were up, Mr. Terry said, "Everyone, hand your pages in to Daisy," and I heard the grumbling around me begin: *Ugh, who else, of course, teacher's pet.*

"She is not my 'pet,' she is my *minion*," said Mr. Terry, grinning. "There's a difference. Look it up." I could feel my entire face blushing from the negative attention as my classmates grudgingly passed their pages my way. "Oh, come on, people, hasn't it dawned on you yet? You are *all* my minions. There will be plenty of time for each and every one of you to do my bidding."

I gathered everyone's papers, but when I got to Vivi, she handed me not one page, but two. The top one was her essay, double-sided, filled with sentences clear out to the margins in her tiny, neat writing. The other was a piece of paper with a stylized drawing of two girls, one clearly Vivi-like, and the other one looking surprisingly like me. They both had the large round eyes and big heads of cartoon characters, but there was something about the way she'd drawn them—the way their bodies occupied the space on the page, the expressions on their faces—that made them instantly recognizable as us. The Vivi girl in the drawing sat in a classroom desk chair with a speech bubble hovering over her head. Inside were four words: *We need to talk.*

I looked at her and she held my gaze to make sure I understood. I nodded my head to say sure, and she took the paper back and added a fifth word.

Now.

three

"Patrick says you can sense him."

We stood outside of Mr. Terry's room as everyone else streamed by us on the way to their next class.

"What?" I shivered. Even in the hallway I felt cold.

"That," she said. "Look at your arms. Goose bumps."

"Yeah? So?"

She looked around us nervously as my voice raised, then grabbed my elbow to pull me to the edge of the hallway, away from prying ears.

"The cold? The feeling you have right now? It's him. He's surprised you're so clear. Most people aren't as open to him as you are."

I was starting to get freaked out. This was just weird. It was one thing to help her in the bathroom, when she was already drugged out of her mind, but watching Vivi lose it right in front of me was something else entirely. The spiraling pit in my stomach made me feel shaky and shuddery, as if I hadn't eaten all day. What was I supposed to do? What's the etiquette for dealing with someone who was going crazy?

I should get Mr. Terry. I should take her to the nurse. I should take her to the cafeteria and make her eat something, drink some juice. I should—another cold wave passed through me and this time it felt like my insides had goose bumps.

Vivi smiled. "He's trying to tell you to chill out."

"Vivi, you're freaking me out. You're not making any sense. *Who's* telling me that? There's no one else here."

She smiled sadly. "I had a feeling you weren't ready. But Patrick said . . ."

I couldn't stand it anymore. I didn't want to set her off if she was really breaking with reality, but I just couldn't contain it, and I was getting colder by the second. My teeth clattered together as I blurted out, "Who the hell is Patrick?"

The bell rang, Mr. Terry's door closed, and students scattered around us, running to class.

"Meet me at lunch, at the tree on the big lawn. I'll tell you what I can." She closed her eyes and inhaled deeply, clutching her books to her chest. As she breathed in, I felt the cold leave my body. Then, as if everything that had just happened was all perfectly normal, she turned and left for her Trig class.

I allowed myself to collapse against the wall and stood there for a moment, feeling the warmth re-enter my fingertips like a lightning bolt, as though the air around me was electrified. *Calm down, Daisy,* I told myself. *Don't do this now.* I focused on my breathing, closing my eyes. What had just happened? Had Vivi totally lost her mind? I'd thought Patrick was her tragic ex-boyfriend, but the stuff she'd said—the cold I felt, the goosebumps—made me think there was something more ominous going on. Was this Patrick person even real? Had the chill I felt been, in fact, some kind of ghostly presence? Or was I cracking up, just like her?

Mr. Terry opened the door to his classroom, startling me. "Ms. Jones? Back for a second helping?" He smiled his wry jokey smile.

I shook my head.

"Better hightail it to class, then," he said. Behind him I could see his third-period class peering at the board, struggling to make sense of the poem.

"Daisy?" he waited, motioning with his hands. "Go!"

I nodded. Through my stupor I heard Mr. Terry address his next class. "Folks: 'Ozymandias.' Crumbled statue in the desert. Anyone care to interpret this for me? Explain it to me like I'm five?"

His voice faded as I turned away and started heading to History. I would be late, and Mr. Dubinsky would give me a choice: answer a question correctly or get a late mark. Today I would take a late mark. I didn't think I could trust myself to speak at the moment. Too many things in my head. Nothing that made any sense.

I shivered again as I headed to the 100 building, but I was pretty sure it was just a passing breeze.

I took my late mark and settled in to my desk. Danielle usually sat in the row across from me, close enough so that we could whisper, or pass notes, or at least roll our eyes or make funny faces if necessary, but today her seat was empty. She hadn't been in English, either, but I watched the door, just in case she might show.

I had really wanted to talk to her before meeting Vivi at the big lawn at lunch. Sophomores weren't technically allowed there—it was the exclusive, if unofficial, lunching place of juniors and seniors, who tolerated the occasional sophomore but never freshmen. I wanted to talk to Danielle about what had happened, and I wanted her to come with me as reinforcement. To keep me grounded in reality, just in case Vivi's crazy was catching.

The cold struck me at the thought and I shivered, strongly enough to roll my pencil off the side of the desk. My not-so-subtle lunge for it won me the attention of Mr. Dubinsky. He folded his arms at the front of the classroom, the entire force of his tall, skinny frame focused in my direction.

"Ms. Jones? Are you volunteering?"

"Um . . . volunteering for . . . ?"

"Answering the question I just asked." He frowned. "The question you were surely paying attention to rather than daydreaming, of course."

"Of course," I stalled. My mind raced, searching for a playback of the last two minutes of whatever American History topic he had been talking about as I had been puzzling over Vivi. Finally I blurted out, "1776?"

He sat on the edge of his desk and sighed, one angular hand raking through his thinning hair. "Questions for chapters 10 and 11 due tomorrow," he barked at the class. "And expect a pop quiz. You can thank Ms. Jones for this. The next student to doze off during class will earn everyone oral reports." He stood up and turned to the board, yanking up the pull-down map of the colonies as the bell rang. The entire class glared at me as they made a break for the door. That made two classes in a row that hated my guts.

The big lawn was actually not all that big, as it was part of a much larger field right in the center of the school, where most of the students hung out during lunch or in between classes if there was enough time to linger. Most people were still in line for lunch or retrieving their bags from their lockers by the time I got there. But I wasn't bothering with lunch; I was too cold to eat. I leaned against the tree where Vivi had said we should meet and waited, trying to keep my nerves under control, trying to seem inconspicuous as people started to filter in.

Sunlight played hide-and-seek with the leaves as I looked up into the branches. As they moved in the breeze I thought about the way they clawed the sky, the way each branch shot out from the other like a network of veins, the idea of my body containing multitudes of tiny branches.

This was the kind of thing Mr. Terry encouraged, finding hidden meanings and metaphors in everything and connecting the dots to everything around us. Which was fine and all. But getting lost in the meaning of everything didn't make dealing with the real world any easier.

In the real world, Vivi wasn't here, and I was getting irritated. I peeked around the tree, scanning the big lawn, but she was nowhere. I took a few steps toward the square, hoping to find her striding toward me, and squinted into the sun.

"Looking for someone?"

I jumped as I heard the voice behind me, and turned around to find a boy standing next to the tree. A cute boy.

I tried to sound normal. "Yeah, actually. But she's not here. I was just going to go look for her on the square," I said, trying to get away before I was escorted back into sophomore territory.

"You're Daisy, right?" He smiled. Maybe he wasn't going to kick me off the big lawn, after all. "You're new?"

"Yeah—well, new *here*. I was at Pacific Junior last year, when we first moved. Came here for tenth grade this year. Obviously. Because it's this year. And I'm in tenth grade." I was babbling like an idiot. What was my problem? I blushed.

For a split second I had a sick foreboding in my stomach as a lightning zap of realization passed through me. *This guy is Patrick. Vivi's not coming, and she sent Patrick to explain things.* But then he took a step forward and said, "I'm one of Mr. Terry's senior TAs. I've read your essays. You're pretty good. I'm Kevin."

Relief flooded my body and I felt myself relax for the first time since I'd gone to the big lawn. "I'm Daisy," I told him. "But you already know that. Because you said my name. Like five seconds ago." I felt my face burning. *Such an idiot.*

But he just laughed. Tall and lanky, with longish dark hair that fell over his forehead and around his face, he set his backpack on the ground next to me with an easy expansiveness as though he owned the place. Which, being a senior, he kind of did.

He pointed to his head, grinning. "That's okay. Short-term memory issues. I need constant refreshers. I was just going to ask you what your name was again anyway."

I suddenly felt even more awkward. "Sorry for the whole-life-story thing. I'm kind of a blurter."

He smiled and waved me off. "What, seriously? That was blurting? I think you need to recalibrate your scale, because that seemed pretty, you know, garden variety conversation-making. Unless you were just about to say something about your recent alien abduction or the messages from the voices in your head."

I laughed. "No, I just mean—"

"You should really consider kicking it up a notch. I mean, if you're going to blurt . . . BLURT!" He was smiling. He had a nice smile, one of those sideways smiles that made it seem like one side of his face was smiling more than the other. I smiled back before I could stop myself, even though I was sure I looked goofy.

"So, your friend?" he asked.

Right. Back to reality. I looked around and still no Vivi. The lawn was full of people, all done or nearly done with their lunches. "Yeah, I don't know what the deal is."

"Looks like the deal is she isn't here." He grinned. "In addition to my short-term memory issues, I possess a stunning grasp of the obvious. It's a gift."

"I should probably go," I said.

"You sure?" He squinted at me.

No, you're not sure. Stay! Danielle would tell me if she were here. But I nodded. "Yeah, I have to try to find out what's up. It was nice to meet you."

"You, too," he said. "Come back to the big lawn and blurt anytime."

"Yeah, right," I laughed. But he smiled as though he meant it.

I smiled, too, a huge broad giddy smile I made sure he couldn't see as I walked away. I probably looked ridiculous to everyone else on the lawn, walking around by myself, grinning like an idiot. But I didn't care. For the second time that day, I felt like a live wire, my whole body bursting with energy. I had braved the big lawn, and

gift

I had talked to a boy—Danielle would positively freak when I told her.

I realized as I got to the edge of the lawn that the cold that had dogged me all morning was totally gone. Not a goose bump in sight.

And no Vivi, either.

four

Normally after lunch Danielle and I had Trig together, and then PE, which this term was aerobics. But with Danielle absent I was on my own. I took down extra-good notes for her in Math to cover what she was missing, and that helped take my mind off what I was missing: Vivi. Why would she tell me to meet her and not show? Was she just being mysterious, or had something happened? After Trig I made a cursory check of all the bathrooms, just in case. But she was nowhere to be found.

I sweated my way through aerobics and once the final bell rang I went back to the big lawn. I stood under the tree for a few minutes, lingering on the off-chance Vivi might finally show, or at least walk this way on her way out of school. And then I gave up and started heading home.

Home was a bus ride away. Not a school bus, a city bus. The most embarrassing kind of bus, especially in Southern California. Standing at the edge of the Castle Creek parking lot with seniors, juniors, even some sophomores laughing it up with friends in their parents' cars, or the cars they were given for their sixteenth birthdays, I burned with the shame of those doomed to public transportation. My bus pass might as well have been a Scarlet "L." Loser. A car of cheerleaders drove past me as I stood at the bus stop and I pretended to be looking the other way, squinting as though I was watching for someone in the distance, or lost in deep thought, or preparing to walk in a different direction. Anything other than waiting for the bus.

The ride was brief, but merciless. High, fuzzy seats, their balding cracks patched with duct tape, made it impossible for my feet to touch the floor. I squeezed into as small a space as possible and embraced my backpack on my lap as my feet dangled below. The cloudy window, scratched with graffiti and grimy with handprints, offered a faded view of the sad facts of the city. The farther we moved away from Castle Creek, edging south and ever closer to the Mexican border, the bleaker it got. Fancy green lawns with sprinklers and potted trees gave way to ice plants and weeds. Houses with circular driveways morphed into gas stations and sketchy 7–11s with smokers and rangy, bike-riding teenage boys laughing in front. We passed mechanic shops and taco stands. One-story houses with plastic roofs. Kids running around in diapers, not a grown-up in sight. Finally the bus deposited me on the busy corner where the freeway met the check-cashing store.

I walked along the edge of the highway, lowriders and trucks whooshing past me, until I came to the entrance: Pacific Breezes Community. A wishful-thinking name. Sure, we were close to the ocean, but the good beaches were at least ten miles north. We had a breeze coming off the bay, but you wouldn't want to take a deep whiff or anything.

Danielle had laughed at first when I told her. *You do not live in a trailer park!* And then her face, so serious, so embarrassed for me. *You do live in a trailer park.*

Well, I had exaggerated a little bit. It was fancier than that. It was a "community," according to the sign out front. More like a tiny subdivision of tiny homes that years ago had actually been trailers but now were more modern, eco-friendly, pre-fab constructions the developers preferred to call "modules." And besides, it was just me and my mom. Why should we pay for some sprawling house in the burbs, when it was just the two of us? This was good enough. This way I would be able to afford college, my mom said. That worked for me. Once I was off the bus, anyway.

I jiggled my key in the lock until it caught and then let myself inside. Romeo, our cat, meowed loudly to protest his long day without food, and I gave him a thorough petting, stroking his fluffy orange fur as I scooped some food in his bowl.

"Gross! Romeo! You've been in the sink all day?" His worst habit was sleeping in the sink. Which wouldn't be so bad if he didn't shed like crazy. So now I had a pile of dirty, hairy dishes to wash. Fantastic.

I started thinking about what to make for dinner as I washed the dishes. I always tried to make something that would keep well so that my mom could just heat stuff up when she got home from her shift. Maybe tonight I'd just do pasta.

"What do you think, Romeo? Spaghetti and meatballs?"

He yowled in response. *Pasta it is,* I said to myself. I grabbed the phone off the wall and called Danielle while I started dinner.

"I took notes for you in History and Trig," I said when she picked up the phone. "Where were you today?"

"Hello to you, too," she laughed. "I had a sore throat. And my mom is an alarmist, so she kept me home. Notes in History *and* Trig? My, my."

"And aerobics."

"Ha. I'm sure that's very, very complicated."

"There will be a quiz!" I joked. "Actually, there will be a quiz in History. Thanks to me."

"Oh, no—what did you do?" she said in a mock-stern voice.

"I was late, and then I wasn't paying attention, and then . . ."

"Mr. Dubinsky freaked out."

"Pretty much," I said. "So listen, two things. First, the weirdest thing happened with Vivi today."

"Wait, hold on," Danielle said. There was a muffled conversation in the background while I stirred the pasta and prodded meatballs around some sauce in a separate pan on the gas stovetop. Romeo tangled himself in the old-fashioned crinkly phone cord, walking back and forth as I cooked. Then Danielle was back. "I gotta go," she said. "My mom is crazy, capital C, nuts, capital N."

"But I have to tell you—"

"She's totally cutting me off here, I have to 'save my throat' if I want to go to school tomorrow. Like I want to go to school tomorrow. But I totally want to hear about it! Call you later?"

I sighed. "I guess."

"Seriously, I'll call you later," Danielle said. "And if I can't, I'll catch you tomorrow at the lockers before first period and you can tell me then."

"Okay," I said, unable to hide my disappointment.

"You know, if you just had a cell phone or a computer or something placing you in the digital age like a normal person, I could text you or IM you or . . ."

"Don't make me feel any more lame than I already am," I said. "Can you just call later?"

"Yeah, yeah, I'll try," Danielle said. And then I heard her say, "All right, I'm hanging up!" to her mom as she hung up on me.

I put down the phone and Romeo jumped onto the counter, perilously close to where the meatballs were cooking. He meowed at me twice, looking extra pitiful, so I caved. "Just one," I told him, forking a meatball onto a plate for him, and he rubbed against my arm like he understood.

Like a normal person.

Danielle had been joking, but she knew my secret. She'd discovered it the first month of school, after we'd realized we had almost every class together and it seemed like we might hit it off. We ate lunch together every day, we did homework together, we hung out. And then just when it seemed like everything was awesome, and I was passing, she handed me her cell phone.

In the hallway between classes she said, "Here, can you grab this, I know I dumped some lip gloss in the bottom of this bag somewhere . . ."

I started to protest, but she didn't hear me as she rummaged through her backpack. Instead she thrust the phone my way, and I yanked my hand back before she could give it to me. The phone clattered to the floor and she picked it up in a panic.

"Jeez, Daisy! You could have broken it!"

But that's just it, I *could have* broken it. If I had touched it.

She set her backpack down and pored over the phone, turning it over, checking for damage, flipping it open and poking its buttons to check that it still worked. Luckily, it did.

"Sorry," I told her. "I'm not good with electronic things."

She looked exasperated as she flipped the top back down. "I wasn't asking you to use it, just hold it."

"I know," I said. "I just—"

And then she thrust it in my hand again, using her hand to close my fingers around it. "Thank you! Just let me get the lip gloss and then I'll take it off your hands! It is *so* not a big deal!"

But I could already feel it happening. My secret unfolding. The buzzing sensation, like my arm was vibrating. The headache moving from the top of my neck over my head and onto my face. And then a zap, like an electric shock to my fingertips and hand.

Danielle stood up, lip gloss refreshed. "See? No big deal." She took the phone from me and flipped it open. My hand smarted as though I'd slapped something.

"That's weird," she said. "It's turned off. Did you turn it off?"

Not on purpose, I thought, but I just said, "No."

"Oh my God, it's not working at all! Maybe it did get totally messed up from being dropped." She punched the keys frantically, trying to revive it.

"Just give it a second," I said.

"What," she said, "you know how to fix this? I thought you were a dork about electronic stuff."

"I am," I said, taking a deep breath. "Just hold it out toward me."
She held the phone in her hand and I placed just one finger on it.
I took another deep breath and felt a tiny charge rush through my
fingertip and up my arm before I took my hand away. "There," I
said. "In small doses, I can fix the things I mess up."

"What?!" She looked at me incredulously. Then her phone
arpeggioed a greeting as it booted back to life and Danielle's
mouth dropped open. "I don't know what the heck just happened, but you are definitely going to have to tell me the whole
story here."

I hadn't ever told anyone anything about it, let alone the whole
story. And in fact any story I could have told her would only be a
halfway story, because the truth is I don't know the whole story
myself. But I did know that I was tired of keeping it a secret. And I
felt like I could trust her. So I told her, the first person besides my
mom to know for real.

I told her how when I was a baby my mom noticed the radio
garbling or going static if she happened to be holding me while
she touched it to switch stations or fiddle with the volume. I told
her how as a toddler I was able to change the channels on our
television when I pressed my hands against the screen, trying
to say hi to Cookie Monster. How anything—everything—electric went on the fritz when I touched it. Cordless phones, digital
watches, microwaves, blow dryers. I told her how it was kind of a
family joke when I was little, or a joke between me and my mom
anyway, since that was all the family we had—*there goes another
toaster, Daisy must have sneezed*—and how for a while that's all it
was: a joke. How as I got older it got more intense. How people
started noticing, how stuff happened at school, how it stopped
being funny.

I told her how when I turned twelve—before I'd learned how to
stay in control—things got crazy, and I didn't have to be touching
things for them to freak out. How it was like I had a cloud of bad
electricity around me. How in junior high I'd walk into homeroom

and people would suddenly complain that their phones had no reception or that their watches stopped working. How some days I'd get frustrated while doing my Math homework and erase an answer from the page really hard, and our apartment would blow a fuse. And then of course there was The Incident in computer lab. I hadn't even been upset or angry, or even a little bit ticked off. I was just feeling antsy, and a little sad, because we'd been kicked out of our place after one too many Daisy-caused electrical problems. And then I logged onto the school network and the next thing I knew all the computers were on fire.

Danielle took it all really well. Better than I expected. She said she wouldn't say anything to anyone. She said it was kind of awesome. She said it was like having superpowers or something. I'd laughed: *Yeah, the power to never be able to use a cell phone or laptop!*

But she said, "No, Electricity Girl, the power to control things with your *mind*."

I'd be happy to be able to just control my own mind with my mind, forget controlling other things with it. I'm working on it, meditating every night and doing yoga every day to keep it under control, to keep it calm. But I'm not quite there yet. Mostly I just want to get through tenth grade without blowing anything else up.

In the morning I woke to Romeo's cold nose nudging my face.

"Okay, okay," I grumbled.

Danielle hadn't called, but hopefully I'd see her at the lockers before class. I showered quickly and grabbed a granola bar for breakfast as I tried to make my exit without waking my mom. She was sleeping on the couch, a book on her chest, her glasses still half on. She must have fallen asleep reading last night after getting home from her shift. I fixed the throw blanket over her a little better and she stirred. I could see she was still wearing her nurse's scrubs, lilac with tiny cartoon pandas.

"Thanks, sweetie," she mumbled.

gift

"*Shh.* Don't wake up. I'm just heading to school. Go back to sleep," I told her as I opened the door to leave.

"Have fun at the party," she called after me in her sleepy voice. I stopped.

"Party?"

She lifted her head from the arm of the couch and took off her glasses. Her hair was a mess and her makeup was still on. "I don't know, you were talking about it in your sleep. Some kind of party? At school maybe?"

I shook my head. "Uh, not that I know of. Bye, Mom. Get some sleep. I'll see you tonight."

She waved a hand in my direction as I left to catch the bus.

The bus was especially crowded, and I realized only after I'd squeezed myself into a seat that I was sitting next to someone with an electronic book reader and a music player. I tried to put my backpack alongside me as a kind of physical barrier and I closed my eyes and breathed in a few deep breaths, repelling the energy I could feel emanating from the seat next to me. I felt the woman jostle, and I cracked one eye open to see her readjusting her ear buds as she pulled the music player from her pocket and looked at it with a frown, of concentration or consternation I couldn't tell. I tensed up as she pressed buttons, hoping I hadn't inadvertently changed songs on her, or something worse, but then she slipped it back in her pocket and returned to her book.

I breathed again.

I was in the clear.

27

five

I have always been like this.

I remember when I was really little, like in preschool, I had this toy, a kind of little-kid computerized reader. It was a book with a special pen attached to it, and if you waved the pen over certain words, the book would speak and say the words to you. But I played with it by ignoring the pen, and simply waving my hand over the pages or touching the special words lightly with my fingers. "Ball," it would say in its mechanical voice as I touched my pinky to the page. "Cat." I thought that was how it was supposed to work.

One day as I was making the book read to me this way, my mom yanked it out of my hands. *No,* she said. *You mustn't do that. You have to use the special pen.* I remember feeling surprised, and worried that I was doing something wrong. *But I can make it talk all by myself.* She put her hands on my shoulders and said gently, *I know that, Daisy. But I need you to try to do things the normal way. If your teachers saw something like that . . .* She trailed off, but she didn't need to finish. I suddenly sensed what she was afraid of. That there was something wrong with me, and that because of it there was a gulf that separated us, a dangerous something that had the power to keep us forever apart.

She never said anything like that out loud, but it was clear to me that this was a secret. My mom covered up for me when we were in public, at the check-out line when the grocery scanner beeped like crazy and the checker couldn't get it to stop, laughing and brushing it off and escorting me to a bench *fast*, within eyeshot while she paid and loaded everything back into the cart. I could see the way she would tense up, or speed up, or make her movements faster, louder, grander, to pull everyone's attention to her and away from me. She seemed calm, but I could see the vein in her neck pulsing, her chest and face beginning to flush slightly, as she hurried me away from whatever I might inadvertently be messing with.

As soon as I was old enough to go to the library by myself, I tried to learn about other people like me. Over the years I read about mind-melders who could guess the shapes drawn on special ESP cards. I saw pictures of a man who could turn spoons inside out just by staring at them with his crazy eyes, his bushy eyebrows and crushing gaze intimidating them into contortion. I learned about people who communicated with spirits and pulled long diaphanous scarves from their bodies as proof of their connections to ghosts. I read stories of young girls who wasted away and became ghostly figures themselves.

I discovered plenty about ESP and telepathy and otherworldly paranormal hoaxes and sad scams and naive believers, hysterical girls who fooled themselves into thinking they'd made contact with the spirit world, con men who tricked audiences into believing they had seen apparitions from beyond the grave.

But I discovered nothing about my particular strange ability, nothing that would help me explain it, or understand it, or above all be rid of it.

"You simply have a gift, Daisy," my mom would say to me when she put me to bed, winding up an old-fashioned alarm clock, not a digital one like the rest of the world had, to set the alarm. "And when someone gives you a gift, you say thank you, even if you don't want it."

My mother did what she could. She tried to make life normal, Daisy-proofing our living space and trying to help me learn how to control things. When she saw the kind of library reading I was doing, she saved up and bought me a book about yoga, thinking I might tame my wild energy through *pranayama* breathing exercises and *asanas,* the physical postures practiced by yogis for thousands of years.

The book is dog-eared now, its pages marked and underlined in places, every chapter well-thumbed from the nights I spent looking through it again and again, desperate for guidance and answers. Now I have it memorized, the poses and breathing second nature to me.

Like the rules my mom gave me, it was a start, a piece of the puzzle. But the rest I am figuring out as I go, living with this gift that, some days, I would rather return.

six

"Whoa. Hold on. Back. Up. You talked to *Kevin Beck*? Kevin Smart-Guy, Dark-and-Brooding, Doesn't-Talk-to-Anyone Beck? Weird Kevin-Who-Plays-Weird-Music-In-His-Weird-Band Beck?"

"Danielle, you're missing my point!" We stood in front of my locker in the 300 building before the start of first period as I tried to fill her in on everything that had happened. "Wait, he's in a *band*?"

"Was he dark? Was he brooding? Was he totally weird? Of course he was totally weird, what am I talking about? *Tell me everything!*" she demanded.

"He—he wasn't the point," I said, exasperated. "He was just there—"

"And he talked to you!"

"No, we communicated through mime."

"That would also be good. I could see him as a mime," she mused. Then she snapped out of it and looked down at me, more serious than I'd ever seen her. "*What. Did. He. Say*?! Spill! I want everything!"

"My God, what is the big deal," I muttered. I paused for a moment before admitting, "He said my essays were pretty good."

"What?!" she sputtered. "How does he know—?"

"He's Mr. Terry's TA or something. And he seemed nice. Not weird."

"Oh my God. He said they were *pretty good*! And you like him," she said in a sing-songy voice as she leaned against my locker,

31

clutching her books, looking dreamy. Which just made me more irritated.

"Danielle! Snap out of it! The point was that I was just waiting there, for like half of lunch, and she didn't show."

"Who?"

"I'm talking about Vivi, remember? She said that creepy stuff, and then she told me to meet her at the tree on the big lawn, and then she didn't show up?"

"But Kevin The-Dude-Who-Thinks-Your-Essays-Are-Pretty-Good Beck did," she said, smiling at me.

"Whatever!" I wasn't smiling back. "Vivi never showed, and after that I couldn't find her. It was like she just vanished."

"Maybe she did," Danielle said. "She's a very strange girl. Maybe she had a sudden impulse to go home. Maybe she hid out in study hall. Maybe she had to go to a party." She looked amused when she said this last part, until she saw my face. "What?"

"Why would you say that?" I asked.

"Say what?"

"That part about a party."

She shrugged. Now it was her turn to be a little irritated. "I don't know. What's the big deal? Why can't we just keep talking about Kevin Beck?"

I shook my head. "It's just kind of random, that's all. My mom said I was talking in my sleep about a party or something."

Danielle looked at me sharply. "Did you have a dream?"

"Of course I had a dream, everyone has dreams at night. I don't actually *remember* my dream, but evidently it was about a party—"

"This is important, Daisy," Danielle said, grabbing my arm. "What did you dream about?"

She held my arm tightly and I began squirming away from her encroaching energy when suddenly I felt it: the dream. The world of it washed over me, small fragments tumbling in my mind like colorful pieces inside a kaleidoscope. An old-fashioned, stiff dress. A green, grassy field. People standing on the porch of a huge house, talking to one another like they were at some kind of garden party. Danielle walking beside me, her arm in mine, looking not like Danielle at all but somehow still Danielle. Storm clouds overhead, darkening the field.

"It was old-timey, right?" She interrupted. "Like everyone was in old-fashioned clothes?"

I felt goose bumps on my arms as electricity pumped through me.

"How do you know that?" I asked.

Her eyes were huge as she told me, "Because I had the same dream."

We stood there, neither of us speaking for a moment, and Danielle steadied herself against the lockers with a shaking hand.

"What does that even mean?" she asked.

"It means he's made contact." Vivi's voice surprised us.

"Jeez, Vivi," Danielle said, nearly dropping her books. "What are you, some kind of ghost? I didn't even see you there."

Vivi stared at me as if I should know what she was talking about and repeated, "He's made contact."

"Who's made contact?" Danielle asked, at the same time I was saying, "Nice of *you* to finally make some contact, where were you yesterday?"

Vivi shook her head, like we were irritating toddlers she had to babysit until the adults got home.

"Let's get out of here," she said. "I can explain what's going on." She started to walk toward the end of the hall, but Danielle stood firm.

"You go on ahead. I'm just going to stay here and continue to freak out."

Vivi turned, clearly surprised that neither of us were following.

"Hello?" Danielle said. "I don't know if you heard what we were talking about before you magically appeared in the middle of our conversation, but Daisy and I just had the same dream."

"I know," Vivi began.

"*The. Same. Dream,*" Danielle repeated.

"I know," Vivi repeated.

"No, you *don't* know! Unless . . ." she paused ominously.

"No," Vivi interrupted. "I didn't have the same dream. But Patrick told me everything."

That was it for me, I couldn't hold it in any longer. "I am so sick of hearing about this Patrick. *Patrick says to be friends, Patrick says you can sense him, Patrick says to chill out.* Only trouble is, I've never *seen* Patrick. I waited all lunch for you and him yesterday and neither of you showed. What is he, your imaginary friend?"

I expected her to be mad, but she just smiled. Placid, calm Vivi, beaming indulgently as though in on some private joke. "In a way."

Danielle groaned. "Enough, okay, Vivi? Total cry for help; I get it. But seriously, can we just move on? Daisy and I have bigger things to figure out right now."

Vivi smiled patiently. "You *don't* get it. I'm here to help you figure things out. And you're going to help me figure things out, too."

"No, *we're* not," Danielle said. "And *you're* not. Look, this doesn't involve you, it's between me and Daisy. It's about us having the same dream. That's what we're talking about right now, and, no offense, but I don't see what your pretend boyfriend has to do with any of it!"

"Actually," she said, "he's more like my guardian angel."

seven

I wasn't thrilled about ditching first period, but after what Vivi had said, Danielle was too freaked out to care. She just wanted to get to the bottom of it. And so, here we were, in the bathroom of the 300 building, sitting on the floor, our backs against the full-length mirror where only weeks before I'd found Vivi slumped and sobbing.

"I really hope you guys don't think I'm weird telling you all this," Vivi began.

"Too late," Danielle said.

Vivi turned to Danielle. "I'm sorry to have to involve you. I hadn't realized you and Daisy were psychically so close. This was just going to be about me and Patrick and Daisy, but Patrick says you're important to her somehow, and besides, now that you've had the dream . . ."

"A thousand apologies for ruining your plans to keep your weirdness to yourself," Danielle said from the corner where she sat, folded in on herself, her knees up, her arms crossed, her head resting on the table her arms made. "Believe me, I didn't plan to mind-meld with Daisy."

"Hey," I said. "I didn't do this on purpose! I didn't plan to have this dream. I didn't even remember the stupid dream until you told me about it!"

Vivi held up her hands. It wasn't even dramatic, and yet Danielle and I reacted to it like she'd blown a referee whistle. Vivi looked at

35

us, making sure we were paying attention, and said, "Why don't you just let me tell you what's going on."

She took a deep breath.

"I first met Patrick when I was just a little girl. One day, I was maybe four or five, and I was at the park, sliding on the slides and swinging on the swings by myself, until a boy joined in. He was bigger than me, like a teenager, bigger than my big brothers, even. But he was so nice. He played tag with me, we went on the teeter-totters, we climbed the jungle gym, he pushed the merry-go-round for me so I could just spin around and around and around. . . . It was the best day of my life. Then suddenly, my mom grabbed my arm like she was mad, and said, 'Why are you always off playing by yourself? Go play with someone, make a friend.' I was confused—didn't she see my new friend? 'I have a friend,' I told her. But she was like, 'Oh really? Where? Because I just see you here, turning around in circles by yourself like a fool.' I turned back to where the boy had been, but he wasn't there. He was just . . . *gone.* I went to the top of the twisty slide to look for him, but I couldn't see him anywhere. Eventually my mom dragged me home. I cried and screamed and fought the whole way, telling her I wanted to wait for my friend. I could tell she was embarrassed. I could tell she didn't believe me.

"That night, I had a dream. In the dream, I was playing in the park with the boy, just like I'd done that day. We were spinning around and around on the merry-go-round, and it was like rainbows of light were sparking out of us. It was the best feeling in the world. And then he spoke. He said his name was Patrick. He said we knew each other from a long time before, and we could play whenever I liked.

"I didn't always see him every day. He appeared mostly when I was by myself, playing pretend. But he was almost always in my dreams. Not always the main part of my dream or anything like that; I just always had the sense that he was there. I felt good when he was there. I felt safe. My parents fought a lot, and my brothers were in high school already, so I was more or less on my own.

When things were bad, when my parents argued or when my dad was drunk or whatever, Patrick was like a shield, protecting me. He would take me away to a safe place, if I just closed my eyes and let myself go. So I did. I'd just go and go, as far away as I could in my mind.

"Over the next few years, I saw Patrick less and less, until I began to think that maybe he had just been something I conjured out of my own imagination. Then, when I was eight, he appeared in a dream, the clearest I'd seen him since that first day in the park. He told me that everything was going to be fine, that it was okay that I didn't see him so much anymore. He told me it was okay to let him go, that even if I didn't see him or think about him, he was always watching over me. He said he would come back again when I was older, when he could explain things better. I didn't see him or sense him or dream about him for almost five years."

"Wait a second," Danielle interrupted. "What does any of this have to do with the dream Daisy and I had last night?"

"I'm trying to explain it to you," Vivi said.

"Well, that's not really working out. No offense, but so far I've just heard some super-creepy story about you hallucinating a guardian angel or something."

"Danielle!" I said.

"I don't mean to be rude, it's just, this is a bathroom, not a therapist's office, and I don't really care about all that stuff. I just want to know how and why we dreamed the same thing!"

"It's because of Patrick," Vivi said. "He's connecting us. He's making you share the same dream. Don't you see we're all connected?"

"Right. We're all connected. Thanks to your imaginary-friend-slash-guardian-angel who for some reason put the same dream in both of our heads." Danielle gathered her backpack from the floor and stood up. "Well. I'm so glad I skipped class for this. All my questions answered. Come on, Daisy. If we leave now we can get by with just a late slip."

I stayed on the floor, my head in my hands. I couldn't understand why Danielle seemed so aggravated, why her energy seemed to be building and building into something so prickly and sharp.

"Well?" Danielle said, holding the door open. "Come on. This is a waste of time."

"I think I'm going to stay," I said. Danielle looked like she was going to explode. This felt big, like I was taking sides, one friend against another. But I felt like it was important for me to stay with Vivi.

"It's okay," Vivi said. "I understand. I'll tell Daisy the rest, and when you're ready, Daisy can fill you in. Or not. It's your choice."

"Oh, nice, like I really need Daisy to hold my hand through this mystical woo-woo nonsense." Danielle eyed her skeptically. "I can figure it out myself. Just stay out of my head, okay?"

Vivi looked at the ground.

"I'll see you in class," I said.

"Whatever," Danielle said, and walked out the door. I had the sense that she was more scared than angry at either of us.

I debated going after Danielle, to calm her down, but I could feel Vivi's weak energy next to me, and I realized if anyone actually did need some hand-holding, it was her.

"So," I said gently, after the echo of Danielle's slammed door had faded. "Patrick went away?"

"When I was eight," she said. "Right after my dad left for good. My mom thought I was crying about my dad being gone, but I wasn't. I was crying because I missed Patrick."

A missing dad, a missing ghost.

"My dad left, too," I told her. "I mean, before I was born. I never knew him. So I couldn't miss him, I guess. It's always been just me and my mom."

She gave me a sad smile. "I think it's better to have a dad you've never met than one you wish you hadn't."

"Maybe," I said.

I couldn't remember a time when I didn't wish that I could have met my dad. It wasn't that I didn't like having things be just the two of us, my mom and me—we made a good team. I just wondered what it would have been like if he were here, whether him being with us would have changed things, what he might have to say about my gift. My mom was diplomatic about the subject, answering the questions I had about him over the years, never making me feel bad for asking. Her answers got more complicated as I got older, but the basics always stayed the same: My father had left my mother before I was born, and he wasn't ever coming back.

The tiled floor was unyielding and my legs were starting to ache from sitting on the hard surface. I felt a cold shiver on the back of my neck.

"Patrick is here with us right now, you know," Vivi said, smiling.

I felt the cold on my back and said, "Let me guess, he's standing right behind me."

She looked surprised. "You *do* sense him."

The cold moved through me until it felt like I was suddenly sitting in a fog of coldness, enveloped, and then, just as quickly, it dissipated. Vivi's eyes were closed, her face beatific. Then she opened her eyes again and looked at me. I must have seemed especially freaked out, because she reached out and put a hand on my knee. Her fingers were so warm.

"Don't worry," she said. "He's just going to be over there, in the corner. He won't make you so cold the whole time."

I looked in the corner and saw nothing, just the dusty grout and tile, smudges on the edges of the mirrored wall. I couldn't sense anything other than a vague creepy feeling of being watched.

"So, Patrick left when you were eight. What did you think had happened?"

She laughed. "I thought I was crazy. I thought maybe I'd imagined the whole thing. You know, invented him."

"So what brought him back?" I asked.

"Basically, I started to draw. I drew all the stuff I remembered from when I was little. And when I couldn't remember anymore, I started drawing things from my imagination. I filled dozens of sketchbooks with stories about him and me. And then one day, when I was thirteen, and I was by myself in the house, just sitting on the couch and drawing, I had a strange feeling. Like a weird *sense* that something was going to happen. My heart started pounding. All the hairs on my arm stood up. I felt like jumping out of my skin. And just when I was beginning to totally hyperventilate from fear, I saw him.

"But it wasn't like I saw a person. It was more like . . . energy. In the corner of the room, near the bookcase, there was this swirling, miniature storm—like a hurricane picture from space. It was all these little dots swirling and swirling, and then getting faster and brighter, and then suddenly it all coalesced into this . . . brilliant shadow. I know that probably doesn't make sense, but it's the only way I can describe it. It was like the outline of a person, or electrical circuits in the shape of a person, and then like a see-through person, like a hologram. And then, finally, a person. A man. It was Patrick. I just knew it was him."

I shivered. "Did he look like he did in your drawings?"

"He was more beautiful than I could ever draw. He looked like . . . like someone from a magazine, like a movie star, like a dream. He was shimmering in front of me, and I couldn't look away, he was just so mesmerizing and perfect. But then I said his name out loud, and as soon as I spoke, he vanished. Everything was quiet, normal, just like before. I sat on the couch and realized I was drenched in sweat. I didn't know what to do. I sat there for hours, waiting for him to come back. My mom came home and yelled at me for sitting around like an idiot in the dark. He told me later it had taken years of stored energy to break through like that, to make contact. He'd wanted to be able to cross through, at least for a moment, but he just wasn't strong enough."

"But he'd made contact with you before," I interrupted. "When you were little. That didn't take energy?"

"Little kids are much more receptive to messengers from the spirit world," she said. "By the time I was seven or eight, I was already closing off, forgetting my connection to previous selves and lives. The human world was taking over."

"Whoa," I said. "The human world is all there is, Vivi. It doesn't take over. We live in it."

"But you know what I mean," she said. "How kids are open?"

"Yeah, I guess."

She scooted closer to where I was. "I believe children are still connected to whatever came before this life. Whether it's a past life or some kind of soul-plane or another existence we can't even begin to understand, just consciousness hanging out in the universe. I was open to Patrick. I didn't consciously remember any past life or connection, but my mind was just fluid enough, I guess, to accept him."

"I don't understand," I said. "Is Patrick, like, a ghost? Do you think he's someone you knew in a past life?"

She smiled at me, and looked meaningfully for just a moment in the direction of the corner where, theoretically, he was waiting. "He's my soulmate."

eight

The bell rang and suddenly the bathroom filled with people. We scrambled to stand up as girls ran in to touch up their makeup or get to the stalls. My head was spinning from everything Vivi had told me and I leaned against the wall, trying to look like I hadn't just ditched class to have a serious conversation about someone's imaginary friend. Vivi stood near the sink and ran a hand through her hair as she looked in the mirror, but it seemed to me like she was staring off into the distance, focusing on something other than her reflection.

"So," I began.

Startled, she shook her head at me in the mirror. "Not now," she said, nodding at the people washing hands, primping, coming in and going out.

"I just wanted to ask where you were yesterday."

She looked blank.

"Lunch?" I prompted. "The tree? The big lawn?"

She leaned against the wall again as the bell rang and the last stragglers headed out of the bathroom to second period.

"Oh, right. Sorry. I wanted to talk to you and explain things . . . but I just chickened out. Because if I *told* you, then you would *know*. And I was a little afraid of what that would be like."

"Well, I know now," I said. "You just told me, right?"

"I know, it's stupid. It's just that this has been in my head for my whole life. I've never told anyone anything about this. I thought it would, you know, change things. Like what they say about making a wish—if you say it out loud, it won't come true."

I nodded. I had felt a little bit the same when I first confessed my own secret to Danielle—as though keeping silent about my freaky weirdness made it stronger, that talking about it diluted its strength.

"But it's all okay," Vivi said as we sat down again. "I told you, and it's fine, and more important he's here, he's still here." She closed her eyes and hugged her arms around herself.

"After that day in the living room, when he almost came through—after that, I couldn't *see him* see him, like when I was little. But I could talk to him. I could close my eyes and summon him by thinking his name, and then this green light would spark in the darkness and I would know it was him. It was so . . . peaceful." She closed her eyes as she said this, and I shifted in my seat on the bathroom floor. This felt like reading someone's diary. So private. I stole a leery glance at the corner, but there was nothing.

"He explained things to me," she continued, opening her eyes now. "He told me we had been together over many lifetimes, and that he'd been watching over me ever since I'd chosen to be reborn."

I shivered. This was just too creepy. "Wait, what do you mean, 'chosen to be reborn'? People can't choose to be born."

She seemed to smile at me indulgently. "Every soul chooses. Patrick told me. You choose your life in this world. And then you forget that you chose it."

"So why didn't Patrick just choose to be in this life with you?"

She seemed near tears as she traced her finger along the grout path of the tiles on the floor, and I wondered if I should have been so blunt.

"I'm sorry," I said, looking over to the corner again. "Actually, I guess in a way he *is* in this life with you. I mean, we're sitting here talking about him, aren't we?" I felt a coldness on the right side of my body.

"He's not in the corner anymore, you can stop looking there,"

Vivi said. "He's sitting right next to you. He's impressed that you're getting this stuff." She paused and tilted her head to one side, as though she were listening for something. "Although he's not surprised. He says you have a powerful gift."

I sat up straighter, drawing my legs in. How could Patrick know that? Especially if Vivi didn't know that? I felt jittery all over again.

"But you're right," she said, her eyes beginning to fill with tears. "He isn't really here in this life, he didn't choose it. And even though he keeps saying all he wants is to come through, to materialize and be with me, it just hasn't happened. When you found me that day, I thought he had left for good. I hadn't been able to feel him for weeks—I hadn't heard him, couldn't sense him. Instead of bliss and peace there was nothing. I took the pills because I thought it could bring me to him."

"Oh, Vivi," I said, taking her hands. She smiled through her tears, and it was like the sun had just come out.

"But then you found me. And you shimmered in front of me like a heat wave. And above you I could see him, clear as day, standing over the both of us, astonished. Daisy, don't you see? You brought him back to me. Somehow, you brought him back."

nine

"So, what does any of this have to do with me? With us, I mean, with the dream?" Danielle asked, picking the cherry tomatoes out of her salad and lining them up on her lunch tray.

After Vivi's unwitting revelation—that my energy had somehow recharged a ghost—I had stayed with her until lunch, but I'd been itching to talk to Danielle and tell her what I'd learned. I'd made Vivi promise to wait for me while I went to the cafeteria, and then I'd tracked down Danielle and told her what I knew.

"I'm not sure yet," I said. Having finished with the tomatoes, Danielle moved on to the carrots, lining them up alongside their compatriots. Then the cucumber bits. Then the onion. When all that was left in the bowl was a few clumps of iceberg lettuce, she sat back and wiped her hands on a stiff, beige cafeteria napkin.

I gestured at the tray. "Uh, *why?*"

She waved me off with a smile. "Oh, come on. *You're* going to tell me *I'm* weird? Besides. Everybody has a thing. This is my salad thing. I like to line up all my salad ingredients *exactly* on the side of my tray, and then eat them *in order,* dipping them into the little thingy of ranch dressing, and then . . ." She looked at me, a self-deprecating grin on her face. "I may be a little more anxious than normal today. Especially after everything you just told me."

"I know. This is all really, really freaky."

45

I watched Danielle eat the tomatoes one by one, then start on the carrots. She was being friendly enough, but I could feel her energy. Not exactly hostile, like when we were in the bathroom with Vivi, but boundaried. Cautious. Orange around the edges.

"Look, I kind of feel like this is my fault," I said.

Danielle stopped, mid-ranch-dressing-dip. "That's ridiculous. Who's the one with mental problems? Hint: Not you."

"No, I know, but I kind of roped you into this."

"How? Listen, unless you're the one who engineered this whole dream-synchronicity thing, this is all Vivi. You're a good person to be a friend to her. I don't hold that against you."

"I don't know, I'm just throwing out theories here," I said.

"Ooh, let's talk theories," Danielle said. "Because I've got a few. About Vivi, I mean. Because, hello, definitely some daddy issues there, right? I mean, seriously. But what else—bipolar? Multiple personality disorder? Schizophrenia? Ooh, what if she has Münchausen Syndrome! You know, the thing where people act like they're all sick or something just for the attention?"

"Come on. That has nothing to do with seeing ghosts."

Danielle shrugged. "You have to admit, it certainly does seem like she wants attention. It's all a big cry for help, I think."

I shook my head. "I don't know that it's as simple as all that." I thought about what she'd said about Patrick being a shield, from her dad, from anything painful or dark. "I think she wants protection."

"I think she just wants to feel special," Danielle said, picking up her tray. "She's a special, special snowflake living in a cruel, cruel world. Well, guess what? It's high school. Everybody feels that way. And ninety-nine percent of us do not have to invent imaginary boyfriends in order to cope."

"What if it's real?" I said.

"What do you mean, what if it's real? It's all 'real,'" she said, leaning in. "I mean, you're real, I'm real, she's real. She 'really' thinks she's 'really' communicating with some spirit from her past life or whatever."

I shook my head. "I mean, what if it's *really* real? What if she really *is* seeing this guy—this ghost, or whatever he is? Really communicating with him?"

Danielle stared at me and then shook her head, like she was shaking off my question.

I shivered as I gathered my stuff and the food I got for Vivi. "Can you just come back there with me? I know it's weird and stuff, and I know it's freaking you out—"

"To say the least . . ."

"But I kind of need you," I pleaded. "I can't deal with this all by myself. What if she's really mental? And—what if she's not?"

Danielle shifted her weight to one hip as she considered the question. "Is she still in the bathroom?"

"Yes," I said, hoping *please please please* to myself.

She narrowed her eyes. "And if I came, that would mean I'd have to ditch Math?"

"Yes!" My fingers were visibly crossed now.

"Done," she said, turning on her heel and leading the way out of the cafeteria. "Come on. Let's go get ourselves some crazy."

We pushed open the door gingerly, having made our way back to the bathroom against the oncoming rush of people heading to fifth period.

"Vivi?" I whispered. "Danielle and I brought you something to eat."

We ventured around the corner and saw her sitting on the floor, her head in her hands.

"They should really consider getting a couch in here," Danielle said, plopping down on the tiles unceremoniously. "At least a bench. I'd even take a folding chair."

"Danielle," I said, pointing with my head at Vivi, who seemed to be lost in her own world.

"Vivi?" she said, too loudly, articulating her words like Vivi was a slow child. "Vivi! It's Danielle. Daisy convinced me to chill out and hear what you have to say. Can you hear me? Are you there?"

Vivi looked at her with sudden clarity. "Of course I'm here. What, do you think I'm crazy?"

I shot a warning glance at Danielle. "No, Vivi," I said. "Of course she doesn't think—"

"Yeah, I think you're crazy!" Danielle interrupted, turning to me. "What, you think it's better that I treat her like a total idiot? I'm just being honest. She deserves as much. Right?"

Vivi looked at both of us and then nodded. "She's right, Daisy. I deserve honesty. I want to know the truth. Danielle's told me the truth."

"*Her* truth," I emphasized. I sat down and handed Vivi the sandwich I'd gotten for her.

Vivi nodded. "What about yours? Do *you* think I'm crazy?" She looked at me with her huge brown eyes, and I tried to think of how I could even begin to phrase my concerns.

"Oh, for crap's sake, of course she thinks you're crazy," Danielle broke in. "We'd be crazy *not* to think you're crazy. You're telling us that you talk to ghosts! Hello? Definition of crazy!"

We sat in silence for a few moments, me fuming at Danielle for being so blunt, Vivi seemingly lost in thought, Danielle looking so bored she'd probably be glad to be back in Math class.

"What is the deal with ghosts, anyway?" Danielle finally said. "I mean, why can't they just come out and be like, 'Hey, I'm so-and-so, I was killed in whatever year, and I'm here to avenge this totally specific thing?' I mean, look at, like, those TV shows where a detective has a psychic follow some lead about a murder from a long time ago, and she's all, 'There's a body of water . . . a stream . . . and I'm sensing red! And there's a horse!'"

"Your point?" Vivi spoke up.

"My point is, everything is totally vague, there's nothing specific, it's all just signs and hints and mysteries to figure out."

"So?" I asked.

"So!" she said, indignant. "So, ghosts—if you believe in them—are supernatural, right? Supernatural. You know, *super*? As in, *awesome*? As in *better than natural*? They can do anything they want, so why would they bother giving a psychic PowerPoint presentation of random stuff when they could just bust out exact details like, 'Hey, I was killed near a lake by a guy in a red shirt riding a horse. And BTW, his name is Reginald Q. Murderer and I can see him at his house over there at 555 Murderer Lane BECAUSE I AM A GHOST!'"

"You want Patrick to give us information," Vivi said.

"I want 'Patrick'—if he exists—to speak to us directly—clearly, plainly, normally, the way we're all talking right now, and tell us why Daisy and I had that random dream."

"That's not how it works," Vivi said.

"Why not?" Danielle demanded. "Why can't it work that way?"

"I don't know, it just doesn't." Vivi said.

"Well, it should," Danielle said.

"Is he here right now?" I asked.

Vivi nodded. "When you left, I couldn't really sense him. But now that you're back, it's like he's come into focus. The nearer he is to you, the clearer I can see him."

That was odd. I could sense a coldness, as before, but I couldn't sense any particular energy. Didn't ghosts have energy? Shouldn't I be able to pick up on that?

"Can you hear him? Like, does he talk to you?" Danielle asked.

Vivi's expression changed. "Yes and no. It's more like I'm hearing the inside of my own head."

"Okay, that's just creepy," Danielle said. "Can he move things? Like, physically?"

"No, but he can affect things—like influence things with energy."

Danielle nodded in my direction. "So, like a ghost version of Daisy, huh?"

Vivi looked confused.

"Daisy hasn't filled you in?"

49

Danielle's aggressive attitude was palpable, her energy bundled like an angry knotted mass.

"Patrick told me she has a gift, a kind of energy, but . . ."

"Yeah, she's kind of a human Geiger counter. She can mess with watches and microwaves and electric stuff."

"Danielle," I said, my voice a sharp edge.

She waved her hand. "Vivi should know about this. Besides, it's not like you're talking to ghosts, right? I mean, on the crazy scale, you're like *here*—" she held one hand out flat, palm down, level with her mid-section "—and she's like *here*." She held her other hand high above her head. Then suddenly her hands were down and her eyes were trained on me intensely. "I have a question for you, too, while we're having a Q & A here."

"Okay," I said. But Danielle's interrogation was beginning to unnerve me. Even though Vivi had shared her own totally private otherworldly thing with us, I wasn't too thrilled that Danielle had let her in on my secret. I had trusted her with that. And here she was, talking about it like it was no big deal.

"Why don't you use your powers all the time? You could be tripping fire alarms during Math tests, messing with the cheerleaders by frizzing out their hair and stuff, zapping the school computers to change our grades to straight As. . . ."

"I've told you," I said. "I try not to do anything like that. I'm trying to keep it in control and be normal."

"Normal. That's a good one." She laughed. "And now a question for both of you. Why the hell am I here? I mean, I'm not psychic, I don't believe in ghosts, I can't levitate or teleport. So, what's the deal?"

Vivi grabbed Danielle's hand and held it firmly. Danielle squirmed and tried to take her hand out of Vivi's grip, but Vivi calmly held on and stared into Danielle's eyes. Then she closed her own eyes, still holding Danielle's hand.

"When you were five you fell into a pond at a family picnic and nearly drowned. When you were being resuscitated you heard your dead grandmother talking to you and telling you it wasn't your time yet, and that it was okay to go back. Since then, you occasionally talk to her in your head when you're falling asleep at night and you believe that she can really hear you, and you sometimes hear her, too."

Danielle yanked her hand away, her eyes blinking rapidly. "How do you know that?" she asked in a harsh voice.

Vivi sat with her hands in her lap. "Patrick told me. He said she's fine, by the way."

"Stop it!" Danielle hissed, fighting back tears.

"She watches over you and sends you her love," Vivi continued, her voice a monotone.

"Stop it!" Danielle shouted.

"I'm just telling you what he said."

"Well, I don't want to hear it," Danielle said, standing up and angrily wiping her eyes.

"Danielle—" I began, but she left before I could stop her.

ten

I spent the rest of the day with Vivi, mostly just trying to keep her grounded in reality, keep her company, keep her together. It was hard to reconcile this eager-to-talk Vivi with the silent, ethereal Vivi who had merely drifted in the corner of my consciousness in class until I'd found her that day and all this strangeness was set in motion. Was she manic, or just glad to have someone to talk to? Should I be reporting this to someone? Was it a bad thing that I kind of didn't want to? I was probably doing everything wrong, but I felt like maybe we should be keeping this whole strange thing to ourselves. So I just tried to keep her going, to keep her talking the way they do in TV shows with witnesses or crazy people or hostage-takers. Eventually the bell rang marking the end of sixth period and the end of the day, and there was no point in our hiding in the bathroom anymore.

I lingered for a while longer, until Vivi felt okay enough to leave, and then I left, hoping to catch Danielle. She wasn't at her locker—nobody was at the lockers by this point—but she'd left me a note in mine. *Sorry,* she'd written in puffy letters. Then in her regular handwriting: *I know you're just trying to help her. I'll catch up with you later.*

I hadn't realized until I saw her fancy-folded note how worried I'd been that something unfixable had happened between us. I refolded the note and slipped it in my pocket, relieved that things seemed to be okay.

gift

I got my stuff and closed the locker door. With Danielle already gone, there was nothing left for me to do besides grab the next bus home. But I couldn't face it yet. I didn't want to break the strange spell this day had been. I wanted to walk around—run, actually, as fast as I could, to feel my heart racing, my lungs straining, my body aching with the effort. I wanted to run out the jumble of feelings I felt, run away from the confusion and strangeness. But I sensed my hands tingling, my body electrifying in that way that meant *danger, freakiness ahead,* and so I tried to concentrate on taking deep breaths instead.

The deep breathing helped calm my spiking electricity—at least until I remembered that I'd missed nearly all my classes that day. I'd never skipped a class before. Ever. If I hurried, I might be able to collect at least my English homework. I walked toward Mr. Terry's room to see if I could catch him before he left.

The door to his classroom was open when I got there.

"Daisy." Mr. Terry motioned me in. "How nice of you to join us. You are a little late, though." He had his serious face on, but even when he was being stern he looked mildly amused. The rumor at Castle Creek was that Mr. Terry was a surfer, or used to be—one of those sandy-haired, "it's all good, man" guys who drove a van to the beach at five a.m. to get the best waves, then spent the rest of the day sleeping in the van. I wasn't sure. He did drive a van, and his hair, though thinning, was sun bleached. He definitely had the casual air of someone who could easily spend the day hanging out doing nothing. But I couldn't picture him actually surfing. Reading a book on the beach, yeah. But surfing?

"I know, I'm sorry," I said. "I, uh, missed your class today."

"Yes, hence my understated reference to your lateness."

"I wanted to pick up the homework, though, if that's okay."

He moved a pile of books and thumbed through some papers on his desk, wincing. "You're out of luck—it was an in-class essay." My face must have betrayed my disappointment because he came around to sit on the edge of his desk and looked at me patiently.

"Listen, Daisy. This isn't like you, missing class. If you have some time right now, and I mean *right now,* you can make it up—write the essay and turn it in before I have to leave in about"—he checked his watch—"twenty minutes. But I'm concerned. Is everything okay?"

I felt my face redden, and I looked down as I answered. "Yeah, it's fine."

He sighed a teacherly kind of sigh. "I don't want to get all 'up in your business,'" he air-quoted, "but it seems to me you've been off your game a bit ever since the . . . incident with Vivi. Which is understandable. I'm not suggesting that you've done anything wrong, or that you're doing anything wrong. But perhaps it's affecting you more than you realize. Would you like to talk about it? With me, or perhaps one of the school counselors?"

"God, no!" I blurted before I could stop myself. No way would I talk to my guidance counselor, Mr. Adams. When I'd first transferred in, he'd taken one look at my records—good grades, but too many school transfers, too many "behavioral incidents" from back in the day when I didn't have things under control—and I could see him mentally filing me away into a folder marked Trouble. Or Loser. Or Someone Not to Be Bothered With. His sense of me as a waste of his time was palpable, and I was glad that I hadn't had to interact with him past that first week of settling in to school as a new student. But Mr. Terry wasn't too far off—hadn't I been asking myself that all day? Whether I should talk to someone about what was going on with Vivi? It would be kind of a relief to unburden myself, even if only to hear from an unbiased outside source that I was right, she was crazy, the dream that Danielle and I had was a fluke, that there are no such things as ghosts. A part of me wanted Mr. Terry to keep asking, to insist I spill my guts.

But he laughed, his hands up. "Okay, okay, just a suggestion."

"No offense," I stammered. "It's just—I'm just—I'm fine. Really. I've just had a weird day. Not weird enough to talk to anyone about, just a regular old weird day. But, if I could, I'd like to try to do the essay now, so I won't be behind."

He crossed his arms, assessing me, then nodded. "All right. Twenty minutes. Compare and/or contrast 'The Road Not Taken' with 'Ozymandias.'"

I sat down in my usual seat and got out my notebook.

"And, Daisy?" Mr. Terry said. I hoped he wasn't going to try to broach the subject of talking to a counselor again. "Don't let the ditching become a habit."

"Right. I won't."

"Seriously," he said, trying to look serious. But he couldn't help it: He winked.

I finished my essay and gave it to Mr. Terry, trying my best to seem normal and chipper and enthusiastic, just like the kind of student who would never ditch class ever again. We walked to the edge of the parking lot together, and then I went to the bus stop while he went toward his van. I waved as he drove away. Theoretically, there could be surfboards in there. I tried to imagine Mr. Terry surfing: board shorts, T-shirt, probably a poetry book in hand, saying to the other surfers, *Come on, people, explain it to me like I'm five.* I smiled to myself, imagining it.

And then: a voice.

"Daisy?"

I jumped, as though I'd heard a ghost, only to find, standing there in the bus shelter, possibly the last person I ever wanted to witness my standing in the bus shelter: Kevin.

"Oh my God, you scared me," I said.

"Really?" He scrunched his forehead. "I've been standing here for like five minutes not being scary."

Oof. How long had I been musing about Mr. Terry's theoretical surfing career? "Sorry, just . . . lost in thought, I guess."

"Really lost," he said.

I felt myself turn red.

"Well, okay, maybe it wasn't *five* minutes," he said. "But I was definitely standing here not being scary for at least three minutes."

If it was possible, I turned even redder. "I just . . . I'm sorry, I've had a crazy day. And I don't mean like wacky-fun crazy, I mean like certifiably crazy."

"Whoa. Sounds intense," he said.

I nodded. "You could say that."

"Wanna share with the class?" he asked. I must have fixed him with a look, because he quickly said, "Yikes, okay, forget I said that. I just thought, you know, sometimes it helps to talk."

"God, you and Mr. Terry," I muttered, shaking my head.

"God, me, and Mr. Terry?" he asked. "Pretty esteemed company, but I'll take it."

I waved him off. "No, I just mean Mr. Terry was trying to get me to *talk*, too."

"Sorry," he said, more seriously.

Now I felt bad. I shrugged. "But, you know, I'm more of a blurter."

He smiled. "Right. It's the only way to go, really."

"It's an art, I think."

"At the very least a craft."

I nodded. As much as I kind of did want to talk, I couldn't actually tell him anything. I mean, I shouldn't. I could hear Danielle's voice in my head: *Are you crazy? Do you* ever *want to go on a date, ever?* Not that I could ever really go on a date with Kevin—I mean, come on—but still, imaginary Danielle had a point. Sharing crazy stories about having the same dream as your best friend and trying to help another friend who's in love with a ghost? Probably not setting myself up as Date Material.

"So, let the blurting begin?" he said.

I smiled, shook my head. "I don't think so."

We stood in silence for a few moments. I shifted my backpack to my other shoulder and watched the trash tangle in the gutter across the street. Picturesque, sunny, Southern California bus stop. Cars blew by, taunting us. I squinted into the distance, hoping my bus wasn't lumbering toward us. What would be worse: telling Kevin about all the crazy, or outing myself to him as a person who rides the bus?

"Okay, so I have this . . . story I'm trying to figure out," I said, finally unable to take any more of keeping silent while standing next to him.

He motioned his hands toward himself. "Perfect audience right here. Try me."

I sighed. "Well. Okay. Imagine there's this girl, right? And she loves this guy. Only . . . he's dead."

He laughed. "Is this like one of those, 'I have a girlfriend, but she lives in Canada, that's why you never see her!' kind of things?"

"I'm explaining this wrong," I said. Maybe this was a mistake.

"So. There's a dead guy," he prompted.

"Well, not really," I said.

"Wait, there's a zombie?"

"No, no!"

"So . . . there's a ghost?" he asked.

"Well, kind of," I said. "I think."

"O-kay . . ."

"Okay, let me start over." I took a deep breath and plunged in. So much for date material. "Imagine there's this guy, and he's dead. But the girl he loves is still alive. So he watches over her. For, like, her whole life. But after a while, he can't stand it anymore, being without her. He wants them to be together again. So he goes to get her."

"Huh," he said, his brow furrowed. "Kind of a reverse Orpheus."

"A reverse Orfee-who?"

"Orpheus and Eurydice. Greek mythology?"

I shook my head.

"Okay, so, Orpheus was like the king of the poets. Not a literal king, just the guy who was the best at singing and playing music. He was the son of one of the muses—you know, the nine goddesses of music and dance? His mother was Calliope, the goddess of elo- quence, and so he was pretty much born to be a musician and poet. He was super charismatic—a rock star, basically. Anyway, he married Eurydice, but right after the wedding she was bitten by a poisonous snake and died. Which, you know—totally common in these types of stories. So Orpheus, being a rock star and a guy who was used to getting what he wanted, set off to the underworld, the place where all souls go after death, to get her back."

"So, *reverse* Orpheus would be . . . ?"

"Yeah, well, in the real story, Orpheus goes to the underworld to bring Eurydice back to the regular world. And it sounds like in your story, the guy goes to the regular world to bring his girl back to the underworld."

Was that what Patrick was doing? Trying to take Vivi out of this world and into his?

"So, in your story, does the dead guy succeed?" Kevin asked. "Does he bring the girl back with him to the underworld, or wherever he is?"

I felt my heart race, my breath become shallow. "I don't know," I said. "I haven't gotten that far into it yet. I'm still trying to figure it all out." I fiddled with my backpack again, shifting it back to my other shoulder to distract from the fact that I was so rattled, and tried to take a deep breath.

"Hey, no worries," he said. "I know how it is—you start talking about a story, and then all of a sudden it's like all the magic goes out of writing it."

"Something like that," I said.

"Well," he said. "You could always go the traditional route. If you get stuck on what to do next, I mean. Just follow the original story."

"What happened in the end?"

"It's pretty tragic. Orpheus went to the underworld and used his powers of persuasion to beg Persephone and Hades, the queen and king of the underworld, to let Eurydice go. They were so swayed by his performance that they said okay—under one condition."

"What was that?"

"He couldn't look at Eurydice until they both made it back to the land of the living. He could lead her out, but if he looked back to see her face and make sure she was still there, poof, she'd be gone. Doomed to remain forever in the underworld."

"Wow."

"I know. And you'd think, well, that's not a crazy-difficult condition to fulfill. But, of course, you'd be wrong."

"And so that's what happened? He looked at her while they were leaving the underworld, and—poof?"

"Pretty much. He started getting paranoid when they were climbing out, thinking that maybe Hades had tricked him, or that Eurydice had gotten lost or fallen behind. So he looked back—and, just like Hades had promised, she was gone, shouting one final word." He paused dramatically. "'Farewell.'"

"That *is* tragic," I said.

He shrugged. "Well, in a way it wasn't all bad."

"Really?"

"Yeah. After he lost Eurydice, he lived in the forest for a while, playing sad music for the animals and stuff. Until one day a bunch of women came along and demanded that he play happy songs—which, of course, he couldn't, being all heartbroken. So, they tore him to pieces. And then they threw all the pieces into the river."

"Uh . . . and how exactly is that not all bad?"

"Well, he and Eurydice were together again. You know, since both of them were dead."

"You really do know how to look on the bright side of things."

"It's one of my many gifts." He smiled, raising an eyebrow.

I saw a bus in the distance and craned my neck to see which number it was, hoping I could avoid having Kevin see me taking public transportation. Luckily, it looked like it was the 64—not mine. Sweet relief.

"Thanks for telling me all that stuff," I said.

"No problem. I hope it helps."

He grabbed his backpack and ran a hand through his hair. "Well, this is me," he said as the 64 pulled up.

"What, seriously?" I said.

He grinned. "You didn't think I stood here *just* to hear your whole reverse Orpheus thing, did you? I mean, granted, it was interesting, and it's always fun to sneak up on you and freak you out in the hopes that you might blurt stuff, but really. You know this is a bus stop, right?"

"Well, yeah," I said. "I take the 56."

"Awesome."

Awesome? Who is *this guy?*

"See you later," he said, stepping onto the bus. "Hope your day gets better!"

I waved and just barely stopped myself from blurting out, "It totally, completely, one hundred percent just did!"

My bus came a few minutes later, but it was more like I floated home.

eleven

A storm is coming.

I breathe in the wind, feeling it fill my lungs, expanding me.

Beside me is a large house with a wraparound porch. Before me, a grassy field, a rocky path. I can feel the wind push my long skirt against me, the material stiff and constricting. I see other people nearby, their clothes old-fashioned, like mine.

I am dreaming.

"Jane! Honestly, you'd think I was talking to myself all this time the way you wandered off like that."

A girl smiles at me as she threads her arm through mine.

Veronica. My best friend.

Suddenly I know who she is, I know where I am and who I am. Suddenly I am not *Daisy* anymore.

"This is such a nice party, Veronica!" I say.

"It is, isn't it?" she says, but I notice a shadow pass across her face.

Storm clouds gather above us as we stroll past the house.

"We should go in soon," I say.

We pass a girl, pale and ghostly, her head down. Instantly, in the manner of dreams, I know something tragic has happened to her.

"Poor Lily," I whisper. "But then, she's always been so fragile."

Veronica stops walking and looks at me, her dark curls whipped by the wind. "The girl was attacked."

61

"I know. But she'll be okay. It will just take some time," I say to reassure her. But she withdraws her arm from mine. "Maybe James can help—maybe he can find out who did it and bring him to justice!" I add.

"My brother?" Veronica asks. "Are you so in love with him that you can't see?"

I'm caught off guard by the tears in her eyes, the anger in her voice. She turns away from me and runs into the field. Fat raindrops begin to pelt the ground.

"Veronica!" I call after her. She shouldn't go too far. The only thing beyond the field is the ocean, and it's too stormy for her to be on the shore alone.

But before I can stop her, Veronica disappears into the long grass. Soon I can't see anything but rain.

I jump as I feel a hand on my shoulder.

"Come inside," James says over the rain. "You shouldn't be out here in this storm."

He ushers me to the porch, his coat over my head to protect me.

"Veronica's still out there," I tell him. "She ran into the field, toward the shore. You've got to find her. She was so upset. We saw Lily and then—"

James is never rattled, but I see his jaw tighten and he runs a quick hand through his wet hair.

"I'll find her," he says. "But let's get you safely inside first."

He takes my hand and leads me into the house. I find myself overwhelmed by detail: the noise of the party guests; my clothes wet and dripping on the diamond-patterned carpet; my fingertips touching the wallpaper, its raised burgundy floral pattern soft as velvet.

No one notices us as we go up the stairs. A window looms above us at the landing to the second floor. I pause, and with a zap I sense a dark energy, tendrils snaking their way through the air.

"Jane," James says, pulling on my hand. "There's not much time."

He ushers us into a room. Bookshelves, a desk, a fireplace: Veronica's study. My heart leaps as he leans in close to speak to me.

"Stay here. I'll find Veronica. I promise."

"Of course," I begin to say, but he is gone.

Suddenly I am chilled, as if the storm has come inside.

Is the window open? Could there be a draft? But the window is closed, and all I can see when I look out is blackness.

Veronica—my best friend, who shares everything with me—is out there, alone. James is somewhere out there, looking for her, hoping to bring her home. What if they should both be lost in the dark? I must tell someone.

My fingertips tingle as I walk toward the door.

I see my hand reach for the doorknob, and in that moment the dream shifts away from itself.

I am waking up.

An ominous dark energy presses down on me, and I sense more than see the vision that comes to me next: Lily, covered in blood, the cold, hard glint of a butcher knife in her hand.

part two

twelve

If you've never been inside a trailer park before, I guess I can't begrudge you for leaping to the stereotype. I know I did. But the one we live in isn't like that. I mean, it's no luxury resort, but it actually looks a lot like other places we've lived. Rows of homes. Streets that connect and intersect. Palm trees.

There is a gate at the front entrance, but no one is ever there inside the shack-like security station, and if you follow the main street, it winds around in a circle and leads you back to where you started. But if you stop about a quarter of the way in, you'll find Palm Drive, and if you hang a right there and go two doors down, you'll find my place.

It doesn't look like a trailer from the outside, mostly because it's dressed up with vinyl siding and a roof—the kind of details that make it look more house-like than trailer-like. In fact, I don't even know if it really qualifies as an actual trailer. There aren't any wheels on it, so you can't pull it around or anything. On the right side is a long carport, essentially a covered parking space. On the left side is the stairway to our front door and a little bit of land enclosed by a fence that separates us from our neighbors. Some people have yards, or laundry stations. We just have rocks, the kind of nondescript filler rocks you can buy at a home store for cheap. I thought it might be fun to fill it up with the kind of colorful rocks you get for aquariums, but my mom vetoed that. Too small, twice the price. Moving here was all about cost efficiency, which is a Mr. Terry way of saying that money is tight.

Inside, it looks even less like a trailer. I was surprised the first time I saw it, because I expected it would look like the inside of a tour bus or something, maybe with some bunk beds and some kind of fold-out table and a place at the front with a giant steering wheel. But it actually looks like a regular old apartment. When you walk in the front door, you're in the common area, which is like a living room, only a little bit smaller. We have a couch, a comfy chair for reading, a coffee table, a rug. We don't have a television, but that's more because of my own particular issues than any economic concerns. To the right is the kitchen, with a sink and oven and nice counters and everything, and a small table where we eat dinner. If you kept going to the right, past the kitchen, you'd go down a little hallway to the master bedroom, which is my mom's. She has the good bathroom, too, with a big tub and a shower. My room is on the other side of the common area, to the left after you walk in. It's about the same size as my mom's, but my bathroom is smaller, just a tiny shower stall, no tub. Overall, it's pretty cozy. Small, but not too small. A good place for us.

But the walls are rather thin.

Which is why both Romeo and my mom raced in immediately when I screamed.

"What is it?" my mom asked, and began taking my pulse, assessing me with a critical eye. Her transition from full-on dead sleep into nurse mode was instantaneous. Sitting up, I could see from the clock on the wall it was six a.m. My heart was racing. I was sweating and cold at the same time. If I closed my eyes, I could still see the knife.

"Daisy!" my mom said sharply, her hands gripping the sides of my arms, grounding me, forcing my eyes open. Romeo marched back and forth across my lap.

My mom looked pale and tired. How many night shifts had she been working? Those were the best-paying ones, she always said. But she looked weary to me, her face lined with tension and worry.

She loosened her grip on me and moved her head down to look me in the eye, gauging something medically, I'm sure. "You were having a dream. But you're awake now," she said, and her voice sounded tight. "Daisy? You're awake now."

"I know," I said. My transition from dreamland to reality was not as sharp as hers.

"Can you tell me about it?" she asked, her arms folded now, her mouth a twisted line.

"I'm sorry, what?" I said, trying to focus on what she was saying. She seemed so nervous.

"Do you want to talk about what happened in the dream?"

"I don't know," I said. "It just all felt so . . . *real*. It was like it was really happening, or maybe like it already happened."

I felt my mom pull away. Not physically, but with her energy. It was as if she'd sucked in her breath and zipped up a dress: All the warm and welcoming energy she usually radiated suddenly retracted. "Mom?" I said.

She sat very still, then reached out and felt my pulse again. "It was just a dream," she told me, leaning close, her face taut with concern. "There's nothing to be scared of. I really want you to believe me. Nothing you dream about can hurt you, or affect you, or change your life. Dreams are just stories your brain tells itself to make sense of the activity that happens while you sleep. Do you understand?"

"Ow," I said, twisting my wrist from out of her grip. She looked surprised and dropped her hand.

"I'm sorry, sweetie. I just don't like seeing you scared." She leaned forward and hugged me, and I could feel her warm, good purple energy again, but now edged with a bright orange flare of fear. The dream feeling continued to float around me, and I could feel my own anxiety mounting as I flashed onto the memory of Veronica running into the darkness, the screaming wind, the vision of Lily wielding the knife. I took a deep breath and tried to concentrate on keeping my energy stable. Somehow I sensed it was important to calm my mom down, to keep my worries to myself for now.

"I'm not scared," I said into her shoulder. "I mean, I *was,* but I'm not anymore. It just all seemed so real—I can't explain it. It was like it was really happening—"

She sat back and cut me off. "But it wasn't, Daisy. It wasn't happening. Dreaming something can't make it real."

"Mom, it's okay. People have nightmares. I know I'm a freak and all, but seriously. Chill."

She looked at me, a smile finally playing on her face. "Okay. Point taken. But you can't honestly expect me to not be slightly concerned when I hear my kid screaming like a banshee at six in the morning."

"I'm sorry I woke you up," I said, giving her another hug.

"And I'm sorry you had a nightmare," she said. Romeo, tired of being the meat in our hug sandwich, wiggled himself free and jumped off the bed. "Now. Can I get you some breakfast?"

"Sure," I said. "But I think I'm going to try to get the early bus. I need to catch some friends before first period." I had to talk to Danielle about the dream. It felt so significant, I was sure she'd dreamt it, too. And Vivi. I caught my breath: What if we had all had the same dream? What would that even mean?

"Oh?" my mom said. "Homework stuff? Or some kind of project?"

"Something like that," I said, and headed for the shower.

thirteen

Come on, I said to myself, my hands restless, my feet pacing, my whole body jangling with impatience. I walked back and forth in front of the main entrance to the school at the 100 building, stopping only for a moment here or there to deflect the raised eyebrows or confused stares of students as they took the stairs two at a time, probably to ensure they'd pass by the crazy pacing girl sooner. *Where are you guys?*

I scanned the clusters of people coming from the school bus stop, or wandering in from the parking lot, or emerging from a parent's car in the semi-circular drop-off zone and hoping nobody had noticed they'd been driven by their mom. Nobody was moving fast enough, walking or running with enough urgency to stand out to me as being Danielle or Vivi. But they had to be here soon. I craned my neck to see the big industrial school clock through the doors of the 100 building. *7:20.* Surely they would be here today. I had to catch them before first period started. I didn't think I could last until we were all in second-period English together, and even then, we would be reduced to passing notes, or whispering when Mr. Terry wasn't paying attention.

I continued to pace. What did it all mean? The dream felt so real. I felt it as surely as I felt the electricity coursing through my body. My pacing seemed to rile me up rather than calm me down, but I couldn't stop. My mind was a movie screen playing scenes from the dream, and not just dialogue and action, but still shots, moments, feelings. I closed my eyes and for a moment I could almost recapture that feeling of being Jane, of being an entirely different person, of following James up the stairs and waiting for Veronica to be found.

"He sent us this one, too, didn't he?"

I opened my eyes and saw Danielle in front of me. She looked serious and worried, clutching her backpack and books like they were her last link to reality.

"Patrick made us dream the other one, and he made us dream this one, too. You dreamed it too, right? Tell me you know what I'm talking about."

"Yes," I said. "I was Jane."

Her eyes widened. "I was Veronica."

We both sat down on the steps in front of the entrance. We didn't look at each other.

"I don't like how this feels," Danielle said, and she sounded like she was going to cry.

"I know," I said.

"It's real, then, right? We had the same dream? Twice?"

"Two different dreams," I said, still kind of dazed.

"You know what I mean."

"What happened in your dream?"

Danielle took a deep breath and turned toward me. "Okay, well. My dad was throwing a party for some reason. I don't know why. I just know I was, like, mad about it. And I was mad at you, a little. I mean, Jane. Anyway, we were walking in this field, and I was really upset about something—I don't know exactly what, just something to do with this girl Lily—and I ran away. I can't explain it, but I felt like something awful had happened. Like something awful was *going* to happen."

I flashed onto the memory of Lily holding the knife.

Danielle looked like she was fighting back tears, and her voice was tight. "I just had this horrible feeling—I *still* have this horrible feeling—and I can't get it to go away."

"Breathe," I said, my hand on her back. "Seriously, take a deep breath. It's going to be okay."

"How do you know that?" she asked in a harsh whisper. *"We are being sent dreams by a ghost.* How is that ever going to be okay?"

The bell rang for first period and we both jumped.

"What should we do?" I asked her.

Mr. Avila, the assistant principal, appeared above us. "Ladies?"

"Sorry," I said, standing up as he moved to close the front doors we'd been blocking. Danielle stood up, too, slowly, as Mr. Avila looked on.

He gestured at the clock. "Don't the two of you have someplace to be?"

"On our way," I said, smiling like a responsible student as I led Danielle down the hallway. "Come on," I said to her, my voice lowered. "Let's go back to the 300 building bathroom. We can talk there. Maybe Vivi's waiting for us."

But Danielle stopped me and shook her head. "I gotta get my mind off this stuff for a while. It's freaking me out. Why don't we just meet up again in English, and then we can see Vivi and figure something out."

"You sure?" I asked.

She nodded. Then she said loudly, for Mr. Avila's benefit, "Okay, well, have fun in French. I guess I'll see you in English."

"Yeah, see you," I said.

She walked off in the opposite direction, and I watched her for a moment, until I realized that Mr. Avila was still standing there, arms crossed.

The doors behind him opened, and he barked, "Late slip!" almost reflexively to the student who entered. It was Vivi. I saw her nod at Mr. Avila and promise to pick up a late slip from the attendance office. I raced over.

"Hi, I need a late slip, too, I'll go with her. Thanks, Mr. Avila!" I said with forced cheer as I steered Vivi toward the attendance office.

"We had another one," I said under my breath.

"Another what?" she asked, looking blank.

"Duh? Dream?"

"Oh, right. Of course."

"We'll talk in English, okay? Danielle wanted to go to class, get her mind off it, but we'll catch up then and figure out when and where we can talk. Sound good?"

"Sure," she said. She seemed like she was moving underwater, swimming through the air like gravity was ten times heavier than normal in her personal atmosphere.

"We have got to find a better place to do this," Danielle said. English had been a bust—we had talked a little, passed some notes, but it was impossible to have a real conversation. So we were in the 300 building bathroom, again. It wasn't ideal, but of all the bathrooms in the school, it was the biggest one. And the best kept. And the least convenient to get to. So that made it easier for us to talk without being interrupted too often. Which was important, since we only had ten minutes between second and third period.

"Maybe we could ask Mr. Terry if we could meet in his room at lunchtime or something," Vivi said.

Danielle laughed. "Oh, right. Like a club. The 'I See Dead People' Society! The 'Girl's Guide to Ghosts' Group!"

"Come on," Vivi said. Danielle rolled her eyes, and we fell silent. Now that we finally had a chance to talk about the dream situation, it seemed none of us wanted to touch it.

"Oh, hey, I meant to tell you, I talked to that Kevin guy again," I said.

Danielle made a funny face. "We went over how he's weird, right?"

"What's weird about him?" Vivi asked.

"He's just . . . you know, dark and broody and stuff," Danielle said, waving her hand. "Plus, I heard he's like a head case."

"Wait, who is this guy again?" Vivi asked.

"Oh, you know, he's that teacher's aide or whatever for Mr. Terry's class?" Danielle said. "He sits in, in like fifth period or something, and Mr. Terry lets him play teacher. Read through everyone's essays and grade tests and stuff." I blushed at the mention of essays and Danielle nudged me. "He thinks Daisy's essays are gooooood."

"Hey," I said, punching her back. "Why do you say that like it's a bad thing? And what do you mean he's a head case? You never said anything about that before. And besides, I don't think he's 'dark and broody and stuff.' I think he's totally—you know, normal."

Danielle widened her eyes and gracefully splayed her hands toward us like she was a hostess on a game show, gesturing to all the wonderful prizes. "Uh, your frame of reference for 'normal' may be slightly skewed, don't you think?"

"Whatever," I said, shaking my head.

She held up her hands in mock surrender. "Fine, fine. Your new boyfriend is neither weird nor a head case. And okay, okay, before you freak out about it, he's not your boyfriend, either. But you should know that he has kind of a reputation. Or, shall we say, a past."

"What is that supposed to mean?" I asked.

"He was locked up, okay?" Danielle said, her voice mockingly dramatic. "Not like *jail* locked up, I mean like psych-ward locked up."

I sat back, shocked. Danielle seemed to take pride in this revelation, and in my reaction to it. Before she'd seemed so excited about my talking with Kevin. Now she just seemed kind of mean. "When?" I asked. "And how do you know about any of this?"

"Hello, everybody knows about it. It's not like I have some secret knowledge or anything. I mean, I'm not like you guys with your"— she waved her hands—"*special powers*. It happened like two years ago. He just, I don't know, went nuts or something. His dad put him in lockdown at the psychiatric hospital. People said he was out of school for a couple of weeks, and then he just came back like nothing happened."

"Well, maybe nothing did," I said. He didn't *act* like someone who needed to be in a psych ward, even just for a visit.

"I don't know the whole story," Danielle conceded, but she sat back with a smug grin on her face anyway. "All I know is, he's weird."

"Well, I disagree. Or if he *was* weird at some point, the weirdness is now in remission. Because he's actually really funny. And really nice." I couldn't help smiling as I remembered our conversation. "And he takes the bus, like me."

"Ha!" Danielle laughed, looking like happy Danielle again. "Unbelievable! You like him! I mean, you LIKE like him!"

"I don't know," I played it off. "Kinda."

"Daisy has a boyfriend, Daisy has a boyfriend," Danielle sing-songed like we were little kids.

"Shut up!" I said.

"You guys," Vivi said, louder than I'd heard her speak in a while. "This isn't helping. We have like three more minutes before the bell rings, and we haven't talked about anything."

"Okay, okay, we'll stop talking about Daisy's real-life boyfriend so we can talk about your pretend one," Danielle said.

I knew she'd meant it as a joke, but the words hung in the air like icicles, brittle and sharp. She closed her eyes and winced, like she was about to apologize, but Vivi waved her hand.

"I know you can't understand it, but he's real," Vivi said flatly. But when she raised her eyes to look at us, I saw that she was more doubtful than she sounded. She cleared her throat. "Though I've noticed something recently. When I'm by myself, he's very weak. I mean, I know he's there, but I can't feel him or see him, or hear him talk to me. When I'm with you, Daisy, he gets stronger."

Both Vivi and Danielle looked at me.

I had begun to notice something, too: Whenever the three of us were together, a strange dynamic seemed to crop up. Danielle became aggressive and mad-seeming. Vivi became more sad and desperate. And I felt—subtly, but nonetheless palpably—that the energy was draining from me.

"Does he seem stronger now?" I asked.

"Yeah. Kind of."

"Because I feel weaker."

I felt a strange pressure on my shoulders, and then a wave of fatigue rolled over me. I felt like I was in the ocean, floating on one of those gentle waves that buoy you up as it rolls past, and I wanted to close my eyes for just a moment, to savor that strangely compelling sensation of displacement. But then I saw Vivi's eyes get very wide and I heard Danielle saying, "What? What is it?"

"Did you see?" Vivi said, pointing toward me. "He was just there—he put his hands on Daisy's shoulders, and then I could see him. He was shimmering, couldn't you see it?"

"Kind of?" Danielle squinted. "Maybe." She looked closer. "Nope, nothing. Once again, it's just you, Vivi. I don't see anything at all."

But I did. Out of the corner of my eye I saw motion, a small ripple of something disturbing the air as it moved, a glimmer or glint of sunlight glancing through the frosted bathroom window perhaps, or possibly a trick of the eye. Or maybe—just maybe—a glimpse of a ghost.

fourteen

"Daisy—didn't I just see you in second period? Is my class so nice you want to take it twice?" Mr. Terry said as I opened the door to his room, peeking in after third-period History to ask about us using his room during lunch.

I blushed. "No—I mean, yes, your class is fine, but—I mean—actually, I just wanted to ask you something."

"No, I'm sorry, you cannot do *extra* extra-credit." He paused to make sure I knew he was joking and then folded his arms. "Go ahead. Shoot. Ask away."

"I just wondered if it was okay for me and Danielle and Vivi to eat lunch in here today."

He walked around to the side of his desk, an amused look on his face. "Yes, I noticed the three of you seemed to have a lot on your minds in class this morning."

"Oh, gosh, I'm sorry, I didn't realize—"

"No, no, go ahead," he waved his hand. "What is my class good for if not stimulating discussion?"

"Well, now I feel terrible."

"Good, that was the goal. Now just promise me you'll stop yapping in class—unless I call on you, in which case your brilliant yapping is more than required. As for your question about lunch, that sounds fine with me."

"Okay, great. Thank you." He nodded at me and then went

back to his desk, rifling through the papers there. I lingered, wanting to talk more but not sure if I was brave enough to take the plunge.

Finally he put down his papers and looked at me. "What? I know you're not staying for the scintillating company. Out with it."

I looked at the floor and then I looked at the ceiling, and then I finally managed to say something.

"Why did you send me to get her?"

"What do you mean?"

"You know, Vivi. The other week? When she . . ."

Mr. Terry sat on his desk and exhaled like he was about to jump into the deep end of the pool. "I very much appreciate what you did for her. And I'm sorry to have put you in that situation."

"I don't mean that, I just mean . . . why did you pick me? Why send me, out of all the students in the class?"

He smiled at me, and it didn't seem like one of those patronizing teacher's smiles. "I thought the two of you might get along. You just seemed to me like you had something in common."

I nodded. "We do, kind of. But how did you know?"

"I didn't. I just suspected you might."

I shifted my weight from one foot to the other. "So there wasn't anything more to it? Something you knew about her—or me—that you thought was important?"

Now Mr. Terry crossed his arms and gave me one of his looks, the one he gives in class where he's slightly amused but more than prepared to put a stop to whatever nonsense is about to happen. "What's going on here, Daisy? Is there something you want to ask me directly, or do you want to keep going on this fishing expedition?"

I smiled, somewhat embarrassed. "No, I just thought—I don't know how much you know about what happened at my old school, or if you knew anything weird about me or anything."

"Ah, no, I can't say that I do," he said, the amused look turning into more of a bemused look by the second. "And, if you don't mind my anticipating your next question, I also don't know anything 'weird' about Vivi, either. I just thought the two of you might get along. That's it. Really." He moved around to sit behind his desk and began sorting through his papers. Then he looked up, an eyebrow arched and ready to strike. "Unless you think there's something I *should* know?"

I looked around us, both to ensure that nobody else was there, and to distract from how utterly nervous and uncomfortable I felt. "I'm not sure," I told him.

He put down his papers. "Is anyone in trouble?"

I shook my head.

"Is anyone in need of help?"

"I'm not sure."

"Is anyone in danger?"

"Oh, no. At least, I don't think so. Oh, God, you know, this was a mistake. I'm sorry to have brought it up, I'll just go now if that's okay," I said as I turned to leave.

"Hold on there," he said, rising from his desk. He had his serious teacher face on now. "I want you to listen to me. You can always come to me, to talk about anything. Now I don't understand what's going on here exactly, but I want you to understand that this is a safe place if you—or Vivi—or anyone else wants to talk. Okay?"

I nodded.

"Okay?" He repeated.

"Okay," I said. He looked at me doubtfully. I sighed. "I promise that when I really have something to talk to you about, I will come and talk to you."

He smiled, looking like friendly surfer-slash-English-teacher Mr. Terry again. "Good," he said, putting a teacherly hand on my shoulder and steering me out the door. "Now get to class. And, yes, come back at lunch, that's fine."

"Thanks," I said.

"And Daisy," he said, "I don't know anything about what happened at your old school. It's a clean slate in here. So, no worries about that."

I nodded my head.

Relief.

fifteen

At lunch, we sat in the corner of Mr. Terry's room, in the "conversation corner," the little hippie space he'd set up with beanbag chairs and a latch-hook rug for "class-time, teacher-approved conversation, contemplation, or composition," as he'd put it. Mostly people used it to catch up on their reading, or work on their assignments during "workshop" days, or as a Mr. Terry–sanctioned way to veg out in class. But we were going to use it, of course, to talk about the supernatural.

Mr. Terry sat at his desk on the other side of the room, seemingly absorbed in grading papers.

"Are you sure this is okay?" I whispered to Danielle and Vivi. "I mean, I didn't think he was actually going to be staying here . . ."

Mr. Terry's voice was bored-sounding as he spoke from behind his stack of papers without so much as raising an eyebrow in our direction. "Ladies, I assure you, I am not eavesdropping, nor am I particularly interested in your conversation. Anything I inadvertently overhear will surely be drowned out by the clamor of my internal screams at confronting the grammatical errors, run-on sentences, and absolutely unacceptable misspellings on these papers. Feel free to proceed."

"Thanks, Mr. Terry," Danielle said. "Besides, you're like our priest here. Or our therapist, or lawyer or whatever—you're bound by confidentiality. Right?"

"Wrong. But in general, anything that happens inside this classroom stays in this classroom," he said without looking up.

"See?" Danielle said, turning back to us. "Just like Vegas."

"Okay, okay," I said. I still kept my voice a whisper, and I turned my back so that I faced away from Mr. Terry, just in case.

"So, how is this going to work?" Danielle said. I could feel her energy vibrant and nervous, a propelling force beneath her chatter. "Can I be the president? I'm the president, okay? Vivi, you can be the secretary, take notes and stuff. Daisy . . . I don't know, do we need a treasurer? Okay, so I hereby call to order the first meeting of the Dead Ghosts Society—"

"It's not a club!" I said. "And keep your voice down!"

"Okay, scratch that. How about—Ghost Hunters. Or we could just call ourselves the Supernaturals. Though that sounds more like a singing group."

"We do not need a name! This is not a club! We're just . . . talking about stuff," I said, exasperated. "Weird stuff."

"You guys are no fun at all," Danielle said, pouting as she crossed her arms. Then she relented. "Fine, whatever. But in my head, I'm going to keep calling us the Dead Ghosts Society."

I rolled my eyes. "Look, I get that this is freaky or whatever, and it's more fun to joke about it than actually deal with it, but since we're here already, can we just start dealing before lunch is over?"

"Fine," Danielle said. Vivi just sat there, placid and blank, as though she were really somewhere else.

I looked over my shoulder to make sure Mr. Terry was still buried in his papers, and then I leaned in, still keeping my voice quiet so he wouldn't overhear anything.

"Okay. So, the dream. I don't know how it was for you, but for me it was all just so vivid, like it was really happening. I couldn't stop thinking about it during my classes, so I started writing down all the stuff I remembered." I rifled through my bag to find my notebook. "I wish I was as good at drawing as you are, Vivi. Everything was so detailed I could totally draw it from memory

85

if I had any artistic ability whatsoever. Although, hey—that's an idea."

"What?" Vivi said.

"You could sketch it for us," I said. "I mean, I know it would be from your perspective and not maybe exactly like what I saw or Danielle saw in the dream, but it would be really cool to see it all drawn out."

Vivi shifted uneasily. "I don't know," she said.

"What is it?" I asked.

She looked at us with a worried expression. "I just—I didn't have the dream."

"What?" Danielle said. "But you were in it! You were Lily, right?" She turned to me, tugging on my arm. "She was Lily, wasn't she?"

Vivi shook her head.

"You didn't dream that you were at some kind of party? Like, in olden times?" Danielle asked.

She shook her head. "I didn't actually have any dream last night." Her eyes were big. Innocent anime eyes, the kind of eyes you see on baby animals or cartoon characters. She couldn't be lying to us.

"Why didn't you say something before?" I asked.

Vivi looked down, defeated. "I was going to," she said. "But then I thought maybe I just didn't remember—that if I heard you guys talk about it, it would all come back to me."

Danielle slumped back onto her beanbag chair. "This makes no sense! Why would Patrick the Friendly Ghost be sending me and Daisy dreams and not cutting you in on the deal? Not that I believe there is actually a ghost talking to you and telling you what to do and putting dreams in our heads and, oh my God, I have been completely infected by you guys and now I am *insane!*"

"Ladies," we heard Mr. Terry say. At first I thought he'd overheard our conversation, but I looked over to see him pointing a finger at the clock without so much as raising his head from his stack of papers. It was almost time for the end of lunch and the start of fifth period. As if on cue, the bell rang.

"Well," I said.

"Yeah," Danielle said, starting to gather her things. "I guess that wraps up this meeting of the Crazy People Who Talk to Ghosts and Other Random People Who Have the Same Dream Club."

Vivi closed her eyes and sighed.

"Come on, let's get going," Danielle said as the door opened and students began filing into the classroom. I stood up and grabbed my bag, preparing to follow Vivi and Danielle as we headed to fifth period, but I was lost in my thoughts, trying to puzzle out the possible meanings of our shared but not-so-shared dream.

"Hey!" Kevin said, surprising me. "Fancy meeting you here."

"Oh, hi," I stammered. I saw Danielle rolling her eyes from just beyond where Kevin stood.

"I'll catch up with you in Trig," she said. "Have fun—" and then she mouthed the words *talking to your WEIRD boyfriend.*

I blushed furiously. "Shut up, I'm coming," I told her, waving her away and trying to ignore her making a kissy face over Kevin's shoulder. "So, what are you doing here?" I said to Kevin.

"This is where the TA magic happens," he grinned. I saw Danielle finally give up trying to embarrass me, leaving with Vivi.

"Oh, right. Well . . ." I paused, suddenly at a loss without Danielle to distract me.

"Still working out your story?"

I was caught off guard. "Story?"

"You know, your reverse Orpheus?"

Oh, right. That. "Yeah, pretty much," I said.

"Any progress?"

"Not that I can really make sense of," I told him. "It's all still just . . . complicated."

"Huh," he said. "Anything new? Or just the same old storyline?"

"Well," I said, moving off to the side, so that we were talking out of the way of the kids still coming into class. "Was there anything in that Orpheus story about dreams?"

"Dreams?" He thought about it for a moment, looking up into

the corner of the room as if there were a movie screen of knowledge visible only to him. He squinted his eyes a little bit. I couldn't help my heart racing as I watched him think. *Oh, man, you've got it baaaad,* Danielle would say if she were still here, looking over his shoulder, trying to make me blush. I blushed a little anyway.

"Yeah, dreams," I said, trying to get myself back on track and focusing on the conversation instead of on how tall and smart and awesome he was, or the way his eyes always looked smiling and sleepy even when he wasn't smiling or sleeping. I felt like Jane in the dream, flitty and flighty when she talked with James. My thoughts raced. How could Danielle think he was weird? What did she mean by all that "head-case" stuff? I shook my head: *Back on track, Daisy.* "Particularly vivid or realistic-seeming dreams?"

"Oh, vivid dreams," he said, nodding his head. "I get those."

"Anything . . . weird?" I winced as soon as I said it, as though he might somehow know about Danielle calling him weird before. But then I had a chilling thought: What if he had had the dream, too? Had he been in the dream? *Oh my God, was he James?* But he shrugged.

"Nah, just the usual—you know: I'm at school, there's a big test but I haven't studied . . . plus I'm naked, I can fly, and all my teeth fall out." He looked at me and then his deadpan face broke into a grin. "Oh, come on, just a little dream humor."

"No, I get it," I said.

"Actually," he said, serious again, "there is something. As it turns out, Hades, the lord-of-the-underworld guy, was also the master of dreams and nightmares." As he said this, all the hairs on my arms stood on end, and my heart raced even more than it had when I'd dreamily watched him think. "Hades controlled these dream demons, called the Oneiroi, who were like the dark spirits of dreams. They would go out at night and plop dreams into people's heads. Sometimes they'd even bring messages from the dead, in the form of dreams."

"So, you mean like—dreams sent by ghosts?" Suddenly I felt dizzy, and I put my hand on the classroom wall to steady myself. I tried to make it seem normal, like I was normal, but I felt like the ground was shifting underneath me, a rolling, ominous earthquake.

"Yeah. Crazy, right?" he said. "Oh, yeah. And get this: The entrance to the underworld had two gates, one made of horn and one made of ivory. So the Oneiroi carrying *true* dreams would go through the horn gate, and the ones with *false* dreams would go through the ivory gate."

My mind was racing. Hades, the king of hell, basically, could send out dreams, true ones and false ones, whenever he wanted, to whomever he wanted. This did not sound good. Was that what was happening to us? Were we being sent dreams from hell? And were they true dreams or false ones?

"Could he make people dream the same dreams?" I asked. "Or send people the same dreams?"

"I don't know," he said. "Could be. I'd have to look it up."

"Wow," I managed. My throat felt like it was closing up. I started turning to walk away before I even realized what I was doing. I just felt like I had to move, I had to get out of there, I had to think.

"You okay?" he asked.

"Yeah, uh . . . I've got to get to class," I said, and I started for the door without even saying good-bye.

"Okay, well. Glad I could . . . help?"

I wanted to turn around and say something to him as I left, but then I remembered Orpheus in Hades, and I thought: *Don't look back.*

sixteen

gift

I'm in a small one-room building, a schoolhouse, gathering books and placing them on bookshelves. Through the window I see a path leading to a field, and beyond that a house with a broad porch.

Of course, I think. *It's the day after the party. I'm in the schoolhouse. I am Jane again.*

There is a heaviness weighing on me, a sadness I can't shake.

Veronica.

She never came home.

"There you are," I hear, as a woman walks into the room. In the dream, I understand she is my mother, and that she is the teacher of this small school, but the part of me that's still Daisy doing the dreaming recognizes her as my mom in real life.

"Remember, we leave in the morning," she says. I know this trip has been planned for a while, but I wish I didn't have to go. As if she knows my thoughts, she says, "With everything that's going on right now, I think we could use a bit of a holiday, don't you?"

She's referring to Veronica, I know, and Lily's attacker—both of whom are still nowhere to be found.

"Of course," I say.

Before she turns to leave, she puts her hands on my shoulders and smoothes my braids. "A weekend visiting your cousins will do us both good. I'm sure by the time we get back, your friend will be home, safe and sound."

"I hope so," I say, but my chest feels tight with doubt.

I watch her through the window as she returns to the house. I wish I could share her certainty about Veronica's eventual return. There is a pit in my stomach that has only expanded since she ran off into the field, since James returned from his search by himself, without her.

I put the last of the books away. Just as I'm about to leave, I glance up at the window again. In the distance, coming toward the schoolhouse, I see Lily. Even from here she seems dazed, walking slowly, as if she doesn't trust the ground beneath her. Suddenly, James is at her side. He grabs her arm rudely. I can see the shock register on her face. I pull back from the window, in case they can see me, and watch as he stands too close to her.

She yanks her elbow away from his grip. Even though she keeps her head down, her eyes on the ground, I can see that she is talking, and that he doesn't like what she has to say.

Then he says something to her and she nods her head. When she looks up at him, I can see that she doesn't look ghostly or insubstantial anymore.

She looks afraid.

James glances over his shoulder, and for a moment I think he can see me in the window. I duck down. When I stand up again, they are both gone.

My heart races. This doesn't make sense to me. Why would James speak that way to her? He must be upset about Veronica, I reason. He must be out of his mind with worry. Otherwise how else could he be so cruel?

As I walk to the door of the schoolhouse, I suddenly feel the warmth leave my body.

I'm waking up.

Again the dream falls away from itself, my surroundings disintegrating into nothingness, a blank landscape, and all I can see is Lily, her pale skin shocked with blood, a butcher's knife in her hand, urging me—commanding me, Daisy, Jane, whoever is there to hear her—

Run.

seventeen

In the morning I waited for Danielle and Vivi at the front of the school again, hoping to catch them to talk about the latest dream. But the bell rang, and then the final bell rang, and still neither one showed. I lingered as long as I could under the suspicious eye of Mr. Avila, and then I finally gave up and went to class. *Maybe they're both absent,* I thought. But then there they both were, in English, like always. Vivi seemed the same as usual, which is to say unusual. But Danielle seemed to be actively avoiding me. I tried to talk to her before class started, but she pretended to be wrapped up in finding a missing homework assignment. Then during class she refused to catch my eye, seeming a thousand percent invested in whatever Mr. Terry had to say. She took so many notes it was like she was transcribing everything that was happening, documenting everything, right down to the pauses and throat-clearings and sounds of marker on white board. Midway through Mr. Terry's lecture about Julius Caesar, I couldn't take it anymore. I passed her a note. I folded it in our special way and everything.

We really need to talk about the dream, it said. *Let's meet at lunch in Mr. Terry's room. P.S. You can be the president.*

She took the note from me but left it on her desk, unfolded, practically out in the open, as she took notes on what Mr. Terry was saying. I couldn't understand what was going on. Finally, I reached my foot across the aisle and tapped the leg of her chair. She looked in my

93

direction with an annoyed expression on her face and gestured with her hands as if to say, *What?* I pointed to the note, and she rolled her eyes and made a big deal out of opening it. Then she scribbled something and practically threw the piece of paper back to me.

So much for our special note-folding technique. Or trying to fly under the radar. I saw Mr. Terry homing in on our side of the room, his eyes like a magpie on the alert for shiny things. Except in his case it was chatter and note-passing. I slid the piece of paper underneath my notebook and tried to appear interested in his lecture, poised to write down anything he might say. He gave me a critical look and then returned to whatever he was writing on the board.

I pulled out the note to see what Danielle had written. It said, *I don't want to talk about it.*

While Mr. Terry's back was still turned, I kicked her chair again, and she finally looked at me directly and whispered, "Just drop it. Okay?"

Mr. Terry, his back still facing the class, said loudly, "Ms. Parker? You have something to contribute?"

Danielle glared at me and faced forward in her seat. "Uh, no. I just . . . didn't hear what you said about that one part you were just saying."

He glanced over his shoulder. "Yes, I find it hard to hear what other people are saying when I am talking while they are talking. But in any case, I had just mentioned the Ides of March. Anyone care to fill Ms. Parker in on what the heck that means?"

An army of hands shot up and Mr. Terry began calling on people. Danielle shook her head at me and whispered, "I need a break. I don't want to talk about it. The end."

I nodded even though I didn't understand.

Danielle continued to ignore me in History and in Chem, just in case I hadn't gotten the message. But I hoped that even if she didn't want to talk about the dreams, we could still talk about what was bothering her. So at lunch I went to Mr. Terry's room, in the hopes that either she or Vivi might show up.

Mr. Terry sat at his desk, again going through papers. Or pretending to. "Everything okay?" he asked, without looking up. It seemed offhand and nonchalant, but I sensed it wasn't an entirely innocuous question.

"Uh-huh," I said, taking a bite of my sandwich. I didn't even feel hungry. "I'm just waiting for Vivi and Danielle."

"Vivi went home sick today," he said, looking up, his hands folded, a red pen sticking up from between his fingers like a flag. I tried not to look surprised. He unclasped his hands and went back to marking errors with his felt pen. Sometimes my papers came back stained with so much red it looked like they had been in battle. You could see where Mr. Terry was emphatic about his corrections, or his praise—the ink saturated the paper in those places, tiny veins of red spidering out from each letter of his underlined remark. The sheer amount of red on my papers had been startling at first, but I soon learned it wasn't always punitive, and it didn't always mean you'd written something bad. His comments were always helpful, and it had become a kind of game with me to anticipate what errors he might find, what conclusions he might think were lazy, what grammatical traps I might fall into. "She didn't feel so hot after my class today—not that I take that personally—so I sent her to the nurse."

"And she went home?" I said.

"That is what I heard," he said, his eyes back on the paper. I hadn't realized the nurse reported stuff like that to the teachers. It made sense, I supposed. But, no offense to Mr. Terry, why hadn't Vivi said anything to me? "You are still welcome to stay here. Even if your note-passing compatriot fails to join you."

I put down my sandwich, my face burning. "Sorry."

He gave a self-satisfied grin. "Ah, it never gets old, making students squirm." Then he made a face at the paper he was attacking with his pen. "Come here," he said, gesturing to me. "I won't name any names here, but can you tell me what's wrong with this picture?"

I set my stuff down and went over to his desk. He held the paper out toward me, the student's name obscured by his thumb. I scanned it quickly, trying to look for what might be the most likely thing Mr. Terry wanted me to find.

"There's a lot to choose from," he said. "Just pick one."

"Well . . . it looks like whoever wrote this uses commas instead of periods. So it's like one giant run-on sentence."

"For three pages!" He sighed and let the paper fall to his desk. "This is why I need minions."

"Like, you mean, TAs? Like . . . Kevin?" I tried to say his name without blushing, but failed.

"Yes, exactly. Like Kevin." He looked at me as he shaped his pile of papers into a neat stack once again. "Or you. You might make a fine TA in a couple of years."

"Whatever," I said, embarrassed.

"You will have to strike that word from your vocabulary, to be sure—and also dial back the class-time note-passing—but yes. You can talk to Kevin about what it's like. Essentially it's a great way to sharpen your own skills and get class credit all at the same time— not to mention help out your favorite English teacher and quite possibly affect the lives of fledgling English students in a positive manner. And, of course, with such great responsibility comes great power." He wagged his pen in front of me. "Your very own red pen."

I smiled.

"Think about it," he said. "It's down the road, to be sure. And first you have to survive not just *my* class without being arrested for passing notes, but Mrs. MacIntyre's eleventh-grade English as well. But I think it could be a fun thing for you when you're a senior."

"I'll think about it," I said.

"Good!"

Just then I heard the door open, and a well of relief opened in me as well. Danielle had finally showed. We could get past whatever this was that was making her shut me out. Before I could even fully exhale a sigh of relief and turn around to see her, I heard Mr. Terry say, "Ah, Kevin, we were just talking about you," and I realized it wasn't her after all. She wasn't coming.

"All good, I hope," Kevin said, walking over to where we stood.

"I was just trying to brainwash Daisy here into becoming a TA when the time comes."

"Cool," Kevin said, and Mr. Terry rolled his eyes.

"Have I taught you nothing?"

"By which I mean to say—excellent idea," Kevin backpedaled.

"You children and your slang. Everything is 'cool' this, and 'gnarly' that." Mr. Terry stopped as we regarded him with confusion. He sighed. "I am old. I am not going to explain 'gnarly.' Just accept that it was something that teenagers used to say. Go, eat your lunch, be gone with you." He waved us off.

I went back to the conversation corner, packing up the remnants of my sandwich while Kevin handed a stack of papers to Mr. Terry.

"You taking off?" Kevin dropped his backpack on the beanbag next to mine.

"Eventually," I said, glancing at the clock above the white board. "I was just finishing my lunch, kind of waiting for Danielle."

"Well, I'm done with my lunch, so I'm just waiting for class to start," he said, sitting down. "Want company?"

I shrugged. "I guess. She's not coming, anyway."

"Ouch," he said.

"No, I didn't mean it like that," I said. "I just—she's mad at me or something. It's all just crazy."

"I think you've used that word pretty much every time I've talked to you," he said.

"Really?"

"Crazy story, crazy day . . ."

"Crazy life," I said.

"How is your story going, anyway?" he asked. "How's that dream stuff going?"

I froze. How did he know about the dreams?

"The Oneiroi? Hades?" he prompted.

Right. *That* dream stuff. "Um, good," I said. "Fine."

We sat in silence for a moment. I wrapped my arms around my legs, resting my chin on my knees and watching the door for Danielle, just in case.

"You know, I guess it's really none of my business," he said, looking down at the frayed latch-hook rug. Some student of Mr. Terry's had made it long ago—maybe so long ago that this student had actually used the word 'gnarly' in conversation with other people who actually knew what that meant. "But it kind of seems to me like there's more going on for you in this than just a story." He looked up, his eyes squinting sympathetically, that one-sided smile on his face. "Not that I mean to pry."

"Oh, yeah, no," I stuttered, sitting up a little. "No, it's not prying."

He looked at me expectantly.

"And no, you're right, it's not just a story. Well, it is," I hedged, "but it isn't."

He nodded. "Like I said, really none of my business. But, well, I guess I just kind of know what it's like to experience what you might call . . . weirdness? So. You know. Just if you ever . . ."

Mr. Terry banged his papers on the desk as he stood them up on end to gather them into a neat stack, and cleared his throat. "Kevin, Daisy—there's about ten minutes until the end of lunch. Can I ask you to keep an eye on the room while I run to the teacher's lounge? Without coffee or some other form of caffeination, it's highly unlikely that I will be able to retain consciousness."

"Sure," Kevin said.

"Excellent," Mr. Terry said, heading for the door. "Carry on."

I was poised on the edge of something, I was sure. I just didn't know what was over that edge, whether it led to a bottomless pit or a safety net. But I decided I couldn't stand it anymore, just waiting there hoping for someone else to give me a push. I decided to make the leap.

"Okay," I said, my body flooding with a yellow-orange rush of energy. I glanced at the nearby clock to make sure I wasn't triggering anything inadvertently and slowed my breathing for a moment to keep myself calm. "You're right. There's more to the story than, well, the story."

"Okay."

"But it's crazy," I warned.

"We've established that."

"And I don't know that I can fit everything into ten minutes."

"It's a start," he shrugged.

"And you're probably not going to believe me," I said.

His mouth twisted into a smile.

"So, I'll just come out and say it," I said.

He made a gesture with his hands like *bring it*.

I took another deep breath.

"It's true that the story is about a girl who's in love with a guy who's a ghost. But it's also true that it's not a story. It's real life. It's Vivi. She's the girl. And she's being haunted by a ghost."

His eyes grew big, but he didn't freak out or run away. So I took another breath and kept talking.

eighteen

Danielle continued to shut me out. She wasn't particularly mean about it or anything. She just seemed exhausted, too tired to care. In class she was a zombie. No wry remarks, no engaging conversation, barely even paying attention. She said hello if I said hello, and she responded to anything I said with minimal, one-word answers, but I felt her energy edging away from me when I was near, and I couldn't breach it. It was like that for two days straight. Vivi was no help. We had half-hearted lunch sessions in Mr. Terry's room, just me and Vivi, but she had no insight into what was going on with Danielle—who wasn't talking to Vivi, either—and she wasn't having any dreams. None at all, in fact. I had them every night, one or the other, the dream of the party or the dream at the schoolhouse, each one ending with that chilling vision of Lily—but hers was evidently a completely dreamless sleep. Mostly we just sat on the beanbag chairs together, with her asking me to be very still so she could listen for Patrick. Who was also no longer talking to her.

Then, on Wednesday, officially day three of the silent treatment, I walked into Mr. Terry's room at lunchtime and saw him tilt his head in the direction of the conversation corner. And there she was. Normally Danielle's energy was a kind of coiled excitement, something waiting to be unbounded, like one of those joke cans with a pop-up snake inside. But instead she sat slumped over on a beanbag chair, her eyes underlined with dark circles she hadn't even bothered to try to cover with makeup. Her hair fell around her face in a way that was practically feral, and her mouth twisted into a nervous frown. Her usual orange vibe of exuberance was replaced by a dull, rust brown of slow pulsing waves I could barely pick up.

"Are you okay?" I asked. "Are you talking to me now?"

She ignored my second question and sighed as she continued to look at the floor. "I'm just really wiped. I haven't been sleeping."

"At all?" I sat down next to her.

"Yeah, no, I mean I guess I've been sleeping. Just not very well," she said. She looked at me and her face was tense. "It's the dreams, you know?"

I knew. The nights I had them, I felt like I barely slept at all, they were so vivid. Now that we were finally talking about it again, I didn't want to say too much, for fear of making her go quiet once more, but I couldn't help saying at least something. "It's crazy. There's just so much going on."

But she shook her head. "It's not that. It's not that at all."

"What do you mean?"

"It's the exact opposite. It's why I wanted to stop talking about it in the first place." She paused and took a shaky deep breath in, exhaling loudly. "I go to sleep, you know, like normal. And then eventually I start to have the dream. The same dream."

"You mean, like the same dream as me?"

"No, I mean like *the same dream*. It happens over and over. We're at the party, we're talking, I get upset, and then I run out into the field. And I just keep running and running. But I never go any-where. It's just . . . dark. Like, blank. And when I turn around to go back, there's nothing. There's no way back. It's all just blackness. And I keep thinking, wake up, wake up, but I can't wake up. I'm stuck there. It's dark and it's terrifying, and I can't wake up. I try to scream, but I can't. I try to move, but I can't. It's like I'm paralyzed, like I'm trapped, and then it's hard to breathe, and—"

She was nearly hyperventilating. She stopped talking and wiped her eyes, tried to breathe normally. I stayed very still and tried to send blue calming waves of energy in her direction, to help her relax. She looked at me imploringly.

"It's horrible. I started setting my alarm for the middle of the night to wake myself up so I won't be trapped there forever."

"You can't get trapped in a dream," I said, trying to be soothing. I probably sounded like my mother.

She laughed, and her voice was harsh when she spoke. "Are you kidding me? You have no idea what you're talking about. You have no idea how scary this is. I wake up from the alarm and I stay up for a little while, totally spooked, but I'm exhausted, so I set my alarm and fall asleep again, and then it happens again, and then my alarm goes off, and the cycle repeats, over and over, until it's time for me to get up and go to school."

"Did you try, I don't know, sleeping pills?" I asked.

"Nothing helps," she said, looking at me pointedly. "If you're even thinking of something to suggest, believe me, I've already tried it. There is a freaking ghost messing with my head. Let me know when they make a pill for that, okay?"

I let the silence pool around us. Mr. Terry made teacherly sounds at his desk. I could hear the second hand of the clock mechanically chugging away as it rounded the dial.

"I'm guessing it hasn't been like that for you," she said.

"Not as bad," I admitted. "I've had different dreams. Well, I've had that first dream, with you and the party and the field, a couple of times. And then this other one, where I'm in the schoolhouse. Every night it's one or the other, and every time they happen the same way. Both of them always end with something really scary."

"Well, that's a relief, I guess. That it's not just me being scared. What about Vivi?"

"What *about* Vivi," I said. "She's like a ghost herself these days. She said she hasn't been having any dreams at all. Just blank. And nothing from Patrick."

"Huh," she said. "I guess I'd take no dreams at all over nightmares."

"Actually, that reminds me," I said, kind of thinking out loud. "I was talking to Kevin about it, and he said—"

Danielle fixed me with a look that was all the more menacing due to the fatigue on her face. "You were talking to *Kevin* about it?"

"Well, yeah, but—"

"No, no, back up. You were talking. To Kevin. About this crazy ghost-dream-psychic stuff?" She sighed heavily. "Are you out of your mind? Why would you be talking to *anyone* about this crap?"

"It's not like I could talk to *you*," I said, before I could stop myself.

"Don't even," she warned.

"No, seriously, listen, it is not a big deal. He's not going to . . . *tell* or anything." I stole a furtive glance in Mr. Terry's direction. "And besides, he's really smart about this stuff. He told me about dreams and nightmares, about mythology stuff, like how people believed that dreams were sent by demons from the underworld, and sometimes they were true dreams, and sometimes they were false dreams—"

Danielle put her hands over her ears. "Stop talking, just stop talking about this."

"Look, all I'm saying is, maybe what's happening now is that you're stuck in some kind of false dream loop or something," I said. "Maybe we just need to find a way to stop the cycle and get you out."

We both looked up to see Vivi striding toward us, moving with a purpose she hadn't demonstrated in weeks.

"I think I have an idea," she said.

nineteen

Vivi held the pen lightly with just her fingertips, dangling it above the page so that its felt tip barely touched.

"What's supposed to happen?" Danielle asked, but Vivi shushed her and shook her head.

Danielle gave me a look of exasperation, but I made a *wait-wait* motion with my hand, and she rolled her eyes and settled in.

Vivi had been totally energized as she explained to us what she'd been reading about: automatic writing. She said it was a way to communicate with the spirit world. And she hoped it might be a way to reconnect with Patrick, who, it seemed, had gone totally silent.

We leaned in closer to see what would happen as Vivi closed her eyes and breathed in deeply.

Suddenly, the pen began to move.

"Is she doing that?" Danielle asked.

"*Shh,*" I said. "Just watch!"

Vivi kept her eyes closed, and her hand wavered above the page. The pen touched the surface lightly as though it had a mind of its own.

H

It looked scraggly, like the handwriting of a child. Or perhaps just the way an H might look if you tried to draw one with your eyes closed. The pen's tip jumped to the space next to the H and began a downward trajectory, a squiggly line roughly the same size as the letter next to it. Then a wavering line extending from the top, another one from the middle, another one on the bottom.

E

We all held our breath as Vivi's pen continued to move. Another downward stroke, another line extending to the right.

L

Then again, the same pattern.

L

Vivi stopped for a moment, and I felt chills all over. *Hell?*

Then, abruptly, the pen circled on the page.

O

"'Hello'?" Danielle read. "Are you messing with us?"

"What," Vivi said, opening her eyes. "What did it say?"

"Like you don't already know," Danielle scoffed.

"Seriously, I really didn't," Vivi said, sitting back and looking at the paper. "I didn't know what was going to come through."

"What did it feel like?" I asked. "Did it feel like when you usually talk to Patrick?"

"No, of course not," Vivi said, looking disappointed.

"What do you mean?" I asked.

"Well, for one thing, I wasn't talking to Patrick. It was someone else. I'm sure of it."

Danielle slumped on the beanbag and exhaled loudly, her voice teary and tired when she finally spoke. "I can't do this anymore, guys. I just can't take it. It's too much for me. You know? I mean, a ghost, telepathic dreams, this automatic writing stuff, now another ghost. . . . I think I'm out."

"What? No, you can't be out!" I said, grabbing her arm.

"Besides," Vivi said. "I think the person or spirit or whatever we were communicating with here wasn't talking to me. It was talking to you."

"To me?" Danielle asked, looking skeptical.

"Yes, I think so," Vivi said, as if this was all perfectly ordinary. "It's just a feeling I got while I was doing it."

Danielle sighed, and I could tell she was weighing her options: bolt from the room and be done with all this nonsense, or stay with us and embrace it.

"Give me that thing," she said, grabbing the pen out of Vivi's hand and swiping the paper from her. She turned it over to the side that was fresh and looked at both of us with determined eyes. "Okay, so how do I do this?"

"Just hold the pen lightly," Vivi said, "as lightly as you can without dropping it. And then just close your eyes and let it happen."

"Just let it happen," Danielle repeated, sounding dubious. But she steadied her hand on the cap of the pen and closed her eyes. Vivi and I watched as words took shape upon the page.

HELP
ME

Danielle opened her eyes, and for a moment she was silent.

"Wow. You guys," she said, clearing her throat to steady her voice. "I mean, I thought about writing all kinds of things. But not that."

"You didn't write it," Vivi said. "Someone else did."

"Who?" Danielle demanded. "Who could possibly be asking me for help? This is freaking me out."

"Try it again," Vivi said. "Ask who's talking to you."

Danielle shook her head like that was ridiculous, but she held her hand out, closing her eyes and dangling the pen above the paper again, and soon we saw more wavery letters appear.

VERONICA

Danielle opened her eyes. Once she saw what was written on the paper, she dropped the pen as though it were on fire.

"Veronica?" She raked her hands through her hair. "That's the girl from the dream. I mean, in my dreams, I'm her, and she's trapped. I'm trapped. How can I help? How can I do anything?"

"Maybe we just need to tell her everything's okay?" I said. "Maybe she just needs to know that someone's heard her."

"What am I supposed to do, write back?" she retorted.

Vivi took my hand in her left and Danielle's in her right, and nodded at me, wordlessly urging me to take hold of Danielle's other hand so that we sat in a small circle, all holding hands, the paper and pen on the floor in the middle of us. Danielle's hand felt shaky and weak in mine; Vivi's felt surprisingly strong. I drew in a breath, closing my eyes, and before I realized it, a gentle wave of energy traveled from the base of my skull down through my shoulders, my elbows, my wrists, my hands, my fingers, and out into each of their hands.

"Everything is okay," Vivi said quietly, speaking to Danielle or to the visiting spirit I wasn't sure. "It is safe for you now. You may go. Be at peace."

I felt a sensation of lightness and a tiny shock to my fingertips as the energy I had sent out zipped back up my arms, retracting. I opened my eyes to see Vivi still sitting with her eyes closed, Danielle barely able to keep hers open.

"Maybe you'll be able to sleep tonight," I said.

"I hope so," she replied, curling herself into a ball on the bean-bag chair. "Did it really work?"

Vivi shrugged. "I don't know. It felt like something was happening. But I can't be sure." She took out another piece of paper from her notebook and held the pen over it. "Now let me see if I can get through to Patrick."

She sat with the pen hovering, poised to write. After half a minute had passed I heard Danielle's steady, even breathing and realized she had fallen asleep.

twenty

Even though Danielle had initially been irritated by the fact
that I'd spilled everything to Kevin, once she finally got a night of
actual deep, dreamless sleep—thanks to the automatic writing ses-
sion—she didn't seem too annoyed by much of anything. When
I told her the next day that Kevin might join us at lunch, she was
more or less cool about it.

I, however, was a little nervous.

"Kevin!" we heard Mr. Terry say, and I felt my heart race crazily
just knowing that he was in the room. I sat facing Danielle and Vivi,
so I tried to keep my face neutral. But when I saw by their expressions that he must have been walking in our direction, I had a hard
time keeping my energy in check. I heard Danielle's phone buzzing
from deep within her backpack, and I winced to let her know that it
was me and not a real call.

I twisted around to see Mr. Terry stand up from his desk and
gesture toward us.

"So, you're joining the ladies who lunch?"

Danielle wrinkled her nose. "Ew. When you put it like that, it
sounds so . . . Something My Mom Would Do." She shivered in
mock disgust.

"Just sitting in for a bit," Kevin said. "If they'll have me."

Vivi and Danielle sat with arms crossed, regarding him with suspicion, but I gestured for him to sit next to me on the floor.

"Well, I'll leave you in their capable hands, then," Mr. Terry said. "I'll be back by the end of lunch, so try to keep things down to a dull roar while I'm gone. No wild parties or anything."

We waved him off.

Kevin sat down next to me. I marveled at his ability to seem so casual. I could never walk into a room of his friends and plop myself down like I totally belonged there. And yet he was so normal about it. I couldn't feel normal, not with him sitting next to me: The left side of my body felt supercharged where his arm grazed mine, and I half expected sparks to fly out of my head just from the effort of trying to stay calm. It all felt so unreal. He was here, sitting next to me, hanging out with my friends.

"So, Mr. Terry brings up a good point," Danielle said. She had uncrossed her arms, but I could still sense the spikiness of her energy. I could tell she wasn't able to resist giving him a bit of a hard time. "About joining us, I mean."

"Yes?" Kevin asked. He smiled his most disarming smile, and I marveled that either of them could just sit there and not instantly succumb to it.

"Why are you here?" she demanded, smiling back.

I was prepared to be defensive on his behalf, but he seemed to take it in stride.

"You mean, like, in general? Or—"

"I mean, like, you're a *senior*. Why would you bother to come here and hang out with *sophomores*? Isn't that, like, against the law of high school? Don't you have your own friends?"

"Danielle!" I said.

"What? It's a question!"

He looked at Vivi, who looked steadily at the floor, and at Danielle, who held his gaze like they were having a staring contest.

"Well," he said, "as it happens, I happen to like hanging out with at least one of you."

He took my hand in his, and electricity coursed through my fingers, up my arm and right into my brain. I looked at him, alarmed, but he was still smiling that one-sided smile of his, as though absolutely nothing unusual was happening.

"Static electricity? Sorry, didn't mean to zap you," he said to me before turning back to Danielle. I felt myself blushing as I felt pulsing electricity zip-zapping along my arms, my chest, my heart.

"And Daisy's told me some pretty intriguing stuff about what's been going on with you guys. Way more interesting than stuff I usually get to talk about. So, if you're up for it, I'd like to help, if I can, or at least hear more about it."

"You do realize you're holding her hand, right?" Danielle asked.

"Uh-oh, have I violated some kind of 'ladies who lunch' rule?"

She fixed him with her serious face, but when he looked down briefly to inspect our held hands, she snuck a quick glance at me to signal with her eyes that this turn of events was unprecedentedly awesome.

He gave my hand a squeeze, then dropped it to hold both his hands up in surrender to Danielle. "Got it, no hands. Any other rules I should know about?"

"Just don't tell anyone else about the stuff we talk about. Though I guess that rule's really mostly for Daisy," she said.

"Though I guess not anymore because he's the only person I told and I'm not going to tell anyone else," I said, mocking her tone.

"Fine," she said. "And . . . I don't know. I guess that's it. Just . . . don't be weird about stuff."

"Don't tell anyone, don't be weird," he repeated. "Done."

"Well? What do you guys think?" I asked.

Vivi finally looked up at us. "He can stay."

twenty-one

After school on Friday, Vivi and Danielle and I walked the mile or so from Castle Creek to Danielle's place. Danielle's post–automatic writing sleep reset had been remarkable: It was like a switch had been flipped for her. She was back to her usual gregarious self, no longer moody or snippy, instead laughing and joking and sneaking best-friendy notes to me in class (*OMG, holding HANDS with you right in front of us! Dude! Who does that?*) as though her silent treatment had been merely another passing dream we'd shared. She really hadn't hazed Kevin as badly as I'd feared she might, and she was even managing to be less sarcastic with Vivi. I'd been surprised but pleased when Danielle suggested we all come to her house after school instead of talking in Mr. Terry's room at lunch. She seemed to think that even though Mr. Terry said he wasn't listening in on us, he was getting suspicious about our conversations. She was probably right. And at her house, we'd be able to speak freely. In private.

Vivi and Danielle walked faster than I did, and I scrambled to keep up. Danielle was a head taller than me, easily, and Vivi was nearly as tall as that. My skin was pale, not the mocha cream of Vivi's or the easily tanned Danielle's, and my hair was long and dark brown, prone to stringiness on cool days, frizz on hot, humid ones. I kept it pulled back, usually, a style that served to both keep it out of my face and off my mind, and emphasize the only barely interesting thing about it, which was its subtle zebra striping of random lighter brown streaks from the omnipresent sun. The sun today was pleasant—hot enough to necessitate us taking off our layers of T-shirts to reveal the tanks underneath, but not so hot that we were sweaty and gross. Which was good, because Kevin was going to be joining us.

"Guys, is it still cool that Kevin's coming?" I asked for probably the fifteenth time. Even though he seemed to have passed the friend test at lunch yesterday, I was still nervous, my energy jolty whenever I thought about him.

"Argh." Danielle groaned, but she did it with a grin. "That's like the twentieth time you've asked us that. I already said yes! One more time and I'm gonna change my mind."

She walked close to the edge of someone's front lawn where the sprinklers jetted, rainbows shimmering in the watery shine, and dangled her hand in front of the spray, disrupting the water's arc and soaking her arm.

"Hey!" Vivi said, backing up so as not to get wet.

"Come on, it's refreshing," Danielle said, switching hands and getting both arms thoroughly drenched.

"I just wanted to make sure," I said. "I mean, really sure."

"We're really, really, and just in case you're going to ask again, *really* sure," Danielle said, rolling her eyes at me. She ducked her whole head down into the sprinkler spray and then whipped her hair back, flinging her wet ponytail around toward us. "So, is he like your boyfriend now or something? For real, I mean?"

I blushed and looked down at my feet as I walked. "No. I mean, I don't know. We just hang out at school. We're friends."

"Aw, *friends*," Danielle taunted. We were passing another set of sprinklers, and she flicked yet more water in my direction.

"Shut up!" I said, but I couldn't help smiling.

"It will happen," Vivi said solemnly.

"The oracle has spoken!" Danielle announced dramatically, holding her arms out like she was onstage. "Seriously, are you, like, channeling this stuff? Do you know the future now? Are the voices in your head accurate at all, because we could buy some lottery tickets . . ."

Vivi just kept walking, like she was in a daze.

"Vivi? Are you okay?" Danielle asked, dropping her arms to her sides.

Vivi nodded absently.

Danielle walked over to her and draped a friendly arm across her shoulder, herding her along the sidewalk. "Come on, let's just get to my house."

I was glad to see Danielle making an effort with Vivi. As I walked next to them, I felt Danielle's orange energy pulsing steadily against Vivi's flat, muddy green vibe. Hopefully Vivi could feel a little of that, too. She could use it. Patrick's silence had unmoored her. She seemed constantly in danger of drifting away, fading.

I felt a cold breeze that lingered as we walked the rest of the way to Danielle's house.

Danielle's room was girlier than you might expect. The first time she had me over, she'd warned me: *Don't. Say. A word,* and then led me into her room without further comment. The walls were light pink with subtle baby-pink stripes. The bedspread and pillows were bright pink and hot pink, respectively. The carpet was yet another shade of pink. The desk and other furniture was white with gold trim and elaborate faux baroque elements, but all the accessories were pink. I followed her directive and said not a word, but I couldn't help raising an eyebrow. She'd sighed as she explained that the girly pink stylings were the result of an unfortunate indulgence on her mother's part to let Danielle pick the paint and decorations when she was nine. Now she was stuck with it.

Danielle dropped her stuff abruptly on her desk and plopped on the bed. "Make yourselves at home," she said. "You have your pick: You can sit on the pink beanbag, or the pink chair, or the pink bed, or the pink shag rug. . . . God, I disgust myself."

"I think it's nice that your mom let you decorate your room," Vivi said as she sat down.

Danielle rolled her eyes. "Yeah, well, the problem is she won't let me RE-decorate it. Seriously, I'm just going to go to the hardware store and get some chalkboard paint, paint the whole room black and then draw on it with neon chalk." She lay on her bed, staring at the ceiling. "Maybe put a bunch of glow-in-the-dark stars on the ceiling and stuff."

"Sounds cool," I said.

"My mom would stroke out if I actually did that," Danielle said. She rolled onto her side and sat up, suddenly back to business. "Okay, so let's do this."

"We have to talk about the dreams," I said. "You haven't been having any more scary dreams, right?"

Danielle shook her head. "No more scary dreams. Not even like halfway interesting dreams, even. Just like, you know, random things—I'm making toast, but when I start to put the butter on it, it's really a shoe. Regular dream stuff. No being trapped in unending darkness or anything. What about you?"

"No new dreams," I said. "Just reruns of the same ones I had before. They're the same, every time. And they always end scary, with Lily showing up, like she's warning me about something. I mean, at the end of the schoolhouse dream, she literally tells me to run."

"Run from what?" Danielle asked.

"I don't know. It always stops there," I said. "Vivi, what about you? Any dreams? Anything from Patrick?"

"No," she said flatly. "Actually, I feel like since the dreams started with you guys, he just kind of stopped talking to me."

"Ugh." Danielle wrinkled her nose. "Worst. Ghost. Boyfriend. Ever. What is up with the silent treatment?"

Vivi crossed her arms. "I don't know. It's not his fault. It must be me. He said before that we were all supposed to be connected, but maybe talking about this stuff isn't helping. Maybe it's making me less connected to him."

"That doesn't make any sense," Danielle said.

"I'm telling you—you guys started having these dreams, and suddenly it was like he just . . . shut down for me," she said.

"Well, maybe he's just gearing up for something, like you said happened before," I said. "Remember? You said he went silent, and then one day, boom, he burst through? Maybe he's about to do that again."

Vivi shrugged and relaxed her arms, but she still looked worried. I felt a chilly wave pass through me, like the breeze I'd felt outside.

"I don't know if you are getting anything right now, but I think he's here," I said.

Vivi looked at me as though I should know better. "He's always here. Even if I can't sense him, he's always here." Then she looked away and her voice became quieter. "Especially when you're around. Your energy seems to . . . recharge him."

"Freaky." Danielle yawned. But Vivi's comment didn't seem casual to me. I looked at her directly until she was forced to meet my gaze.

"Vivi, I can't see him. I can't hear him. I don't *want* him around me. I just want to help you."

"I know," she said. But she looked doubtful.

"Wait a sec," Danielle said, her hands out like a traffic cop. "Are you saying you think Daisy is trying to steal your invisible boy-friend?"

Vivi's face reddened.

"Hey!" I said, my own face reddening.

Vivi cleared her throat. "It's just—you have to agree—wouldn't it be difficult for you if suddenly the person who was supposedly all yours only 'came to life' when he was around your friend?"

"That's not—" I started, but Danielle interrupted.

"There are at least two problems with that scenario: A, he's not a person, and two, he's not alive."

As soon as Danielle saw the stricken look on Vivi's face, she dragged herself off the bed and onto the floor with us. I felt a subtle energy shift, a calming blue edge on her normal orange vibe, as she became more serious than she had been all day.

"Look, I'm sorry," she said to Vivi. "I don't know why I get all jokey and mean about this stuff whenever the three of us are together. I swear, I want to help us all figure out what the heck is going on. It's just, I don't know. Every time we're together, I feel all weird. And then I find myself saying things that are way harsher than what I mean."

"Guys, I think it's him," I blurted out before I realized what I was saying.

Vivi looked perturbed. "What do you mean?"

"I mean, this whole dynamic. The silent treatment for you, Danielle's weird angry energy, my feeling so drained—I think it's Patrick. I think he's messing with us."

Vivi crossed her arms again and leaned back. "I don't think so. Whatever is happening, it's not Patrick's fault," she said.

"That's not what I mean," I started.

"No, you don't understand. Patrick isn't a bad spirit."

"Okay, I get that," I said, but Vivi shook her head.

"No, you don't. Otherwise you wouldn't be suggesting that he's 'messing' with us, or however you want to say it. He doesn't 'mess' with anyone. He just presents himself to people differently, in a way that is most accessible to the people he's trying to reach."

"What are you saying?" I asked, feeling a little bit attacked.

Vivi looked determined and serious as she focused her eyes on me. "I'm saying, maybe you're feeling like he's 'messing' with us because that's the way you think. Maybe he's presenting himself like this to you because you're suspicious—you *are* skeptical, so that's how he comes across to you. If you could just open your heart to the idea of him, stop thinking so judgmentally, you'd see him the way I see him: as a force for good. As a good spirit. A helpful spirit."

The creeping coldness that had begun before now enveloped me, and I could feel my energy sapping. But despite my sluggishness, I snapped back, "Did you ever think that maybe *you're* the one he's fooling? Maybe he's presenting himself to you the way he is because that's the way *you* think. You need a guardian angel. So he shows up as one."

The chill seemed to expand through the room, and I saw Danielle rub her arms like she felt it, too. Vivi sat perfectly still, as though she were encased in ice. I felt so drained. I wondered if Danielle would mind if I just lay down on her pink, pink floor and slept for a few days. Vivi's face was still a mask, but I watched her eyes fill, a tear roll down her cheek. I felt a strange thrum of energy in the room. I couldn't tell if it was coming from me or not. If only I wasn't so tired.

"When's Kevin coming, again?" Danielle asked, breaking the silence.

"Hopefully soon," I said. I was so cold, my teeth were chattering. "He said he was just going to check something out at the computer lab and then bike over here."

"He'll be here at 3:45," Vivi said, not looking at either of us, her eyes blank like she was in a trance. Then her eyes came back to life as they narrowed at me. "I just heard Patrick. That's what he told me. Despite whatever you might believe."

Danielle and I looked at each other. Then the doorbell rang. Kevin was here.

It was 3:45.

twenty-two

"You guys aren't going to believe this," Kevin said as he walked in the room, Danielle leading the way. Vivi sat on the floor, morose and angry at me for suggesting Patrick's presence was anything short of angelic. I had stood up as soon as I'd heard the doorbell ring, suddenly no longer tired but nervous and jittery that Kevin had arrived, unsure of where to stand or how to be.

"Whoa," he said, taking in the pinkness of his surroundings once he was inside the room.

"Not a word," Danielle said, holding up a hand as she walked past him and sat on the bed. She took Vivi's hand and gently pulled her up so that she had no choice but to sit on the bed, too. Kevin looked around and then rolled Danielle's puffy pink desk chair toward the middle of the room, sitting down to face us, sheafs of paper threatening to fall out of his hands. I solved the problem of where to stand by sitting on the edge of the bed on the other side of Danielle.

"Hey," he said, acknowledging me briefly with a quick smile, but he was focused on the papers he held, shuffling to get them in the proper order.

"So, you're not going to believe this, but I did some research at the computer lab, which is why I'm late, and . . ." He grabbed one of the papers from the middle of his stack and thrust it my way. "Look at this."

"What is it?" Danielle asked, peering over my shoulder.

gift

I felt all the fine hairs on my arms stand on end, and a chill washed over me. "It's . . ."

Danielle took the paper from me, her hands shaking. "Oh my God."

"It's the house, isn't it?" Kevin said. His eyes flashed with excitement. "It's the house."

"It's the house," Danielle said.

"And it's only like ten miles north of here," he said.

The paper was a printout of a web page. HAUNTED CORONADO, the banner read. The sidebar listed links to tours and houses in the area and event dates. Below the banner: STONE HOUSE—LEGENDS OF A HAUNTED HOME. And then some text, which I couldn't really read due to the buzzing in my head. And then the blurry black-and-white picture: a two-story house with a porch that wrapped around one entire side. Three wide steps up to the deep covered porch, the double door of the main entrance just beyond that. It was the house from the dreams.

I looked up at Kevin. "How did you find it?"

He shook his head. "It was a hunch. You described the place in so much detail—it just rang a bell for me. I visited the place once when I was a kid, did one of those haunted house tours." He looked apologetic. "It was my parents' idea. Anyway," he continued, handing us his stack of pages, "it doesn't look like that anymore. That's an old picture of the original place. They built a new house on top of the old grounds. Twice, actually. But I did some Googling and found a couple of local historical society–type sites, including that one with the picture of what the original house looked like."

"It's really the house," Danielle said in astonishment. She passed some of the pages to Vivi, but they seemed to have no effect on her.

"I haven't gotten to the best part yet," Kevin said.

I leafed through the pages in my hand. More text, a few old-fashioned pictures. A woman, long hair. A man, looking stern. Did they appear familiar to me? I was afraid to look closely.

"So, get this," he continued. "The guy who owned the house was Jeremiah Stone. He had a son and daughter. The son's name was Jameson, and the daughter was Veronica."

119

andrea j. buchanan

Haunted Coronado

Stone House—Legends of a Haunted Home

Old Town

Visit Stone House

Stone House History

Haunted Stone House

Restoration

Stone House Shop

Contribute

Jeremiah Stone was an entrepreneur, drawn, like so many men of his time, to California by the promise of glittering gold. Julian, located about an hour east of what is now San Diego, was one such promised land. Though now Julian is most well known for both its delicious apples and its reputation as a popular mountain retreat, between 1870 and 1880, it's estimated that over $5 million in gold was procured from Julian's quite generous mines.

The Stone House, circa 1950.

Jeremiah was one of the lucky ones: he had the resources and the sense of adventure to marshall a crew of miners and discover veins of quartz that quickly led to gold. He made his family's fortune in those mines, and soon enough was able to retire to the beautiful beach town of what is today Coronado.

He built his family home in 1878 on several acres of land. Today, the house sits in the middle of a busy street, but in his day, it was secluded, with a large field that ran all the way to the sandy shores of what is now Coronado beach, and enough land to include both a separate residence for miners working on his crew and a one-room schoolhouse, where his children and others were taught. But all was not happy at the Stone House: his wife, Elizabeth, died in 1883, shortly after giving birth to

Jeremiah Stone

Jameson Stone

Jameson's widow, Jane Stone

http://mysterious-california.org/stone-house-haunted

120

Danielle gripped my hand with such intensity I thought it might break. "Oh my God."

"And the legend is that the place is haunted by the ghosts of Veronica, who went missing and was presumed dead, and a servant girl, Lilian, who evidently died in some kind of household accident—"

"Oh my God," Danielle repeated, her hands at her mouth now, shaking. I remembered the way the dreams always ended: Lily, covered in blood, a butcher's knife in her hand.

"—and the ghost of Jeremiah, who was reportedly so despondent after their deaths that he hung himself."

Nobody said anything for a moment. We were all too stunned.

"It's all right there," Kevin said. "I printed out all the stuff I could find. There are some conflicting accounts of what happened—some people thought Jeremiah was actually the girls' killer. He lived under a cloud of suspicion for some time, it says."

"And what about James? Or, rather, Jameson?" I asked.

Kevin held up a finger and consulted one of the papers I'd handed back to him. "Jameson took over his father's business and continued to live in the house, even after his father's death. He and his wife, Jane, lived there until the fire."

Jane.

"The fire?"

"Yeah, in like . . . what was it . . . oh, here. 'In 1905, a fire on the property destroyed the main house and the smaller carriage house on the grounds, leaving Jane Stone a widow.'"

"A widow?" I echoed.

"Yep. Evidently Jameson died in the fire."

"So what happened to Jane?" I asked.

"I couldn't find much," Kevin said. "The sites I was looking at were mostly concerned with the ghosts and the hauntings, and evidently Jane lived a normal, boring life after the fire. She took over her husband's business, I think it says. But she didn't die tragically or anything. So there wasn't too much info."

"Daisy, look at this," Danielle said. "This is totally you. I mean, seriously. Update the hairstyle? Spitting image."

She held out a page with an oval portrait of a woman, her hair pulled back in a severe style. She stared out of the photo, calm and expressionless in the way of old-time photographs, no self-conscious smile.

It was Jane. And she looked like me.

Next to that picture was a grainy photo of a man. He was handsome, with a hint of a smile on his face, and the text identified him as Jameson Stone.

At once, I felt myself thrust into the memory of the dreams. For a moment it seemed that if I closed my eyes, I'd be back there, walking in the field with Veronica, standing in the schoolhouse watching through the window, seeing Lily talking with James. . . .

With James.

There was something I was close to remembering—something that made my heart race and gave me chills all over my body. I saw flashes of the dreams: the field, Veronica's study, the window, Lily, the butcher knife, *run.*

"This is wild," Danielle said. "Can we keep these?"

"Sure." Kevin sat back in the chair. "Can I just point out that this room is incredibly pink?"

Danielle shot him a look.

Vivi suddenly thrust the papers in her hand back to Danielle. "Take these," she said, her voice tight.

"Sheesh, all right already, you're going to give me a paper cut," Danielle said as she combined Vivi's with the rest of what Kevin had brought.

"Something's happening," Vivi said, and we all looked at her.

For a moment, nothing at all happened. The sunlight streamed through Danielle's window, finding a gap between the pink blinds to illuminate Vivi's head like a halo. Her eyes closed, and her face was calm and perfectly relaxed, as though she was asleep, and she sat with her legs crossed, her body still except for the rise and fall of her chest as she breathed.

gift

The coldness surged around me, making my teeth chatter, and I sensed Danielle's energy straining to bounce around the room as we waited for Vivi to say something. The fatigue descended upon me again, as though I was being smothered by a hundred paperweights.

Then, suddenly, Vivi's eyes flew open and she gasped, her eyelids fluttering while her eyes themselves seemed to roll back in her head, her arms reaching out toward us, and then she slumped back against Danielle's pink pillows like she was dead.

twenty-three

"Vivi!"

I couldn't stop myself from flashing back to the first day I'd found her in the bathroom. She looked exactly the same as she did then: out of it, her head lolled back. Unconscious. All thoughts of the dreams vanished as I ran to her side.

Pulse. Breathing. Vivi had both, but she was passed out cold. It was as though she had just suddenly fallen asleep. What was I supposed to check next?

"Is she okay?" Danielle asked.

Kevin pushed us out of the way, assessing her like he had a clue about what to do. "Vivi? Can you hear us?" He snapped his fingers next to her ears, clapped his hands in front of her face. No response.

The coldness that had trapped me before and made me feel so sluggish was now replaced by a wild rush of energy. *It's just adrenaline, it's just nerves,* I told myself. *Keep it together.* But I could feel myself bristling with electricity that I wasn't sure I could control. I grabbed Vivi's hand. It was like a block of ice. I touched her arm: also cold. Her legs, too.

"Maybe it's Patrick. I always feel freezing when she says he's around. And now she's an icicle. Maybe he . . ."

Kevin shook his head, agitated. "We've got to get her to a doctor."

"Come on, she's just out of it," Danielle said.

"She seems stable, but I've seen this before, she's got to get checked out. I'm telling you guys."

"Well, what do you want us to do? Take her to the ER on your bike? Tell the doctors, 'Hi, we think our friend's possessed by a ghost'?" Danielle's voice was dripping with sarcasm. "We don't even know if she has insurance, or some pre-existing medical condition or whatever. Besides the voices in her head, of course."

I sat down on the bed next to Vivi, shaking her leg to rouse her, but she didn't move. "What should we do?"

"We can*not* call 911," Danielle said, beginning to pace. "My mom would freak. Look, she's breathing, right? She just passed out. Maybe she'll just wake up? Daisy, can you call your mom? She's a nurse, right?"

Kevin's jaw worked as he thought. "Call your mom. But we also have to call her parents."

"Are you kidding me?" Danielle exploded. "They are the last people we should talk to!"

"No," he said calmly, "they are the *first* people we should talk to. They are the ones that could get her help. I don't think you guys realize—she could have something legitimately wrong with her."

"Like what," Danielle demanded, her arms folded across her chest.

"Like," he paused, gesturing with his arms while he searched for the words, "like, I don't know, because I'm not a doctor. Listen, she could wake up and be totally fine, or she could be totally *not* fine. Do you really want to take that chance?"

Now the three of us looked at each other.

"I'm serious," Kevin said. "I'll call her parents right now."

"It's just her mom," I said. "She told us her dad left a long time ago."

"So I'll call her mom," he said.

We all looked at Vivi on the bed, a sleeping beauty. Kevin gently used a finger near her eyebrow to raise her eyelid, but it didn't wake her.

"What's the number?" he asked us.

Danielle sighed. "I'll get it for you."

"I'll call my mom, too," I said.

The sunlight shone through the window in Danielle's room, bearing down on us like a warning. How long would Vivi stay asleep? Was she even really sleeping? Maybe we should have just called the paramedics. What would I say to my mom? *My friend is in a trance and she can't wake up?* Is that what Kevin was going to say to Vivi's mom?

He paced Danielle's room, holding his phone to one ear and plugging his other ear with his free hand, as we sat there on Vivi's bed. I held her hand, squeezing it even though she didn't squeeze it back.

Suddenly, he stopped his pacing.

"Hi, Mrs. Reyes?" His eyes darted over to us, suddenly full of questions. "*No habla Ingles?*"

No English?

"Oh, okay," he said, "Uh, I'm . . . *Soy amigo de Vivi.*"

"What's going on?" I whispered to Danielle.

He paused and held up his hand to stop us from talking.

"*Si, Vivi—su hija?*"

I was beginning to regret my decision to sign up for French instead of Spanish this year. His voice sounded tense, and I looked at Danielle to see if she understood what he was saying.

"I know—I know she's not there right now, it's just, we're—*estamos preocupados por su,*" Kevin said.

He began pacing again.

"*Ella no está bien,*" Kevin continued. "We think she might be sick—*ella está enferma.*"

He stopped suddenly and took the phone away from his ear, looking at it in disbelief.

"What?" I said, as he jammed the phone back in his pocket. "What did she say?"

Kevin's face was grim.

"She said Vivi is the Devil."

twenty-four

I felt myself prickle all over, whether from Kevin's information or from my own unbridled electricity I wasn't sure, and then I felt Vivi's hand weakly squeeze mine.

"Vivi!" I said. Her eyes were still closed, but I could see movement beneath her lids, as though she were having a particularly active dream. Kevin came to her side.

"Vivi, can you hear us?" he asked.

She began to move her head, and slowly her eyes opened. She blinked a few times and her eyes filled with panic as she struggled to sit up.

"Take your time," Kevin said. "It's okay. You're at Danielle's house. You were just a little out of it for a few minutes."

Had it only been a few minutes?

She looked at me and seemed to recognize who I was, as she visibly relaxed, sinking back into the hot-pink pillows and taking a deep breath.

"Is she okay?" Danielle asked. "She seems a little dopey."

"She's a little out of it, but that's normal for coming out of . . . something like that. Whatever it was," Kevin said.

"You sound like you have some experience with this sort of thing," I said.

"What, trances and ghosts?" He sounded light, but his face was serious as he shook his head.

"What happened?" Vivi whispered.

"You tell us," Danielle said. "You, like, freaked out. We were about to call 911."

"Danielle!" I said.

Vivi rubbed her arms. "I'm cold."

I grabbed a hot-pink blanket from the end of Danielle's bed and placed it around her.

"I don't know what happened," she said, her voice flat and expressionless. "You were talking about the house, and then I had this very strange feeling, and the next thing I remember, I was hearing someone speaking Spanish. I think."

"That was me," Kevin said.

"Why were you speaking Spanish?" she asked.

Kevin looked at Danielle and me before answering. "Um, I was talking to your mom."

Vivi sat up, fully awake. There was a flare of something in her eyes—anger, irritation, frustration, fear. Whatever it was, it made me happy: She was reacting. She was out of the trance.

"Why would you do that?" she snapped.

"We're sorry, Vivi, we were just really worried," I told her, reaching my hand out to her arm, but she yanked it away before I could touch her.

She wrapped the blanket around herself tightly and closed her eyes in frustration.

"Vivi, she seemed really—concerned about you," Kevin said.

"'Concerned.' Right. So I take it she shared her theory with you? That I'm possessed? That she thinks I'm the Devil?"

"That can't be for real," Danielle said.

"You don't understand, my mother is very religious," Vivi said. "To her, people who talk to ghosts are possessed. So she thinks I'm possessed. I didn't need you to go snooping around behind my back to figure that out."

"We weren't snooping, Vivi, we were scared," I said. "We didn't know what happened."

Her eyes narrowed. "Do you know what it's like? To have your own mother hate you?"

"I'm sure she doesn't hate you—" I began, but she cut me off.

"She is terrified of me. She took me to a priest, begged him to cast the demons out, or hire an exorcist who could. Do you know what that does to a person, to have your own mother believe you are something from the depths of Hell? And what did you think she would do when you called? Come to rescue me? Actually try to help?"

"I don't know," Kevin shrugged. "Maybe take you to a doctor?"

"I can't believe you would talk to her without asking me. She doesn't know me. She doesn't know anything about me. I don't even live there anymore!"

Kevin and Danielle and I shared a glance.

"What are you talking about?" I asked. "Of course you live there. It's your home."

She laughed through her tears. "No, it's really not. My mom kicked me out. I'm the Devil, remember? The stupid crucifixes and shrines and stuff weren't enough to repel my evil presence, or cleanse her soul or whatever. So she kicked me out."

"When?" Kevin asked.

"I don't know, two weeks ago, two and a half?"

I shook my head. "You're telling me you've been living on the streets for half a month?"

"No, no," Vivi said, suddenly hesitant. "Of course not."

"Do you need a place? Do you want to crash with me?" I said.

"Yeah, or here?" Danielle offered.

Vivi shook her head no. "Really, guys, it's okay. I'm fine. I . . . have a place."

"So where do you live, then?" Kevin asked.

"Well." Vivi seemed very careful with her words. "In like a month I'll be able to move in with one of my older brothers."

"But where are you living now?" I asked.

She looked at me directly. "For now, and I mean just for now, Mr. Terry has been nice enough to let me stay at his place."

Mr. Terry. Poetry lover, English teacher, surfer, and now rescuer of troubled homeless girls? I was shocked, but I supposed I could see him helping a student at risk. My thoughts were interrupted by Danielle's harsh laughter.

"Oh, man, you should see your faces, you guys!" She laughed, pointing at me and Kevin, barely able to get the words out as she imitated us. "*Oh no! We're not Mr. Terry's favorites anymore! OMG! What are we going to do?*"

"That's not true," I said angrily. I looked at Kevin, who seemed irritated more than jealous, but also clearly caught off guard by Vivi's revelation.

"Seriously?" Danielle said. "It *so* is like that. You can*not* sit here and tell me you guys weren't like, *Oh my God I love Mr. Terry why did he not let meeeeee live at his house!*"

"Danielle," Kevin said sharply.

"No, whatever," Vivi said. "I know it's a little unorthodox."

"Unorthodox?" Danielle laughed. "It's more like 'against the law.' Isn't it?"

"I don't know," Kevin said. "I don't think there's any rule about helping a person in trouble."

"Unless she's an adorable, vulnerable minor," Danielle muttered under her breath.

"It's not like that," Vivi said. "He has an extra room, he's letting me stay there. It's just temporary, until my brother can help me out. And besides, it's better than being on the street. Or trying to live at home, against my mom's will, having her cross herself and throw holy water at me every time she sees me."

Vivi was all alone, I realized. No mother, some brothers, evidently, but too old and busy to do anything about her crisis. And Patrick was slipping away from her, she said. Suddenly I felt the overwhelming urge to lie down again, to sleep for as long as everyone would let me.

Vivi looked at me. "It's happening. Hold my hand."

"What?" I stammered.

"Take my hand," she insisted. We sat facing each other now, her hands gripping mine so tightly I found myself wincing from the intensity. She closed her eyes, and I saw a smile bloom on her face. *This can't be happening again,* I thought, squeezing her hands back, trying to hold on and hold her here with us.

I felt a blast of energy, the cold again like a brain freeze, except up my arms and into my chest. My body felt alive, thrumming with a bright blue force.

"Uh-oh," I heard Danielle say as her clock alarm started going off, her television zapped on, the cell phones in the room started buzzing. It felt like a wind was whipping around us.

"What the hell?" Kevin said.

Vivi opened her eyes, radiant. "Can you feel it?"

I nodded.

And then I *really* felt it.

Not just the electronics in the room blaring out of control. Not just the energy, the vibrational waves emanating from me, sine waves and oscillations and spiraling electricity. Not just the aliveness, the sudden intensity of alertness and strength.

I felt his presence. All around me. And then I heard a whisper, coming from the depths of my mind.

Daisy. I know you can hear me.

twenty-five

It took me a moment to free my hands from Vivi's grasp. The energy at first tensed me so that I was stuck like a person with her finger in a light socket, gripping Vivi's hands tighter and tighter as the energy coiled around me. When I finally broke free, I opened my eyes to see Kevin running from the room as Danielle frantically tried to unplug everything electronic that was going haywire.

"Kevin!" I called, but he was out the door. Vivi lay back on Danielle's bed, still serene and beatific with that goofy smile, like she was soaking in a delightful bubble bath rather than the chaos that swirled around us. But she was conscious. She was awake. She was definitely alive.

I got up and ran, following Kevin.

He was outside, sitting on the sidewalk with his head in his hands, breathing heavily.

"Are you okay?" I said. I was still shaking from what had happened, still trying to shake the feeling of having that voice in my head. *I know you can hear me.* It had been a whisper, sinister and creepy and made all the more disturbing by how intimate it felt. Like he was right next to me, breathing in my ear. I shivered and my heart raced. I could hear the high-pitched whine of the electrical wires above us stringing from the telephone poles that punctuated the street.

"Hold on," Kevin said, and I realized he was seriously pale and struggling to stay calm. I sat next to him and started to put my hand on his back, but he shot his arm up quickly to ward me off. I leaned back, surprised, and moved myself over. In a moment, before I even really had time to process the fact that he had almost literally pushed me away, he raised his head and looked at me with a pained expression.

"I'm sorry, it's not you, I just—" he began, wincing, taking another deep breath. "I just had to get out of there. Give me a minute, okay? I just have to breathe."

"Okay," I said. I looked down at the ground. *I know you can hear me,* I thought, but suddenly I wasn't sure if I was remembering that moment or if the voice was whispering to me again. I felt myself go clammy all over. And not just because of what I'd just experienced with Vivi. I felt shaky and breathless as it hit me that I was going to have to tell Kevin the truth about me. About what I could do. About what I'd done in there, with the electronic storm.

"Sorry," Kevin said again, from inside the crook of his elbow. He sat with his knees drawn to his chest and his arms cradling his head.

"No, I'm sorry," I said. "It got kind of weird in there—"

"You don't understand. There's something you don't know about me."

I sat back, cautious. "There's something *I* don't know about *you*?"

He raised his head and looked at me. "Yeah. I was going to tell you, I was just waiting for the right time."

"The right time," I repeated. "Wow. That's kind of a coincidence."

"Really?" he said. "Why?"

"Because there's something *you* don't know about *me*. And I was waiting for the right time to tell you, too." I hugged my knees to my chest, sitting just like him now.

"Huh," he said. "What do you know? We even have *that* in common." He smiled, but he still looked shaky.

"Should I go first?" I asked.

"No, that's okay. I might as well tell you, because I don't know if I'm doing a good enough job of staving off this trigger," he said. He took another deep breath in, closing his eyes as he inhaled through his nose and then opening as he exhaled. "I have a kind of . . . thing. It's like an electrical disturbance in my brain—What?" he asked, taking in the shocked look on my face.

"It's just—I have kind of the same thing."

He laughed in disbelief. "You're kidding me," he said. "You have epilepsy?"

I was confused. "No, I just . . . can . . . you know, zap things. Without meaning to. You know, like back in there? But, wait—is that what *you* have? Epilepsy?"

He shook his head. "No. I mean, *yes*. I do have epilepsy. But—what did you just say? Did you say you could *zap* things?"

"Well, yeah," I said, wincing a little. This wasn't exactly how I'd imagined breaking the news to him that I was a total freak. Though if I were being honest with myself I would say that I had been kind of hoping that I would never have to break the news to him that I was a total freak. Hoping that one day I would wake up and this "gift" of mine would be gone. Hoping eventually I'd just grow out of it and be normal. "I've kind of always been like this, and I just—"

Before I could even make sense of what was happening, Kevin pulled me to him, wrapping his arms around me and kissing me like I'd never been kissed before. Probably because I'd never actually been kissed before. Was this what it was like? A surging of royal red and purple energy flowing through me, from my core right through my fingertips? A literal electrical storm on my lips, a static fuzz in my brain, a delicious flowering of good feelings that enveloped me from head to toe?

Just as suddenly, he pulled away, a huge grin on his face, his hands holding mine.

"I don't know *what* you have, Daisy Jones, but you just saved my life."

"What are you talking about?" I asked, surprised I could even manage to form words, let alone enunciate them clearly enough for anyone to understand.

He kissed me again, and I felt that delicious spark. "You zapped my brain. You got me back to normal."

I must have looked confused still, because he shook his head and laughed at me. "You stopped a seizure."

twenty-six

Kevin tore into his food, ravenous after the episode at Danielle's house.

Danielle had been perturbed to find us on the sidewalk outside her house. *Seriously?* she'd said. *THIS is what you guys are doing right now? I'm in there dealing with a poltergeist-possessed-electronics situation, and you're out here smooching?* She'd stood on her front lawn, arms folded across her chest. I scanned her face for a glimpse of the best friend who should be happy for me to have gotten my first kiss right there in front of her house, but I couldn't find it. Vivi had floated into view behind her, looking lost and frightened, oblivious, as always, to what had just taken place. And then Danielle's mom had pulled up, alarmed to see so many teenagers congregating in her driveway, and Danielle convinced her to drive Vivi home. To Mr. Terry's house, I supposed. *I'll call you later,* I'd said to Danielle as she got in the car with Vivi. *See that you do, and I expect a full report,* she'd replied, jokingly, but she still seemed annoyed. After they'd left, Kevin grabbed his bike and informed me that we would be going to Fakeburger so that he could eat something before he died. And here we were.

I watched him eat, my own veggie burger and fries sitting limply on the plastic wrapping I had spread out as a feeble attempt at a placemat. He had warned me this would happen, the sudden post-seizure hunger pang, and I watched in awe as he devoured practically his entire meal before I'd even had a chance to crack open my straw.

"So, who goes first?" he said.

We looked at each other.

"Fine, okay, me. I'll start," he said. "So. How does it work? Do you have triggers? Do you take medication? Is that why you don't have your driver's license? Or a cell phone?"

"Hey, I thought *you* were going to start!"

"I am starting. I'm starting with questions!"

I smirked at him. "Mine is weirder. Can we do yours first?"

He shrugged, taking a long drink from his soda. "Sure. I mean, I guess you probably heard something about me?"

"No," I said, unconvincingly. He looked at me. "Okay, maybe I did hear something."

His face looked cloudy. "Yeah, that happens. I don't know what the deal is with that place. Word just spreads. Everyone's just always craving drama."

"You mean Castle Creek?"

"Yeah," he smiled. "But I guess I mean everywhere. Human nature, right? So, but yeah, I was drama fodder at school for a while."

"What happened?"

"Well, basically, almost two years ago, I started having these symptoms—it was epilepsy, but I didn't know that then. Because I wasn't having convulsive seizures. That's what I thought epilepsy was—somebody flailing around on the floor, foaming at the mouth or whatever." He looked away, watching something out the window I couldn't see. "I had these . . . well, at first it was just these weird feelings. Like, have you ever had the feeling like someone is standing right behind you? I mean like *right* behind you? But you feel like if you actually turn around to check, something terrible might happen? It was like that. And then I'd kind of space out. Like, I'd just be totally out of it."

"Like, blacked out?" I asked.

"No," he said, "Like, absent. More like Vivi after she's been 'talking' to Patrick."

137

Finally I understood his urgency about getting her to a doctor. "Do you think that's what's going on with Vivi? That she has some form of epilepsy?"

"Could be. Could be vitamin D deficiency, could be a brain tumor, could be . . ." He shook his head. "Could be that she's really communicating with a ghost."

"So, wait, how did you figure out what the deal was with you? Did you get diagnosed or something?"

"Ha," he smiled. "Well, that took some doing. I started having more and more of these weird episodes—feeling, like, ominous portents of doom or hearing music that nobody else heard, or having everything around me appear super colorful and bright. And they started happening at school. So that was awesome, because, you know, hello, way to blend in."

I nodded my head in sympathy.

"But what was worse was that it started happening at home. Like, when I was at my dad's."

"That sounds . . . like a not-good thing?"

He shrugged. "My dad is . . . well, he's my dad. My mom is like this total crunchy granola person, all yoga and Zen and health foods and hippie stuff. She's awesome. You'll have to meet her."

At this he grinned, his first genuine, happy smile of the whole conversation. My stomach flipped. *He wants you to meet his mom,* Danielle would gawk if she were here.

"Anyway," he was saying when I tuned back in, "My dad is a decent guy. He's just not quite the compassionate flower child my mom is. Opposites attract, I guess is the saying, right? Until they get divorced. Anyway, so he's this very buttoned-down kind of business guy. Very disciplined, very controlled, very kind of . . . distant. So when all this stuff started happening, it wasn't like I could go to him and be all, 'Hey, listen, I think I'm seeing and hearing things that aren't there.' And so I didn't."

"Did you tell your mom?" I asked as he paused to eat the last of his fries.

He grinned, then his face sobered. "I should have. I just didn't want her to be worried. I thought I could handle it, I guess. And I kind of didn't really want it to, you know, be real. Anyway, so, yeah, space case at school, barely keeping it together at home. And then one night when I'm at my dad's and he gets home from work, I have one of these things come on. I hear someone talking to me who isn't there, all the color in the room gets turned up to vivid, and I feel that horrible dread, like something terrible is going to happen. And I freak out. And I have my first actual seizure that someone else noticed."

I must have looked worried, because he quickly held up his hands. "Not like a horrible one or anything, but evidently—I don't know, my eyes rolled back in my head, I started shaking. . . ."

"Oh my God."

"And my dad thought it was because—wait for it—I was on drugs."

"No."

"Yes. Because I was so spacey all the time. Plus I wore black. I know, shocking, I didn't have the awesome fashion sense I have now," he said, gesturing to his black T-shirt and so-dark-blue-they-might-as-well-be-black jeans. "Plus I had just started playing guitar and stuff. . . . You know, it all added up."

"So what did he do? Did he take you to the ER?"

He nodded. "Yep. And then he had them put me in a forty-eight-hour psychiatric hold for observation."

As casually as he told his story, I could tell it still affected him. The muscles in his neck were tight and he gripped the napkin in his hand like a stress ball.

"How long did it take to figure out what was really going on with you?" I asked.

"You mean a diagnosis? I guess in retrospect not all that long. I mean, it took a couple of months of tests, but then I had a name for what was causing all the space-out stuff and hallucinations and whatnot: temporal lobe epilepsy. But first they had to rule out all kinds of other things: brain tumor, mental illness . . . you know, demons. It wasn't pretty. I had CAT scans and PET scans and MRI scans and every other kind of scan, and then eventually a doctor who specialized in epilepsy and kids put all the puzzle pieces together, and that was it."

"And your dad?" I said. "How did he take it?"

"Like he takes everything," he said. "Which is to say, not well. Actually it was my mom who really freaked out. But in a good way. She was really upset with him for having me 'institutionalized,' as she put it, even for just a night or two. And she was livid that he had ignored what was going on and seemed to have no interest in helping me figure out how to deal with it myself. So, she had me move in with her full time."

"Wow," I said.

"I know. Kind of a guilt trip. I mean, I felt bad for my dad. But on the other hand, it was nice to have my mom be so fierce about helping me. It made me feel better, in a weird way, you know?"

"Yeah, I kind of do. Your mom sounds a lot like my mom, actually."

"Huh. And your dad?"

"Not in the picture," I said. "But he never was. I mean, he left before I was even born, so it's always just been my mom and me. And she can be pretty fierce when she needs to be."

"That's good. I mean, I'm sure it's annoying sometimes, but it's good."

"Yeah." I smiled. "But, so, after you moved in with your mom, did things get better? Did you start medication or something to get it under control?"

He grinned. "Uh, I said I moved in with my *mom*. The anti-establishment 'all you need is love' person? So, yeah, in the beginning, we tried a few different medications, doctor's orders. And they were . . . okay. But they made me just as spacey as if I were having those blank-out seizures all the time. And they didn't really do much to stop them from happening. So after a while my mom was like, enough. Forget Western medicine, we're trying something else. So, then it was all acupuncture and Chinese herbs, and meditation, and gluten-free food, and drinking chlorophyll and stuff."

"Hence, the burger and fries," I said, gesturing to our food.

"Uh, you mean *veggie* burger and *potato sticks* sprayed with coconut oil and baked instead of fried?" he said.

"Fine, fine," I conceded. "But did any of that stuff actually help?"

He grinned and stole a fry from my still-plentiful stash across the table. "Actually, the mindfulness stuff did a little. At least in terms of dealing with the stress. But then she found this doctor who had this non-traditional approach to treating epilepsy, and once I started going to him, things started to shift a little for me. He recommended some medication, to keep things under control, but he also recommended something along the lines of what I'd learned about with the meditation and mindfulness and breathing."

"*Pranayama*," I said under my breath.

"Yeah." He looked at me quizzically. "Exactly. See, this guy had the idea that what's happening in my brain—in a brain prone to epilepsy—is that electrical switches are getting tripped. But electrical switches get tripped in your brain all the time, and you're not always having seizures. So he was like, what makes those moments different for people with certain kinds of epilepsy? He thought if we could look at what triggers those moments—and not just, you know, flashing lights or foods or other external triggers, but what's happening emotionally as well—then maybe with breathing techniques and mindfulness stuff and just simple awareness and preparation, some of the episodes—not all, but some—might be able to be prevented."

I sat back, taking it all in. It sounded just like the way my mom and I had come up with dealing with my situation. It was uncanny how similar we were, in a way, both of us struggling to keep calm to avoid triggering the electrical craziness in our brains.

"Did it work?"

He shrugged. "Not at first. I mean, I needed to be on medication. And even then I still had some episodes. But I started trying to keep track of when they were happening—was I stressed, was I angry, was I hyper, that sort of thing. And then I started trying to do the deep breathing or calming exercises the moment I felt that stuff, before the onset of anything. And eventually, I got pretty good at it. Or, good enough. I was able to step down the dosage of my medication, and now it's super low—just, like, maintenance. The plan is that, eventually—if I can go for a really long time without any incidents—I would stop the meds completely."

"Wow," I said.

"To be honest . . . I guess this might sound kind of weird, but . . . even though it was scary and all, not knowing what it was and then figuring out what it was and everything . . . in a strange way, I kind of miss the feeling I used to have when it happened all the time. It's hard to explain, but the feeling afterward—sometimes it was almost transcendent. Like, mystical. You know? Like when you have serious déjà vu and it feels so . . . profound? I'm not saying I want to go back to having blank-out detachment-seizure activity all the time. But I do kind of miss that feeling of being somehow directly plugged in to the universe." He looked at me with a self-deprecating grin. "Well, whatever. Like I said, strange."

"No, I get it," I said. "There's an upside to everything, I guess."

He laughed. "Well, that fits with what my mom always says. Which is that something like this doesn't necessarily have to be a bad thing. Sometimes the thing you think is getting in your way isn't really a roadblock at all. Sometimes it's a new way to go."

He sighed and looked at me, but he didn't seem to notice me marveling at everything he'd just said. "Well, whatever, today kind of blew that progress, anyway. Gotta start the 'this many days without a seizure' clock again."

"Sorry," I said.

"No, what do you have to be sorry about? You helped stop it from becoming full blown."

"Yeah, but I also kind of started it in the first place. That electrical storm in there, with all of Danielle's stuff freaking out? That wasn't just Vivi's ghost. That was my doing. I was the trigger."

He sat back, his arms draped across the back of the booth, an eyebrow raised expectantly, smiling his one-sided smile.

It was my turn to talk. And as I told him my story, I realized that, of anyone I'd ever known, he was the perfect person to share it with. For the first time ever, I was talking to someone who really understood what it was like, even a little bit, to be me.

twenty-seven

Afterward, we headed south toward my neighborhood and found ourselves walking along the beach. This was the breeze that Pacific Breezes aspired to: the salty forceful wind that whipped off the coast. And this was the beach I loved: at dusk, in springtime shadows, its pounding surf sounding like so much white noise, the sand firm and cool in the waning daylight, the only swimmers still braving the waves the crazy surfers who would also be there the next morning just after dawn.

"I love the beach like this," Kevin said as we sat down on the sand.

"Me too." I held out my embarrassingly pale arms. "Though I guess you wouldn't know it."

He shook his head, smiling. "Where did you come from?"

I made a face at him. "You know, I was at that other school, and then we moved here, and—"

"No, I mean, *where did you come from*? Like, how do you even exist, how do you do what you do?"

I dragged my fingers through the sand. "That's kind of a weird question, don't you think? Or series of questions?"

"I'm just marveling at your awesomeness is all." He ran his fingers through the sand until they ran into mine. "Seriously."

I looked up at him, and he did seem serious. I dared myself to hold his gaze without blushing or looking away, but it was like looking at the sun. I was blinded by the angles of his cheekbones, the green of his eyes, the fundamental sweetness of his expression. The way his hair curled around his ears and face now that we were here in the moist sea air. The crooked tooth that peeked through when he smiled a certain way. I felt energy surging inside me that was both unsettling and exciting.

"Show me," he said.

"What?" I faltered.

"I want to see what you do! Here," he said, grabbing his messenger bag and taking out his cell phone. "Do your stuff."

"Are you sure? I don't want to break it or anything."

"Oh, come on," he scoffed, nudging the phone toward me. "Just take it."

I let him place it in the palm of my hand, and I closed my fingers around it. Zapping the phone would be simple; I could have probably crippled it from across the beach with all the jumbled electricity I had scrambling around me. I felt the shock almost instantly and handed his phone back to him.

"That's it?" he asked, his face skeptical.

"What, you expected an explosion or something?"

He turned the phone over in his hands. "It doesn't seem like anything happened. I mean, it feels warm . . . but that could just be from you holding it."

"I don't know what I did to it exactly."

He fiddled with its buttons, slid its top layer off to reveal a tiny keyboard underneath, pressed a series of keys. "Huh. Well, I don't know, either, but it's definitely messed up. Yeah, no, this is definitely dead."

"Sorry," I said, not quite managing to suppress the "I told you so" tone in my voice. "It'll be fine in a few minutes, though."

"This is amazing. Do another one." He looked up, smiling, revealing the slight gap next to that one perfect crooked tooth. *Keep it together, Daisy,* I told myself.

"Really? You want me to just keep messing up all your stuff?"

"Are you kidding? Totally worth it. Let me get my MP3 player."

"No," I said. "I can do it from here."

I took a deep breath and closed my eyes. This was like the reverse of what I normally had to do to stay in control. Instead of summoning my energy to remain calm, I needed to direct it. I felt the fiery orangeness of barely restrained energy swirling around me, and I let it grow stronger, building and growing and generating outward in concentric circles of force. The sound of the surf built in my ears until it seemed like the sound of my own thoughts, and then, finally, the tinny muffled sound of music broke through from Kevin's messenger bag. I opened my eyes to see him scrambling to shut it off, and by the time he got to his music player, I had already done him the favor.

"You could have let me pick the track," he said, looking sheepish.

"What, I liked it," I said. "What was it?"

"Just something stupid I wrote."

"Seriously? You write music?" I asked, moving closer to him. "Let me hear!"

He held the music player up just out of my reach. "Just one more thing."

"What?"

"I want to feel it. Just . . . barely." He took my hand in his and looked at me. This time I looked back.

"There's nothing really to feel," I said, blushing as deeply as the reddish sunset that was just now beginning to dip into the horizon.

"Uh, my cell phone and music player beg to differ. Also my brain?"

I looked down at our hands. My hand lay palm up in his, and I turned it over and drew my fingertips along his hand until it was just my fingernails resting on the tips of his fingers. The energy I was feeling felt bigger than anything else I had ever felt—bigger than the feeling I'd had when I blew up the computer lab at my old school, bigger even than the feeling I'd had when we'd kissed on Danielle's front lawn—and I was afraid to let it overpower me. I didn't know what it would do if it actually overtook me, and more than that: What about Kevin? What if I triggered something too big for me to undo? I found it hard to breathe deeply, and I felt my chest rise and fall with shallow breaths as my body electrified with sensation. I blinked my eyes for just a moment and felt a rush shiver down my arms and to my fingers, where it buzzed and zapped at the point where we made contact.

"Wow," he said. "Just . . . wow."

I looked up to see him smiling, looking at his fingers as though he expected to see smoke coming out of them.

On the way home, I sat on the handlebars of his bike, the wind in my face, as we rode away from the beach.

"I feel like a little kid," I said.

"Just hang on," he laughed.

When we got to the place where the beach road joined the freeway, he slowed so I could hop off and then we walked along the bike path back toward my house. It was getting dark, and I realized with a sudden urgency that I had been due home long ago. My mom had a rare evening off, and the plan was, when that sort of event occurred, that I would be home waiting for her. Like always. Without a cell phone, our routine involved my utter and total predictability: coming directly home after school unless I had something to do that she knew about. And here I was, not home, not anywhere I was expected to be, not anyplace where she could even make contact with me. I tried to send a silent wave of "be home soon" energy in the general direction of my place, but I knew it was half-hearted, and, more than that, futile. She would be freaked. There was no getting around it.

We walked for a while in silence broken by the occasional force of sound and wind as a car raced by us.

"Thanks for being so cool about all this weird stuff," I said, trying not to look at him so I could sound as though all of this—everything that had transpired over the course of this strange day—was perfectly normal.

"Are you kidding? This has been great. Really."

"Really?" I asked. I couldn't help the goofy grin that took over control of my face, so I turned my head, pretending to scan the traffic.

"Really-really," he said. "I hope this is just the beginning of us getting to hang out together on a regular basis."

My face composed, I turned back to him. "Pinkie swear?"

He held out his pinkie, and I grasped it with mine. "Pinkie swear."

And then before I knew it, we were at the entrance to Pacific Breezes.

"Well, this is me," I said. "Yeah, it's a trailer park, but I figure after everything you've learned about me today, the fact that my mom and I live in a trailer park is probably the least of the weirdness."

"Nah, that's cool," he said. "You guys have a tricked out RV situation?"

"No, not at all," I laughed. "Want to see?"

"I would," he said, smiling. "But I have a long ride back to my place, and it's already dark, so I should head out, I think."

"Okay," I said, trying not to sound disappointed. I knew it was irrational, but I felt as though once this day was over, everything would disappear. Everything would go back to normal, and he wouldn't like me anymore. Or everything would change.

"Hey," he said. "Seriously. Today was great. Thanks for telling me all that stuff, and listening to me ramble about my thing."

"*Pshh,* whatever," I said, digging my hands into my pockets. Was this the good-bye part where we were supposed to kiss again? What if he didn't kiss me? What if he did?

"I really mean it," he said, laughing at me. He took my hand and electricity spiked up my arm.

"Did you feel that?" he asked. I nodded.

And then he leaned forward and lightly, sweetly, tenderly, just barely kissed me on my lips, his hand on my hair, a gentle shock. I felt chills, and the nervous excitement in my stomach blossomed into all-over fluttery euphoria.

"Does this always feel this amazing?" I blurted, then immediately regretted.

But he looked at me with his serious, sleepy eyes and shook his head.

"No."

Then he got on his bike and waved a hand, that half-smile playing on his face again. "See you at school Monday."

I just waved back. I didn't trust my voice to speak.

twenty-eight

I heard her voice as soon as I put my key in the door.

"Where were you? I was worried sick." My mom was frantic with anxiety and relief as I walked in.

"I know, I know, I'm really sorry," I said, trying my best to look contrite.

"You know? Really? Then why weren't you home?"

"Mom, I'm sorry, I was just with some friends—"

"Really? Because your friend Danielle called here looking for you, so I know you weren't with her!"

She stood with her hands on her hips. The anger on her face was slightly offset by the SpongeBob-patterned scrubs she wore, but she was an imposing figure nonetheless.

"Mom. I *was* at Danielle's. It just took me a while to get home from there."

She sat down on the couch, one hand on her forehead as she willed herself to stay calm. I could tell that as mad as she was, she was almost ready to give up the interrogation, let go of her anger at me. After all that worrying, she was worn out.

"I'm sorry," I said. "I really didn't mean to be so late. I just lost track of time when I was with Danielle and Vivi—"

"Vivi?" she said. "Who's Vivi? I've never heard you talk about anyone named Vivi."

"Mom. Chill. She's a friend from school. I didn't realize I had to get your personal approval on every friend I have."

"Well, is there anyone else I should know about?"

I couldn't help it: I blushed, and my heart raced, and suddenly her beeper went off. She jumped up to answer it, but I shook my head, holding out my hand. "Sorry, that was just me."

She turned the pager off and looked at me, comprehension slowly dawning on her face. "There's a boy."

"No," I said.

Her face broke open into a huge smile and she pointed her finger at me. "There is! There's a boy!"

I shook my head again, but I could feel my face blazing red. When I looked at her again, she was back to being super-serious and concerned.

"Wait, Daisy, is there a boy?"

"Mom! Stop it. This is totally embarrassing." I sat down on the couch next to her and buried my face in my hands. I could feel her energy gathering, piggybacking onto mine, and so I finally blurted out, "Yes, there's a boy."

"Oh my God," my mom said slowly.

"And he's amazing," I continued, my face hidden but smiling so hard it felt as though the smile itself could break open and take over my whole body. "He's just . . . perfect."

"Nobody's perfect, Daisy."

"Mom, you don't even know—he's so smart, and he's so funny, and he's . . ."

She put her arm around me and gave me a sideways hug. When I looked up I could see that her anger had morphed into some other kind of motherly emotion, and she was shaking her head.

"Daisy."

"What?" I asked, feeling defensive.

She looked at me with such sadness in her eyes, and I felt like she was about to tell me something, but she stopped herself.

"Nothing. I'm just glad everything's okay," she said. Then she stood up, running her hands through her short hair, and sighed. "But I'm exhausted. Waiting for you and worrying that you might have gotten hurt or burned down the school or fried something inadvertently is more tiring than you might think."

I knew that she'd been worried about me, but her words stung. Didn't she see, didn't she know, couldn't she *tell* how hard I worked every day to keep myself in control? To make sure I *didn't* do anything, even inadvertently? It took so much effort for me to keep my energy in check all the time, smooth and unobtrusive. Had she really not even noticed?

But she laughed with relief as she continued to talk. "Who would have thought it was something normal keeping you out late. A boy!" She paused to give me her Serious-Mom look. "Don't think we're done talking about this, though."

"I know," I said, battling my irritation and disappointment. "But can we just talk about it all tomorrow?"

"What's this kid's name again?" she asked as she moved toward the kitchen, ignoring my question.

"I never said in the first place. But it's Kevin."

"And he's a . . . sophomore like you? Someone from one of your classes?" She took a plate out of the oven.

"He's a senior—"

"A senior!" she said, taking the plate to the table.

"Mom! Tomorrow?"

"Okay, okay," she said, holding her hands up in surrender. "We'll talk about it tomorrow. Here's dinner—I kept it warm, but you'll have to see how it held up. I'm going to take a shower and get to sleep. I have to go in early, so I won't see you till tomorrow night." She looked at me pointedly. "Here. On time."

"How many times do I have to apologize?" I asked.

"Just once more," she smiled.

"Okay, I'm sorry," I said.

She gave me a quick squeeze before she headed off to the shower.

"Eat up and get to bed. And prepare yourself psychologically, because we *will* continue this conversation later."

Ugh. More talking, I thought as I sat down to eat. Romeo eagerly butted into my calves, nudging for scraps. But really that was no big deal. A tense interrogation from my mom I could handle—even if it was about a boy.

But tonight, I had a bigger problem to deal with. One she couldn't see, one she couldn't protect me from.

One that I'd pushed out of my head all day in favor of being with Kevin.

One that I'd been too scared to confront.

One that I'd been avoiding thinking about since that moment in Danielle's room when I heard him whisper into my soul.

A ghost.

part three

twenty-nine

My plan was simple, if slightly irrational: I would stay awake all night. Surely if I remained vigilant, I reasoned, I could prevent Patrick from making contact. He couldn't come through if I was actively preventing him from trying, could he?

His slithery voice still echoed in my brain: *I know you can hear me.* It gave me chills just to remember it. I sat on my bed with Romeo, a stack of books on my bedside table. I crossed my legs into half lotus and focused on my breath. Simple *pranayama* practice: covering one nostril while breathing deeply in and out through the other; then switching sides and breathing in and out through the other nostril; then, after a few rounds of that, breathing in as deeply as possible through both nostrils, then holding in that long deep breath as long as I could stand it, and finally, thankfully, exhaling through both nostrils. I felt clear after that, clear and expansive and focused. The buzzing sensation in my arms and legs told me my energy was ready and waiting, but controlled. The purring sound from my lap told me that Romeo approved as well.

It is hard to stay awake with a sleeping cat on your lap.

I read for a while, careful not to disturb Romeo while still using him as an efficient way to prop up my book, stopping every now and then to check on the time. 11:15. 11:37. 12:02. 12:43. And then, as Romeo's peaceful purring began to infect me with drowsiness, it seemed like an eminently good idea to just nap for a little while.

There had been no whispering ghost voice, no spooky presence, no attempts at communication from the spirit world. Perhaps falling asleep wasn't such a terrible concept after all.

I dropped my book and turned off the light.

I'm in Veronica's study, upstairs on the second floor, looking out over the field. The long grass bends in the wind and the tree leaves ruffle like the feathers of giant birds. Clouds loom. A storm is brewing.

I'm Jane again. Looking out the window, awaiting Veronica's return. But this is not the night of the party. I feel older. A ring weighs heavily on my finger.

With a sudden certainty I know it's been five years since Veronica's disappearance. Five years since I left with my mother for a weekend visit with family and returned to the news of Lily's tragic accident. Five years since the suicide of Veronica and James's father. Four years since I accepted, in the depths of my grief, James's proposal.

We are married. But Veronica is gone. Lily is gone. James is gone, too, for the moment, away somewhere on yet another trip, more business to take care of before he returns. I am alone in the big house, sitting at what used to be Veronica's desk, and I still miss her.

I take out a small wooden box from the bottom drawer. The box had been a wedding present from James, something he'd made himself. He had meant it to be for jewelry, but I'd filled it with mementos of Veronica—small things to keep my memory of her alive.

The box smells of lavender as I open it. It comforts me to look through the familiar contents. There is a ribbon I'd saved, a piece of embroidery. Fragile, dusty flowers, a daisy poised to crumble at my touch. A spool of thread. A cloth napkin from the party that fateful night when she disappeared.

James says I'm maudlin, holding on to these things. Angry that I still mourn the memory of my best friend. I'm angry that he isn't still mourning the memory of his sister. *You're entirely too dramatic,* James chides me when we argue about this. *She was never happy here. You know she fought bitterly with our father. She probably just ran away—struck out on her own. You know how independent she was.*

But I know in my heart that can't be true. Veronica would never do something that drastic without telling me. And anyone who knew her knew that she'd never run away from a problem. How could he believe that, even for a moment?

I tell myself that he does so only because it enables him to live with his own sadness about what happened.

And he is sad, I know, though usually his sadness comes out as anger. Like that day after Veronica first went missing, when I saw him and Lily from the schoolhouse. He'd been so harsh with her, and when I confronted him about it, he'd told me he'd felt as sad and helpless as I did, and it made him lash out at one of the last people to see Veronica alive. And then she, too, was gone. It was hard for him to live with the guilt. And so, unlike me, who embraced it, he pushed it away. That was his sadness: dismissal.

I close the box and return it to the drawer, but as I do I notice something curious. The back of the drawer seems to have given way. I take the box out and place it on the desk. Perhaps I have damaged the drawer somehow, forced the box against it and pushed the wood out of joint. But as I inspect it more closely, I see there is a false panel. And there, between the loose, false panel and the true back of the drawer, is a small, leather-bound notebook.

With shaking hands I withdraw it.

Veronica's flowing handwriting fills the pages. Through tears I pick out phrases in her elegant cursive as I thumb through the book, but my sadness turns to shock as I try to make sense of what she's written on the last few pages.

Lily came to me last night and told me about the attack. I don't want to believe it, but deep down I know she is telling the truth. I told her I would speak to Father immediately—make him cancel the party and attend to this—but she begged me not to. She's frightened for her life. And I am terrified as well, now that I know her secret. But what else can I do? Father must know. Something must be done about James.

I jump as I hear the door open.

"Jane?"

It's James.

He's home.

I sat up in bed, a cold dread washing over me. My heart raced in a flood of panic and the lights in my room flashed on before I could even think to stay calm. Romeo stirred at the foot of my bed, meowing in protest at the brightness, and I squeezed my eyes shut and zapped the lights off. I could feel my stomach lurching, a pit of unsettling, jumpy butterflies, and my body alive, every nerve ending raw and firing.

Something must be done about James. What did it mean? Veronica had been writing in her diary about Lily, about telling her father about the attack. What did James have to do with anything? The dream ended so abruptly, but this time without any warning from Lily, just a feeling of terror that I couldn't shake.

Romeo rolled back over to his other side and flicked his tail comfortingly over my leg. But I stayed sitting up, my body pulsing with my racing heartbeat, entirely on edge.

I had the distinct sense that someone was watching me.

I looked around the room, trying to interpret the looming shapes and shadows. And then, in the right-hand corner of my room, I saw it: a vaguely greenish glow.

"Who's there?" I said sharply, disturbing Romeo again. He turned over with a start, facing the light in the corner, then suddenly arched his back and hissed, leaping off the bed to run out of the room, squeezing himself through my barely open door. Now the panic was back, a dread that made me feel cold and shaky.

In the corner, the green glow pulsed, a small nebula on the edge of my room. It was translucent, almost neon, and formless, an ever-shifting shapeless energy I felt desperate to convince myself was some kind of trick of the eye, a waking nightmare, some kind of odd hallucination.

gift

I stayed in my bed, barely breathing, as it remained there, in the corner of my room, oscillating, pulsing, sometimes green, sometimes an icy blue, sometimes barely visible at all. I found myself mesmerized by it—as panicked as I was, I couldn't stop myself from watching it, rigid with fear. I should turn on the lights, I thought, and I tried to send out a flare of energy to zap them back on and banish this . . . whatever it was I was thinking I saw. But I found, to my shock, that I couldn't. I couldn't summon any energy at all. I felt frozen—not just stuck, but literally cold—as I realized what I was looking at: my own energy, materializing outside of me.

Not quite, I heard a voice say.

But *heard* is the wrong word, because I didn't hear it. I felt it. That same voice creeping into my head. Patrick's voice.

This isn't just you. It's me. It's our energy, combined.

"I don't understand—" I began. And then the greenish, pulsing light grew larger as it moved closer to me, enveloping my bed entirely and bathing me in its glow. I felt a sensation of absolute bliss wash over me, as though the tide of my energy that had washed away was now back, filling me with a gentle strength as warm and calming as a bubble bath.

A feeling of peace opened up, and I felt myself blossoming into sleep. Everything felt so absolutely right, so overwhelmingly beautiful, the panic faded away, the frightening dream now absorbing itself into the amnesia of sleep.

So this is what it felt like being visited by a ghost.

How could I have been so afraid of this?

We have a lot in common, you and I, I heard the voice say. *I have my energy, you have yours. Shame neither of us can use it fully.*

I was drifting in an energized haze, and I could barely think, but I felt myself resisting his implication.

True, you are not trapped the way I am, Patrick said, as though he had heard the inside of my head. *I am trapped here on the spirit side. But you are trapped here, in your life.*

—No, I thought through the fog. The green energy swirled now, shapeshifting into no form at all, a looming glow hovering over me, bathing me in its light.

You are right, perhaps trapped is the wrong word. You are hobbled. Unable to use your full powers, your energy kept on a constant leash. And yet your mother still doubts you.

I remembered the conversation earlier, when my mom had been so angry with me for being late—not because she'd been worried I was gone, but because she'd been worried I'd done something. Lost control.

Did you ever think, perhaps, that your mother's desire for you to control your power is less about helping you cope and more about helping her cope? Keeping you in her control? Keeping you so repressed and tamped down that perhaps eventually your ability might disappear, shrivel up and fall off from disuse?

I fought to stay out of the fog, but it was too compelling. The energy surrounding me beckoned me to give in.

She babies you, Patrick said. *She can't even tell you the truth about your own father.*

"What?" I croaked, my voice a sleepy whisper.

Shh, he said. *Don't talk. Sleep.*

I shook my head, trying to free myself from the delicious-feeling energy that surrounded me. "I don't want to sleep," I said. "Dreams . . ."

Forget about the dreams, I heard Patrick say. *This energy is more powerful than any dream you might have.*

And I felt like I had no choice as I gave myself over to it.

I breathed in the greenish, blueish energy around me and floated to sleep, completely unafraid.

thirty

If this was what it was like for Vivi, no wonder she staggered around in a daze all the time. All weekend I was in a fog, sleeping more hours than I was awake, dizzily aware of being wrapped in green-blue energy, snug as a blanket, as I slept. I was no longer frightened by the idea of Patrick communicating with me—it wasn't scary in the least. The dream I'd had Friday night—the dream of being in the study, discovering the diary—that had been scary. But the energy rush I'd experienced when Patrick had spoken to me? That had simply been amazing. And it pushed the dreams right out of my mind.

Was he right? Was I allowing myself to be hobbled, holding my powers in check all the time? I wasn't sure I totally agreed with what he'd said about my mom, but I had to admit, he had a point. It was easier for her—for everyone—if I abided by the rules, kept myself together, stayed in control. But was it easier for me? And what had he meant about my father?

I woke up slowly Monday morning, the light from my window filtering past the curtains like the warm embodiment of happiness. Everything felt delicious. My legs under the weight of the blanket, my arms over my head, resting on the pillow—all over I felt that sleepy relaxation that made my body feel so distant from my mind, as if I was floating, unencumbered by any physical shape or form, just existing, a haze of myself.

Then Romeo pounced on the bed, landing on my foot, and I felt myself come back to myself again, waking up fully. He meowed pitifully and walked up my leg to sit on my stomach, where he kneaded and glanced pointedly toward the door.

"Okay, okay, breakfast, I get it," I said, rolling over to my side so that he was forced to jump down. I sat up, looking around the room. In the daylight it just looked like my normal room, strewn with clothes and books and shoes, nothing in its proper place. No hint of any greenish miasma or ghoulish force. Maybe it had all just been a dream. I felt a cold shiver as I got out of bed, and I wrapped my robe around me as I made my way to the kitchen to attend to Romeo.

When I got to school, Kevin was at my locker, talking to Danielle as he waited for me.

"And here she is," Danielle said, a sour look on her face, by way of a greeting. "I was just filling Kevin in on what happened after you guys took off like freaks on Friday."

"What? You took off, too," I said, "and all we did was—"

"Ew," Danielle said, holding her hands up on either side of her face to block us out. "So not interested in hearing the sordid details."

I tried to protest, but Danielle kept talking.

"So, there I was, right, having to deal with my mom in the car playing Twenty Questions with Vivi—who are you, how are you, why are you here, are you okay—and Vivi not having the sense to respond like some kind of normal person. Seriously, we need to get her back to her home planet or something, because who doesn't know how to answer questions like that without being weird? And she freaking *told my mom* she was staying at Mr. Terry's house—like she couldn't have said 'Oh, I have to drop off an extra-credit assignment,' or 'I'm babysitting his kids tonight' or whatever. No, she had to go with, 'My mom thinks I'm possessed, so she kicked me out, and now I'm living with everyone's favorite English teacher.'"

She paused to stare at us, making sure we were getting the sheer ridiculousness of what she'd had to endure.

"Okay, she didn't say it exactly like that, but still . . . she said she was staying there! And then so of course my mom is freaking out, and she interrogates me all the way home, and she wants to call Social Services or whatever on Vivi, or at least talk to the school board about Mr. Terry. But I calm her down and cover for all the weirdness, and she pretty much buys whatever the hell I was saying—I don't even know what I was saying, I was just babbling at that point to get her off the trail. But then we get home and she sees what happened, and . . . let's just say it wasn't pretty."

"What do mean, she saw what happened?" I asked.

Danielle's eyes grew large as she glared at me like I was an idiot. "Hello? You didn't see it? You didn't happen to catch the whirlwind of destruction all over my house thanks to your stupid magical powers?"

I stepped back. "What do you mean?"

"Oh, I'm sorry, I forgot, you guys were getting married on my front lawn," she said, rolling her eyes. "How could you have possibly been expected to witness the minor apocalypse going on in my bedroom?"

"What? I thought—"

"I think you were there for the part where my alarm clock went crazy and my TV practically exploded and everybody's cell phones had a party," she said. "But maybe you missed the part where the entire house shorted out and everything stopped working?"

I felt jolted by the news, and I looked at Kevin. I couldn't read the expression on his face, but I suspected he might be reconsidering his previous statement about wanting us to hang out more often.

"Did everything eventually *start* working?" he asked.

Danielle shrugged. "Eventually. But the place looked like a tornado hit it." And now she glared at me. "And so, thanks to you and your freakish abilities, I am now under house arrest and phone restriction, and you are banned from ever coming over. Ever. Again."

Danielle must have seen the look on my face because she softened a bit and said, "Her idea, not mine."

"I don't know what to say," I told her. "I'm so sorry. I didn't mean for any of it to happen. I swear."

I opened my locker, hiding my face to try to compose myself as I took my books out, and when I closed it again I looked up to find not one annoyed friend but two. Vivi stood there, her arms crossed, glaring at me with a look even more intimidating than Danielle's.

"What?" I asked, trying to steel myself against whatever was coming next.

"Patrick," she said, as though that explained everything. I slumped against the locker, sighing, as she continued. "I know he came to see you. I know he made contact."

Kevin and Danielle looked at me expectantly.

"So what if he did?" I said, sounding more defensive than I would have liked. "Friday night I had more of the dream, and then . . . he was just . . . *there* when I woke up."

"Whoa," Kevin said.

"What happened? What was it like? Did he look like a person? Was he all ghosty?" Danielle asked.

"No, it wasn't like that," I said. I reached for Vivi's arm, but she pulled it away. "Really. It was just this green . . . presence in my room. That's all."

"What did he want?" Kevin asked.

"I don't know."

Vivi's eyes narrowed as she looked at me, and I thought she was still mad, but when she came closer I saw that really she was desperate. "Just do me a favor," she said quietly, so Kevin and Danielle had to strain to hear her. "The next time he comes to you, please. Just send him back."

Before I could even respond to her, she left.

"Okay. Weirdness," Danielle said as we watched Vivi disappear down the crowded hallway.

"Whatever," I said. "Give her a break. She's obviously having a hard time."

"What about you?" Kevin said. "You okay? I mean, after your . . . weekend visitation?"

"Yeah, I guess," I said. "I feel a little out of it, but, you know, I guess that's normal."

"Whatever that means," Danielle said, and slammed her locker shut.

thirty-one

School passed with a drowsy interminability. Teachers' voices droned as I fought the urge to give in to delicious sleep, the sensation of which still lingered in me from the morning. And any moments of clarity—seeing Kevin at lunchtime, walking with Danielle between classes, even Vivi glaring at me with suspicion—seemed to fade into blurry softness as soon as I found myself sitting once again in a plastic classroom desk chair. I felt drugged, almost. I had the sense that I wasn't really there, no matter where I was, whether I was being called upon in class or walking through the halls or standing at my locker. I was numb, and it suddenly just seemed so clear to me that nothing really mattered, nothing at all.

After school Kevin found me at my locker and steered me toward the big lawn. We sat, the sun fierce on my back, warming me through to my bones.

"Hello?" Kevin said, waving his hand in front of my face, and I realized he had been speaking to me. "You've been such a space cadet today."

"Hmmm," I said.

He gave me a look. "I hope that ghost didn't, like, steal your soul or anything."

"Hmmm," I said again.

"Very funny," he said, thinking I was joking. He shook his head.

170

"Okay. Well, anyway. So, I have a theory about these dreams of yours."

"That's interesting," I said. "So do I."

He wrinkled his forehead. "Okay, you first?"

I shrugged, and it felt like I was shrugging underwater, like I could make ripples through the air; that's how heavy it all was. "Maybe it's nothing. But I feel like—especially with all the info you found—I don't know, like I lived it. Like I actually lived the stuff I've been dreaming about."

"Huh." He leaned back, thinking. "I guess that could be one explanation for it."

That jarred me enough to focus my attention. I felt myself sliding from dreamy and suggestible to edgy and defensive. "You seem skeptical."

He put his hands up. "I'm not saying it's not possible, and I'm not saying that you're not experiencing what you're experiencing. I just think—with everything I've read—I just think there may be some other way to explain all this stuff."

"Like what?" I said. "I mean, go for it. Spell it out for me. Tell me how crazy I am."

"You're not crazy," he said. "But I mean, let's look at this logically. Don't you think it's possible that . . . well . . . at some point, you came across the house—read about it somehow, maybe even went there on a tour when you were little, like I did—and just forgot that you ever knew about it? And then these dreams cropped up, from your subconscious, and it seemed like it was all something you'd *lived* before, but really it was just something you'd *learned about* before." He winced in anticipation of how well I would take his theory.

"Uh-huh," I said, crossing my arms. "So it's all just a case of overactive imagination. Got it."

"I didn't say that exactly."

"But then how do you explain Danielle and I *both* dreaming about it? We can't have *both* learned and then forgotten about some creepy old haunted house story or whatever, and then fabricated it into some kind of crazy shared dream."

"Well," he shrugged, "I don't know, I'm just putting it out there. I mean, it's not entirely out of the realm of possibility that these dreams are a kind of . . . I don't know, group hallucination or something."

I stared at him. "You're serious."

"I'm just trying to stay grounded in reality," he said.

"And I'm not?"

"Look," he said, and he put a hand on my knee. Electricity rippled up my thigh. "I was just thinking maybe it would be good to take a field trip."

"What?"

"Maybe we should go to the house, in real life. Check it out. See if it triggers anything."

"Oh." I sat with my arms folded still, his hand still resting on my leg. "So you're not saying I just dreamed this all up for no reason."

"No. I'm saying, maybe if we go there and see it in person, it might put all these dreams to rest for you."

I slumped a little and let myself relax. He traced his fingers lightly along my arm.

"I mean, you seem kinda wiped."

"Uh, yeah," I said. "Who wouldn't be, after the last couple of days."

"Okay, see?"

"See what?"

"I'm right," he grinned.

I rolled my eyes. "If by 'right' you mean 'annoying,' then yes."

He stood up. "Come on, let's get to the bus. It's just about that time."

I followed him, and as I walked the drowsy, dreamy feeling settled over me again, the rhythm of my walking lulling me back into that dulled, pleasant state. Beneath it, though, was a thrum of doubt. Could he be right? Could all of these dreams just be the work of an overactive, over-empathetic imagination? It didn't seem possible. And yet as annoyed as I was, a part of me hoped it might actually be true. Because if it wasn't, what was the alternative? That we were all being haunted by a ghost?

It was hard not to feel sluggish. At the bus stop, Kevin's smile washed over me like the crest of a dream wave, and I leaned into him as we sat waiting, a faint vibration in my arms and legs reminding me I was still there, beneath the fog.

Kevin seemed content to let me be quiet, but my mom was a different story. I could sense that her radar was tripped, and she pestered me with questions all through homework and dinner, trying to draw me out. The fog feeling gave me that sense again that nothing mattered and everything was okay, so I answered her, even the questions about Kevin, and steered myself toward sleep. I could barely keep my eyes open.

In bed, finally surrendering to the fatigue that had wrapped itself around me all day, I felt myself floating, suspended, weightless, and when I forced open my eyes I saw that I was bathed in a greenish glow, the energy pulsing around me, lighting up my body like a circuit board. It felt like I was plugged into some kind of huge energy source, regenerating and recharging me as it shifted and recreated itself, spinning out and out and on and on. I was drunk on this expansive, powerful sensation of light and force, turned in on myself, a wire vibrating, creating harmonics, overtones, sound so pure it sounded like silence.

Daisy, I heard from somewhere very far away. *Daisy, I know you can hear me.*

I fought my way to the surface of my own thoughts and saw, on the edge of my bed, a ghostly form, gradually taking a human shape as it swirled and shifted before my eyes.

Take your time, Patrick thought into my head. *Your energy is becoming stronger. Give yourself time to adapt.*

He waved a ghostly hand, a glowing arc trailing in its wake. I could see his features now, shimmering in and out of focus, and I was mesmerized, powerless to resist as his hand reached out toward mine. My arm was enveloped in a smoky green mist, and I felt a bolus of electric energy discharge into my body. I felt every cell of my body dancing, alive with intention. The lights in my room flickered on. The lights outside my window flickered on. It looked like the neighbor's lights flickered on as well.

Do you see the power you have?

Suddenly I was jolted awake, able to think clearly for just a moment, remembering guiltily about Vivi's request for me to send Patrick away the next time he appeared.

"Turn it off!" I said, yanking my arm back. He dissolved into a translucent swirl, and the neighborhood once again plunged back into darkness.

You can't run away from it forever, Daisy. I couldn't see him anymore, but felt the chill that seemed to accompany him whenever he was near.

"I'm not running away from anything," I said, but I suddenly felt exhausted again, the world submerging me as I went under.

Shh . . . I heard him say, and then everything faded away until the morning.

thirty-two

"It's weird," I said to Danielle as we sat in the corner of Mr. Terry's room on Tuesday at lunch. I hadn't wanted to tell anyone, really, about the true details of my ghostly visitations, but it was too freaky to keep to myself. Of course I couldn't tell Vivi. But Danielle was my best friend, after all. And here we were, eating lunch together. So I couldn't really *not* talk about it. "I'm not sure exactly what's happening. But—and this is the weird part—it doesn't exactly feel terrible."

"Really," she said.

"Yeah. I thought I would feel more scared, you know, having a ghost encounter. But when he shows up, it actually feels kind of . . . amazing. Like I'm in a battery charger or something. Getting my energy re-energized."

"Well, I guess that's good," she said. "But, uh, I wouldn't exactly share that information with Vivi. She's a little tense about her ghost boyfriend being friendly with anyone else."

"Yeah, I got that."

"But the dreams," she prompted. "You're still dreaming, right?"

"Yes," I said. "I finally had a new one. But it was later in time. This one was, like, five years after you—I mean, Veronica—disappeared. And it ended kind of scary. I think."

"What do you mean, 'you think'?"

"When I woke up, Patrick was there, and then there was all

175

this . . . energy. And it kind of wiped away the exact details of the dream. Or nightmare. Or whatever it was."

"Huh." She picked at her sandwich, deconstructing it on the napkin she'd spread out as a placement. Bread, then turkey, then lettuce, then tomato. Once it was fully disassembled, she started eating its components, one by one.

"You know, I've started having the dreams again, too."

"Wait—dreams? Or *the* dreams. Like, Veronica dreams? "

"*The* dreams. Yeah, they were gone for a while, but . . ."

"But?"

She stopped eating. "I did some more of that automatic writing stuff."

"You did? I thought you were freaked out by all the woo-woo superpower craziness." I crumpled up my bag of chips and aimed for a clean basket into the corner garbage can.

"I was," she said, leaning over to grab my badly shot chip bag and dump it into the trash for me. "I mean, I am. But. I don't know— Vivi talks to Patrick, *you're* evidently talking to Patrick. Why can't I talk to a ghost, or a dream person or whatever?"

"Well, did you?"

"Yeah," she said, looking serious. "I talked to Veronica. And once I did, I don't know, I was just able to start dreaming again."

"So, is it okay? Is it the over-and-over bad stuff you were dreaming before? Did you dream my same dream, the five-years-later one?"

"No. It's weird, actually. It's lots of different stuff—it's more like . . . memories almost. Like, sometimes I'm younger, and you and I are playing—I mean, Veronica and Jane, but you know what I mean. And sometimes it's the party dream again, just the beginning of it, before I run away. And sometimes it's just me and James." She shivered. "Sometimes I get a bad feeling about that guy."

"Me too—that's one thing I remember about this last dream," I said. "There was something bad about James. Even though I was married to him."

"You were what now?"

"Yeah. Well, you know—it was all there in the stuff Kevin printed out for us about the Stone House. Jameson married Jane . . ."

The other facts hung in the air around us, unsaid: Veronica, missing; Lily, dead under mysterious circumstances; Jameson, killed in the fire.

"You know," I say, after a pause. "Kevin kind of thinks we're all just hallucinating this stuff. Like we somehow read about it and then forgot about it and are imagining it or whatever."

"Seriously?"

"Well," I shrugged. "Maybe not exactly. But kind of. I mean, I guess his point is, what's more freaky—that we might be imagining it, or that it's real?"

She smirked. "You tell me. You're the one getting supercharged by someone else's personal ghost."

"Keep it down," I whispered, looking over in Mr. Terry's direction.

Danielle looked there, too, and then lowered her voice to a whisper. "Don't you think it's weird?"

"What?"

"You know. The whole Vivi/Mr. Terry thing."

I shook my head. "They do not have a 'thing.' It's not like that."

Danielle arched her eyebrow. "You have to admit . . ."

"No, I really don't!" I said. "And neither do you! Besides, like Vivi said, it's just for a few weeks. It's no big deal."

"Then why is it so hush-hush?" Danielle asked. "Why are we whispering about it? And I mean, come on. She's in love with some old-timey-dude ghost, right? Total daddy complex, right? So, hello, there's Mr. Terry, totally old and dad-like, right?"

"Ugh," I said, putting my hands over my ears. "Stop saying words."

Danielle leaned back and smiled. "It's pretty sad when you're more comfortable talking about ghosts and psychic dreams than actual real-life drama."

"That's just it," I said, standing up and getting my stuff together. "It's someone *else's* drama. Stop loving it so much!"

"I'm not *loving* it," she said, talking louder now. "It's just . . . fascinating."

The bell rang and we headed out toward fifth period.

"Glad I could provide some fascination for you ladies," Mr. Terry said as we walked out the door.

"What?" I stammered as I turned around to see him at his desk, arms behind his head as he leaned back in his chair.

"I just heard the word 'fascinating' and assumed you were talking about me," he smiled.

"Yep, always, Mr. Terry," Danielle said and herded me out the door.

I was uneasy as we walked to class.

After school, Kevin came up behind me at my locker and put his hands over my eyes.

"I'm kidnapping you," he announced.

I gestured to Danielle putting her books away at the next locker, and to the hordes of people around us. "There are a million witnesses here. Kind of a fatal flaw in your plan."

"Well, except that I don't care about you being kidnapped," Danielle said.

I grabbed his hands, a small shock zapping my palms as I did so, and pulled them away from my eyes. "Some friend you are!"

"Eh, I trust him," she said. "He's all responsible and stuff. His kidnapping will probably involve a sedate walk to a reputable dining establishment, a square meal with plenty of vegetables, then perhaps a viewing of one of the many popular moving pictures on display at the local cinema, and a nice chat with your mom after he brings you home at a reasonable hour."

Kevin shook his head. "Man, you are harsh."

"Oh, you have something wild planned?" Danielle asked.

"What if I did?"

"Well, that would run counter to all my theories. Back to the drawing board, I guess." She slammed her locker shut and nudged me. "Hey, so give me a call later, if you survive your kidnapping."

"Deal," I said as she walked off. I turned to Kevin. "So?"

"So?" he asked.

"The kidnapping?"

"Ah, yes, the kidnapping," he said.

"Where exactly are you taking me?"

"It's a surprise." Kevin smiled.

"I hate surprises."

"Man, you're grumpy today," he said, but he didn't look unhappy about it. He slung his bag and his guitar case over his shoulder and held out his other hand for me to take. "Come on."

I wasn't exactly grumpy. But it's true that I felt like something had happened with Patrick's contact. My energy felt bigger—more unpredictable. Jumbled and jumpy and wilder than it used to be. Harder to control. I had tried doing yoga this morning, to help connect myself with my own breath, but it had been a struggle. In school I'd noticed people having problems with their phones when I was around. The clock in first period had jumped ahead by fifteen minutes when I sneezed. Even holding Kevin's hand now I felt a sharp and annoying tingling sensation running up the nerves of my arm. I shook my hand free.

"You all right?" he asked.

"Yeah," I waved him off. "Just . . . energy overload right now."

He nodded. "That's good, though, right? I mean, you've been kind of out of it lately."

"I know." It sounded sharper than I meant it, so I attempted a grin to take the edge off. "So . . . where are we going again?"

"Nice try. You'll see when we get there."

thirty-three

We took the bus to downtown Coronado, and once there he led me along touristy streets near the beach. I could hear seagulls cawing in the distance and smell the sting of salt water in the air. "We're not going to the fancy beach, are we? Tell me we're not going to the fancy beach."

He made a face at me. "Nah. I know you like your beaches like you like your friends: moody and unkempt and free of tourists. We're almost there, so just stop your guessing."

We walked through the palm tree–lined streets of the shopping district until, amidst the drugstores, Mexican restaurants, and snow and surf shops, we found a nondescript-looking building with a modest banner over the front door. "Historical Society Museum." Kevin stopped walking and gestured toward the building.

"Seriously?" I said.

"Seriously," he said, opening the door. "I told you we were going to take a field trip, right?"

The cramped space was lined with old-timey photographs and turnable kiosks, every flat surface populated with knickknacks. An old woman stood behind a counter stocked with brochures and maps.

"May I help you?"

"Yes," Kevin said. "We'd like to take the Stone House tour."

"You do know that if you want the 'haunted tour,' you'll have to come back around Halloween," she said, peering down at us over her glasses.

"Yes, we know," Kevin said.

She nodded approvingly. "Well, it's just a few blocks away from here. Down Orange and then left on Main. You'll see the signs out front. The next tour is at 4:30, which you can make if you hurry."

"Thanks," I said, and we made our way through the thicket of tchotchkes back to the entrance.

"Are you sure this is a good idea?" I asked Kevin.

He shrugged. "Why wouldn't it be?"

The house was unremarkable from the outside. A little old-fashioned looking compared to the low-slung modern retail stores that surrounded it. But it mostly just looked like a regular old place. Nothing spooky or haunted. Nothing like the house from my dreams, either.

The tour guide was lackluster when he greeted us on the side-walk, perhaps because we were the only ones who showed up for the tour and he didn't want to waste his Stone House knowledge on a couple of teenagers. He droned half-heartedly about stuff we'd already read about from the website, thanks to Kevin's research, and mostly confined himself to facts about the Stone family before any of the "haunted" stuff had supposedly happened. After fifteen minutes standing outside in the hot sun listening to his lecture, I was ready to leave. But Kevin seemed into it, so I tried to appear interested.

Eventually the guide walked us up the front steps and paused before he opened the door. "Now, keep in mind, this is not the original house. The original Stone House was badly damaged in the 1905 fire and had to be rebuilt from the ground up. Its owner at the time, Jane Stone, instructed the builders to re-create the original house down to every last detail, from the wallpaper to the carpeting to the kitchen cabinets. The only thing she changed was the upstairs: She redesigned the floor so that there were no longer any windows on the west side. A strange request, but she was a grieving widow, and so the builders did what she asked. However, when the historical society redid the house, in the early 1970s, they kept it truer to the original plans, with windows. But, as you'll see, they also built internal wooden shutters, which they keep closed to honor the wishes of Mrs. Stone."

"Why did she not want any windows upstairs?" Kevin wondered aloud, more to me than the guide.

"The field," I whispered, suddenly remembering being Jane, looking through the window onto the field, waiting for Veronica to come home. "It used to overlook the field. She didn't want to see it anymore. She didn't want to be reminded."

The guide cleared his throat and led us into the house, where we put down our things in the welcoming cool of modern air-conditioning.

"When the historical society renovated the house, they did make a few changes. None of the furniture here is original, for instance, and other structural elements have been altered as well—you'll notice, for instance, if you compare the current house to the photographs inside, that where we were standing a moment ago was once a porch that wrapped around the house. And of course now there is no porch. There's also no land. The house used to be on grounds that extended about a mile to the west and north—mostly just rough grassland and, eventually, the shoreline."

"And what about the schoolhouse?" I asked.

"Ah. You've done your homework. There was a carriage house on the property that was used as a school for the Stone children and for the children of prospecting families who passed through here during the mini gold rush of the late 1800s. But that, too, was destroyed in the fire and never rebuilt." He handed us each a few more brochures about the house and the historical society. "Feel free to look around. If you have any more questions, I'll be down here."

Kevin looked at me. "Well?"

I glanced around us. We stood in a small entryway, a replica of an antique chandelier looming above us. Before us lay the parlor, smaller than I'd expected, and sparsely furnished. Grand, tall windows were flanked by heavy curtains. To the left stood a stairwell with a graceful curving banister that wound itself up and around the corner to the second floor. The stairs were narrow, and the wallpaper not quite right. But I felt a frisson of recognition.

"Let's go upstairs."

The stairs were narrower and steeper than the stairs I'd dreamed about—everything, in fact, seemed smaller, as though I myself had been shrunk in size and was now walking through a doll's house—but something about them seemed familiar to me. When I reached the curve of the banister at the landing, I paused for a moment at the window. Its circular pane framed what was now a scene of modern life: a bustling intersection, a smattering of people, a series of low, one-story buildings. But for a moment I had a flash of what it might have looked like long ago, what it had looked like in the dream.

Kevin stood next to me on the landing. "Anything?"

I turned toward the smaller set of stairs that completed the transition to the second floor. They led to a narrow hallway with a banister on the left, overlooking the main room of the entrance below, and a series of doors on the right, just as I'd remembered from the dreams.

"Remember, none of this is totally accurate," Kevin said. "It won't look the way the house did when people actually lived here."

I knew that, so I wasn't bothered to find the first room on the right utterly unfamiliar. A solid bookcase lined the north wall; a small, prim armchair sat next to a reading table; a dusty-looking rug hid the floor. I didn't even go in. I wanted to move on to the next room.

Veronica's study.

Like the other room, it looked nothing like what I'd dreamt. But unlike the other room, this one felt like a place I knew. A place I'd been before. The shutters on the large windows were closed, and the room was dark because of it, but I felt an eerie clarity as I stood before them.

"Well?" Kevin asked.

"This is it. This is the house I dreamed about."

Just saying it out loud made my arms break out in goose bumps. We stood in the middle of the room. I faced the windows, remembering a dream version of myself looking out the window to the grounds below, waiting for Veronica, watching with unspeakable sadness for a sign.

Kevin nodded.

"Want to get out of here?"

I sighed with relief and realized I'd been half holding my breath ever since we'd come in the room.

I followed him out, looking down the hall toward the last doorway on the second floor.

"Wait a second," I said to Kevin. He stood on the landing, his head framed by the circular window there. "You go ahead. I just want to check something out."

"Sure. I'll meet you downstairs."

I turned back toward the end of the hall, a surge of nervous energy in my stomach. I tried to quell it with a deep breath and went through the doorway.

It was a small, simple room—again, its west-facing window covered by a solid wooden shutter. A four-poster bed dominated the space. There was a small writing desk in the corner, with a plexiglass case covering its surface. Inside were old-fashioned pens, photographs, and other artifacts from a long-ago time.

And then I saw it.

A beautifully carved wooden box, about the size of a cigar box. The box from my dream. The keepsake box that James had made, that I—that Jane—had filled with mementos of Veronica.

gift

Suddenly I was filled with a feeling of dread, and the memory of the last dream came flooding back. I'd been putting the box away when I'd discovered the false panel in the desk drawer. I'd found Veronica's diary. I'd seen what she had written. And then James had walked in. I felt my heart racing, my breath becoming shallow. The box seemed like a portent of something terrible, something violent. Something I hadn't dreamt about yet.

I ran down the stairs.

"The box," I said, interrupting the tour guide's conversation with Kevin.

"Excuse me?" the tour guide asked.

"The wooden box, in the case on the table in the bedroom upstairs. Is that the original?" I said.

"No, not exactly," he said. "The original was destroyed in the fire. But when the historical society did their renovations, they came across a number of quite detailed sketches Mrs. Stone had made of this wooden box in her later years. They figured it must have been important to her, and so they hired a woodworker to make it based on her plans. An homage to Mrs. Stone and to the house's history."

I gripped Kevin's hand tightly to stop my hands from shaking and hoped he could sense how badly I wanted to get outside, away from the energy of the house. He raised an eyebrow at me, but took his cue and said, "Well, thanks again," to the guide.

"You okay? What was up with the box?" he asked once we were out of the house.

"I dreamt about it. And seeing it here gave me a creepy feeling."

He gave my hand a squeeze as he smiled, trying to lighten the mood. "Just FYI, you do know dreams aren't actually real, right? We're clear on that?"

I dropped his hand and punched him in the shoulder. "What are you, my mom?"

"Ow, okay, okay," he said.

But his hand quickly found mine again, and for a moment we didn't talk.

It was about a thousand degrees outside and the air was heavy with impending rain. I looked up at the second floor, the shutter-blocked windows. In the dream, the house had seemed so impos-ing—perhaps it still would, if it had its original grand porch and surrounding land. But out here it looked small: Even two stories high it seemed almost apologetic next to the modern architecture around it. As the darkening clouds gathered over us, I couldn't help but think of the storm from the first dream, with Veronica running away into the darkened field.

"Listen, thanks for this. I really appreciate it," I said, swinging our hands back and forth. "But if it's okay with you, can we get the heck out of here?"

"Absolutely," he said, and he led us back to the bus stop just as the first drops of rain began to fall.

thirty-four

"Can you stay?" I asked Kevin. The trip to Stone House had truly spooked me. He'd been patient with me on the ride home, arm around me as he listened to me talk about the house and the dreams, braving multiple bus transfers until we finally got to my house. But now that we were here, I was worried. I didn't want to be alone.

"Like, for dinner?"

"Like for tonight," I said. "It's just . . . I'm so freaked out. My mom's working the night shift, and what if I have another dream?"

"Would your mom be okay with me staying?" he asked.

"We can call Danielle, make it a sleepover, whatever. I'm just afraid to be here by myself."

"Hmmm," he said. "Let me think about it—okay, yes. I'll stay."

"Really?"

"Sure."

"There's no TV," I said.

He nodded. "Realized that."

"And no computer or Internet thingy."

He smiled his one-side-of-the-face smile. "Noted."

"And there's really nothing to do that's not totally boring."

"Are you trying to talk me out of staying here with you? You did just ask me to stay, right?"

I put my hands on my forehead, closing my eyes against the realization of my own idiocy. "I'm sorry. I'm such a freak show."

He put his arms around my waist, holding me low. "Hey, I like freak shows. Freak shows are cool. You get to travel around, see the world, make money from tickets and stuff. . . ."

I rolled my eyes, partially to keep myself from crying. I had been trying to stay calm, but I could feel tears gathering.

He saw me blinking them back and said, "Hey, *shh*, seriously, it's okay. Everything's going to be okay. I can stay." His hand on my hair sent sparks charging down my back.

"Seeing the house in real life just freaked me out more than I expected."

"I know," he said, pulling me into a hug. We stood that way for a moment, and I tried to concentrate on how I could feel him breathing, could feel his heart beating, and I slowed my own breathing down to match his, until I was calm. Then I looked up, wiping my eyes, to find him grinning at me.

"I have an idea," he said. "Something to take your mind off ghosts and bad dreams."

"Really?"

"Yeah. Sit down." He gestured to the couch and I sat as he grabbed his guitar case and took out his guitar.

"No," I said. Was he really going to play for me?

"Oh, yes," he smiled. He sat on the chair across from me, holding the guitar easily, one arm cradling its neck, the other draped over the side, his fingers idly resting on the strings. It looked so natural for him, like the instrument was an extension of himself, and it suddenly seemed impossible that until now I had never before seen him in that pose.

"I figured it was probably time," he said. "You should hear for yourself what you've gotten yourself into."

"Right. I'm sure it'll totally change my mind."

He laughed as he fingered a few chords. "It's a chance I'll have to take."

I sat cross-legged on the couch. "So, what are you going to play? Do you take requests?"

He shook his head. "Nope. No requests. I'm going to play something I wrote."

"An original!"

"Something I wrote for *you*, actually."

"Are you serious?"

"Yes, I am," he said.

He ducked his head, his fingers softly strumming the guitar strings, and I was glad he wasn't able to see me blinking back more stupid tears. After a moment he looked up and raised an eyebrow at me, then flattened his hands against the strings to tamp the sound.

"Ready?"

I nodded.

"It's called 'Don't Look Back.'" A satisfied yet slightly embarrassed grin broke out on his face. "You know, like, Orpheus?"

"Oh, right, the rock star."

"I know, I know, it's cheesy. But you'll have to just deal with it."

I held up my hands. "I'm dealing."

He smiled. "Okay then. Well, here goes."

He began to play. I took it in in pieces, like looking at fractured panels of stained glass. I focused on his hair, the way it fell across his face, the way his eyes glanced up at me hesitantly, expectantly, hoping to find some encouragement. The way the tendons in his hands moved as he shifted through chord progressions, the way his voice reverberated sweetly in the cramped space of my living room, the way his knee bounced to keep time. I couldn't let myself assemble the pieces into something whole. If I let myself really feel what I was feeling as he sang, I didn't know what might happen. I might set off every car alarm in a fifty-mile radius. I might explode the neighbors' satellite television. I might fully, really, honestly, for the first time feel the full range of what I was capable of. Instead, I held myself back. I focused on my breathing. I tried not to think about how my heart felt like it was going to race out of my chest.

Then suddenly the final notes faded and he dropped his head.

"Well?" he said, not looking up.

"I love it," I said, nearly catching myself about to say *I love you*. I cleared my throat, hoping he hadn't noticed my almost-slip.

He lifted his head, looking, for the first time, earnest and vulnerable rather than self-assured. "I haven't written a song in a while, so it's kind of rough. And it's not really my normal style—I've been told the music I usually play is kind of . . . weird."

"Are you kidding me? It's the most beautiful song I've ever heard."

He put the guitar down in its open case and came to sit next to me on the couch. He reached out for my hand and I was shaken off balance by the contact. I pulled my hand back sharply, protectively, working to breathe. I was a live wire, completely electrified.

"What is it?" he asked, concerned.

I turned away from him. "I've, uh, got a lot of . . . electrical activity going on right now. That I can't control. I don't want to trigger something for you."

He gently turned me back toward him, his arm a fiery jagged lightning strike of energy along my back as he leaned in close. "I'll take my chances."

You shouldn't be holding yourself back.

I sat up on the couch, suddenly awake and terrified. "What? Who said that?" I looked around me, panicked, and then I saw it: a bright blue glow in the corner armchair, where Kevin had sat earlier, serenading me. The glow radiated coldness, iciness. It began to take the shape of a man.

Kevin lay on the floor near me, completely asleep. Danielle snored, sprawled in a sleeping bag on the other side of the room. She'd come over after dinner and we had stayed up well past midnight, talking and playing board games (or "bored games," as Danielle called them) and doing our best to stay awake, but eventually sleep had won. Startled back into consciousness, I felt a coldness surround me, and my heart raced.

gift

What you could do with your abilities if you only embraced them.
It was Patrick.

You don't have to talk out loud, he said, just as I was going to say something.

—I don't want to talk to you, I thought.

But you must. Do you not sense how expansive you have become? I know you are aware of the increase in your energy.

The icy blue shifted to green, and I saw the shape of him more completely. As he materialized, I felt a little of the calming presence I'd experienced before with him, when he was just a glowing pulse in the corner of my room, lulling me into submission.

You don't even realize your potential. There is so much possibility for you, and you're not exploring it. You could be doing anything—controlling the electrical grid, destroying Internet communication—really, the possibilities are limitless.

—I don't want to be doing any of that stuff.

You could be kissing your boyfriend.

I glanced down at Kevin.

I see I have piqued your interest. Yes, I see how you are holding yourself back. And not just from your new romance. From everything. Tell me, with all your concentration on remaining calm and your deep-breathing exercises, when do you actually breathe?

—What do you mean?

I mean, when do you fully inhale and fully exhale—fully, without holding something back, hanging on to some reserve, keeping yourself in check so as to stave off . . . what, exactly? Some stopped watches? A malfunctioning cell phone?

—How about setting the computer lab on fire? Or frying everything in my friend's house?

I didn't say you didn't need to master your powers. Of course you must. But in order to do that, you must know what you are fully capable of.

I felt myself grow panicky. Wasn't that what I had been wrestling with earlier? The fear of learning what fully experiencing my emotions might manifest? I looked at Kevin and Danielle, who continued to sleep as if nothing was amiss.

Don't worry about your friends. I have ensured that they are deeply asleep.

—How?

Well, thanks to you and your energy, I have some energy of my own to spare at the moment. REM states are easy to induce. You could be doing this. Right now. Total mind control—don't you see? Isn't that extremely compelling to you?

—No, it's extremely not.

You can't tell me you don't want a little control. I can feel you trying to control me right now, putting up a force field around you so that I can't tap into your energy as directly.

Was that what I was doing? I had instinctively tried to gather my energy around me, pull myself together. How had he sensed that?

Do me a favor. Just let yourself feel your true energy.

—What do you mean?

You know exactly what I mean. Stop holding your breath. Feel it. Feel yourself be alive. They don't want you to feel it, but you deserve to, don't you think?

I was enveloped in the swirling glow, and before I realized it, my fear fell away and in its place was fire. A snaking line of electricity moved up my arms and legs, and I felt a burning, buzzing vibration pulse through me. I felt my heart beating faster, my lungs expanding and contracting, the blood rushing through my veins. Greenish undulations rippled out from me as I held out my hands, and I wasn't sure if it was coming from me or from Patrick. I felt as though I were soaring above myself, gliding along a massive wave of energy that some part of me realized might easily pull me under at any moment. Danielle and Kevin slept on, oblivious, their breathing even and deep.

—I don't know if I like this.

You don't have to like it. You just have to realize you have a choice. You can stay locked up in this straitjacket of a life, afraid to set off the alarm clock. Or you can acknowledge what you have and start honing it.

—I have a choice.

Yes, you have a choice.

I fought against the fog and said aloud, "Well then, my choice is to make you leave."

I closed my eyes and summoned every bit of the energy I had allowed myself to feel, channeling the wave into a brilliant white light that enveloped me like a giant glowing bubble. I pushed it outward, farther and farther until I felt it extend to the corners of the room, and until the entire house was surrounded by its peaceful protection. When I opened my eyes, I saw a flash of neon blue light near the chair where Patrick had been sitting, and then suddenly the room was silent.

Kevin sat up, nearly knocking into me, startled out of his sleep.

"What was that? Is everything okay? Did you have another dream?"

"It's nothing," I said. "I'm fine."

He moved himself up onto the couch next to me.

"You sure?"

"Yeah," I said. "Just stay with me?"

"Absolutely," he yawned as he put his arm around me. "Got to keep the ghosts away."

thirty-five

"Oh God, we're late."

I ran to the bathroom, brushing my teeth quickly before anyone would have to be confronted by my morning breath. I came back to the living room as soon as I was done. "Hello? School? We've got to run."

"Right," Kevin said, stretching.

"Ugh. Can someone turn off the sun?" Danielle moaned from within her sleeping bag.

"Come on, get up," I said. "We have to get to school."

"Ugh. Can someone turn off the school?" She sat up, her hair covering her face in a sleep-tangled mess. "Okay, okay, I'm up, I'm up."

"Do you have an extra toothbrush?" Kevin asked.

"I think so," I said from my room, yanking my shirt over my head, quickly changing my bra and underwear and grabbing the nearest T-shirt from the pile on the end of my bed. I took off my leggings and pulled on some jeans that were on the floor. My neck hurt from sleeping on the couch. "Check in the bathroom."

"Okay," he said, his voice closer.

Then he poked his head around my door, smiling. "You sure are cute when you're all rushing around in the morning," he said, before heading off in search of a toothbrush.

Danielle came into my room to change. "'You sure are cute

194

when you're all rushing around in the morning,'" she mimicked in a goofy voice.

"Shut up," I said, but she was smiling, and so was I, a stupid grin that felt like it was going to break my face off. "I couldn't tell you last night, because, you know, Kevin was like, *right there,* but—he wrote a song for me," I whispered to her as she got dressed.

"Shut up!" she said, whispering, too.

I nodded, unable to stop smiling. "And he sang it for me, too."

"Shut *up!*" she said again, speaking louder. Then she looked serious. "Was it horrible? You can tell me if it was horrible. Remember how I told you about that guy in ninth grade who was cute until he tried to write poetry and stuff to me and I had to shut that down fast because it was just so, so bad—"

"Seriously, shut up," I said, shushing her to keep her voice down. "It was totally the opposite of horrible. I mean, at least I think it was. I was too nervous to listen."

Danielle made an "awww" face. "Yeah, his music is kinda weird and all, but he's actually pretty good," she said. She looked at my uncomprehending face. "What? He's on YouTube. See, there's this thing called the Internet. . . ."

"I know what the Internet is," I said impatiently.

"Okay, fine. So he's on YouTube. Which means, by the way, if you could actually, you know, use a computer without it exploding, you could watch his videos all the time and hear him sing whenever you want."

"So—you've seen them? I mean, you've heard him sing already?" It was inexplicable, but I felt disappointed.

"Well, yeah, everybody at school has. It's kind of a thing. People use the Internet. People watch YouTube. That's why he's like weird but still not totally unpopular." She caught the look on my face and said, "Don't worry, you still win! Hello, live performance!"

I leaned on my dresser, somewhat mollified, and watched Danielle put her makeup on.

"So, you must have had sweet dreams last night," she said, blinking her eyes as she applied mascara.

I hesitated, and a current surged through me as I remembered my encounter with Patrick. Did that count as a dream?

"I guess," I said quickly, hoping to change the subject. "Thanks again for keeping me company and stuff."

She turned around, zipping up her makeup bag. "No problem. It was kind of fun, being a third wheel with you guys."

"I'm just glad it's not messing up us being friends. You know, me hanging out with Kevin."

She laughed. "You think you getting a boyfriend is more of a friendship-killer than, um, nightmares and spooky ghosts?"

"I guess not."

"You worry too much," she said. "I know you have to, like, keep it all together and stuff, but seriously. You need to relax."

As she turned to put her things back in her backpack, I caught my reflection in the mirror. I looked cautious, worried, stressed, a little flushed. Danielle was right. And wasn't that exactly what Patrick had been saying? That I was constantly holding myself back? Constantly tense, constantly on the lookout for how I might mess everything up? *I have a choice,* I'd said last night. And I'd used it to shut out what Patrick was telling me. But hadn't he been right? Didn't I deserve to stop myself from holding back? I felt a blast of electricity spark through me and this time I didn't breathe deeply or tamp it down. Instead, I walked out of my room and into the bathroom, where Kevin stood, still sleepy, absentmindedly rinsing a toothbrush.

"Yes?" He had one eyebrow raised, his mouth half-smiling in amusement, looking down at me indulgently, but I couldn't let myself become distracted or shy. I was not going to hold myself back. I kissed him full on the lips, feeling as much as I wanted to feel, with so much intensity there was no room in my mind for anything except the sensation of his lips on mine, the energy transfer between us.

"Whoa, whoa," he said, bracing himself with his hands as he leaned back against the sink. "A little warning maybe?"

I felt myself about to apologize, but I pulled the words back in before they could escape my mouth. Instead, I watched our reflections in the mirror as he suddenly turned away from me, his head down. He stood very still for a moment, and then put my toothbrush back in its holder.

"Okay, I'm good," he said, shaking his head. "It's all good. Though . . . maybe we need some ground rules? I mean, like, literally *ground* rules. Like one of has to be grounded? Electrically? Before we spontaneously combust?"

"Probably a good idea," I conceded.

"Okay," he said.

"Okay," I repeated.

"So, I will get right on that," he said.

We stood for a moment in an uncomfortable silence, and then I turned back toward the door. "Okay," I said. "I'll, uh, see you out there."

Stupid, stupid, stupid, I thought to myself. *What were you thinking?* But my heart was racing, and it didn't feel exactly unpleasant. In fact, it felt good.

Baby steps, I thought I heard Patrick's voice say from somewhere. I looked around me, but saw nothing. No blue light, no energy. Perhaps it had just been my own thoughts.

Danielle came out of my room with her stuff and rummaged through the fridge, drinking some orange juice straight out of the container. "Ready?"

"Just about," I said.

Then Kevin emerged, looking normal again, and grabbed his bag and guitar case. "We good to go?"

"Yeah," I said.

Danielle headed for the door as I grabbed my backpack, and just as we were about to leave, Kevin nudged me.

"Hey, so we survived the ghost onslaught last night, right? No supernatural contact? No dreams?"

"Oh—right." I was struck again by hesitation, and I only realized I was making the choice to keep last night's conversation with Patrick a secret from him, too, when I heard myself say, "No. No dreams. No ghosts. None that I was aware of."

I shivered as I closed the door behind us, and then a light zap traveled up my spine as Kevin put his hand on my back.

"And about in there," he said. "We're cool. No worries. We'll figure this stuff out."

"Yeah?"

He held out his hand, his pinkie finger crooked. "Pinkie swear," he smiled.

thirty-six

All day, I felt oddly exuberant. Patrick was right. Not holding myself back felt liberating to the extreme. I walked around school without holding my breath, didn't restrain my energy for fear of screwing up people's e-readers or phones or MP3 players or anything, didn't reel anything in at all. It felt amazing to breathe deep and just thoroughly *not care* whether something terrible happened, whether I was exposed as being weird, whether or not someone else was inconvenienced or shocked, literally or figuratively. All day, I just let myself be. I inadvertently shorted circuits, I accidentally messed with AV equipment, I unintentionally shocked people as they brushed past me. I wasn't obvious about it or anything; I just let myself exist with abandon.

And it felt amazing.

After school, at the bus stop, Kevin looked at me curiously. "You okay?"

"Yeah, why?"

"I don't know," he said. "You just seem particularly . . . electrified. It's like static cling whenever I get too close to you."

"Huh," I said, feeling the electricity ripple around me, running off my skin like water. "I guess I'm just having one of those days."

"Keep this up and I'll have to start wearing dryer sheets around my neck. Like, you know, garlic to ward off vampires?"

"You want to ward me off?" I smiled, grabbing his hand. There was an audible sizzle as our skin touched.

"Yeouch," he said. "Well, maybe? Okay, I'm kidding, but . . . wow. That's some serious static electricity."

His bus pulled up to the stop, and he made a show of touching one hand to the metal bus shelter before giving me a quick hug good-bye. I watched him wave as the bus drove off, and I realized how great it felt to stand there radiating sparks, breathing like a normal person. Not holding back. Free.

thirty-seven

I am in the upstairs study, Veronica's diary in my hand, the wooden box of mementos on the desk, my heart racing. James has just come home.

It's the next part of the dream.

James is unnervingly calm as he looms over me, leaning so close that in other circumstances I might be preparing for a kiss.

"And what do we have here?" he says, taking the diary from my hand. I watch his face change as he realizes what he's holding.

"She wrote down everything. She wrote down what you did to Lily," I say, my own voice surprising me. "You're the one who attacked her. You're the one who violated her and left her for dead and lied about it for years. How could you? You're a monster."

He lunges forward, grabbing my jaw harshly with his strong hand.

"What did you say?"

"You're a monster," I say through clenched teeth, and I look him in the eye as I say it. Have I ever spoken to him like this? Have I ever been so terrified?

He releases my jaw and for a moment I think he will strike me, but instead he brings his hand down on the wooden box, breaking its lid and bloodying his hand.

"You have no idea," he says, his eyes like ice.

He turns away for a moment, and I see that the lid of the wooden box is now a collection of thick splinters on the desk. I take a sturdy piece of it and place it in my lap, hiding it in my skirt. I run my thumb over its rough edges, gratified to discover the way it narrows into a sharp, splintery point.

He rips pages out of the diary and holds them over the flame of the kerosene lamp on the mantle. He watches the fire devour the thin paper and doesn't flinch when it reaches his fingers.

"I hoped it wouldn't have to come to this," he says, dropping the burned paper to the floor.

"You can burn her diary, but I've already read what I need to know," I say. "You're the one who attacked Lily. And Veronica knew. She was going to tell your father."

He drops more torn pages into the well of the lamp. The fire blazes.

"Such a shame she never got to," he says with a chilling smile.

I feel a yawning dread as I realize what he's telling me.

"You killed her," I say. I grip the fragmented piece from the wooden box, splinters digging into my hand. "You killed your own sister?"

"I had no choice," he says, shrugging a shoulder as though we are talking about something trivial, not the murder of his sister, the friend I've been mourning for years. "Lily wasn't supposed to survive. But she escaped me. Never had that happen before. . . . And then Veronica knew, and we couldn't have that. So it was easy enough for me to find her that night, alone the field, in the storm, and just . . . solve the problem."

"That's all she was to you? A problem?"

"And Lily, of course—another problem. But then, thankfully, while you were away for the weekend, she had that tragic accident. So clumsy with the knife."

The way he says it makes me feel as though the world is slipping sideways, tumbling me into understanding.

"Are you telling me it wasn't an accident?" I said through clenched teeth.

He holds more pages from the diary over the lamp, waving them as they catch fire, and a brilliant smile transforms his face.

"That's the beauty of it. Who's to say what really happened?"

My heart races. I feel like I can barely breathe.

"And your father's death?"

"Clever girl. You're catching on."

The terror spreads over me like a creeping frost.

"I wondered how long it might take you. If one day you might snap out of your mourning, put it all together and see the truth. But of course that's been part of the game. Seeing how long I could get away with it before you knew."

"Why did you do it?" I ask.

"Why not?" He laughs. "Lily wasn't my first. And my father wasn't my last. You just haven't been paying attention."

He tears another fistful of pages from the diary, holds it over the flame of the lamp.

"Of course, that's why I chose you. Aside from your obvious affection for me. It just made sense. Who could suspect me of anything if I was married to you? You were my sister's grieving best friend, and at least a sympathetic acquaintance of Lily's. You would never knowingly marry their killer. And so it's worked out quite well, I must say, over the years. I've even grown almost fond of you."

He looks at me with something approximating pity. I edge myself farther back in my seat, my hand still gripping the long splintered piece from the wooden box like a talisman.

"So it pains me to have to do this, Jane. But you leave me no choice."

He sweeps his arm across the mantle, sending the kerosene lamp to the floor, the liquid splattering in an arc that leads straight to me. A cruel smile crosses his face as he watches me, his once-beautiful eyes now terrifyingly ugly. He deliberately drops the burning pages he's been holding, and they erupt into a blaze as soon as they come in contact with the kerosene. The fire streaks toward me, and I understand, finally, what he's intending.

I bolt up from the chair. I can see the expression in his eyes shift from cruelty to shock to begrudging respect that I'm fighting back, to cruelty again. He thinks he can win, that I will become one more tragic accident, one more secret for him to keep.

But he is wrong.

I am fueled by the fire, suddenly attuned to its crackling energy in the air, suddenly able to channel its dangerous, unpredictable power.

Before he can fully react, I run toward him, my arms overhead, holding the sharp, splintered edge of the box in my hands like a wooden stake, and stab it into the side of his head. As he staggers, caught off guard by my blow, I strike him again, stabbing the sharp end into the side of his beautiful face, right into the tender spot, the vulnerable space between cheekbone and brow where his hair curls perfectly. He screams, a horrible, primal sound, as he falls.

He clutches the side of his head, which I see now is bleeding. The fire gathers around us, catching onto his clothes, singeing my skirts, and I force myself not to flinch as he screams. The smoke stings my throat and eyes, and I realize with a panic that his plan for me to die a fiery death might come to pass after all if I don't escape immediately.

I lift my skirts above the flames as I run to the door, ignoring his writhing body as he cries out for help. Before I leave, I pause to look back at him and he reaches out his hand pitifully, crying, "Jane!"

"You showed no mercy," I tell him, "and now you shall have none."

I close the door as the curtains go up in flames, and I run down the stairs, bloodying the banister with my hand, now raw and splintered from the force of gripping my weapon so fiercely, nearly tripping on my own dress as I push open the doors to the great porch, running and running, away from the burning house, out into the field, out into the dark, out where Veronica still runs in my mind, forever and ever, far far away from home.

thirty-eight

I woke up screaming.

Sobbing and shaking, more hyperventilating than breathing, I clutched at my pillows, trying to find something to protect myself with, trying to muffle my cries. But I couldn't stop the lights from flashing on in my room, or the rest of the house, or the houses around us. I heard my mom bolt from her room on the other side of the house, and then she burst through the door.

Sounds came from my mouth, but I couldn't speak.

My mom tried to soothe me, to talk me down, but eventually she resorted to sitting on the bed with me encircled in her arms and rocking me like a baby, saying *shh* and patting me on the back and being her calm, stable self until my sobbing subsided.

My head felt like a swollen balloon, and my eyes were so sore from crying I could barely keep them open.

"You're okay, you're okay," my mom kept repeating. Then finally she released me from her hug and looked me in the eye. "What's going on?"

"It's real," I said, "the dream. It was real." At this I saw her face subtly shift from a look of concern to fear.

She squeezed me in a hug that ordinarily would have been far too tight but tonight felt welcome and safe. I wanted to stay like that forever, with her holding me together. But I was unprepared for what she said when she finally let me go.

"I was afraid this might happen."

I stared at her. My head throbbed from crying. My hands still shook from the shock of the dream. "What are you talking about?"

"I should have told you," she began.

"You should have told me what?"

"Your dad . . ." she said.

My mind flashed back to the conversation I'd had with Patrick. *She babies you.*

"There's something you should have told me about my dad?" My voice was icy, but I couldn't help it. *She can't even tell you the truth about your own father.*

"Daisy," she said. "Calm down."

"I am calm," I said, my voice raw from sobbing. "Don't tell me to be calm."

My mom looked like she was fighting back tears, too. "I just didn't want to worry you, but now . . ."

"Now *what?*" My voice was raised, and I was getting panicky. Patrick's words pulsed in my mind. *She babies you. She can't even tell you the truth about your own father.*

"He was like you," she said, blinking her eyes quickly, looking up toward the ceiling to force the tears back. "He had a gift."

I grabbed my pillow again, hugging it to my chest tightly, a barrier between us. I didn't know how to make sense of what she was saying.

"And you just kept this to yourself all these years," I said. "You never thought this might be, I don't know, useful information to share with me? You never thought, huh, this might help Daisy feel like less of a *freak?*"

"Lower your voice," she said. "Let me explain."

"Oh, sure, *now* is a perfect time to explain! Please, unburden yourself. Tell me the things you should have told me *years ago!*"

I couldn't believe how angry I felt. I couldn't believe that Patrick had been so right.

"It was dreams, Daisy," she said, her voice cutting through my tears. "Your dad's gift wasn't like your thing, with energy or electricity. It was with dreams." She looked at me, trying to gauge my response. "I didn't want to tell you—I didn't want you to worry that it might happen to you, and up until now I didn't think your particular gift had anything to do with dreams. Everything else I've told you is true."

"So what *didn't* you tell me?"

She sighed. "He had prophetic dreams. They started when he was still a teenager, and by the time we met, they were, well, intense."

"Like, nightmares?"

"Dreams about things that came true. He couldn't control the dreams, or what he dreamed about, and he couldn't stop them. And they were never about good things, like winning lottery numbers, or a lost little girl finding her way home. It was always tragedy, always something terrible. And he couldn't save any of the people he dreamed about. It was really hard on him. He tried staying awake, he tried knocking himself out—he thought he might be crazy, so he went to doctor after doctor, had test after test, took medication after medication. I tried to help him." My mom was crying now, the tears coursing down her cheeks. "But nothing helped. And eventually his dreams got the best of him."

"What do you mean?"

My mom swallowed hard. "He took enough pills to stop the dreams for good. He killed himself."

I blinked back angry tears. Now it all made sense, why she was always so alarmed when I had a nightmare, so insistent about telling me that dreaming a thing doesn't make it so, that dreams are just the after-effect of a still-awake brain making sense of a sleeping mind.

She gripped me tightly in another fierce hug and her voice sobbed out in a panic, "Daisy, you have to tell me if that's what's happening with you, you have to tell me if you're thinking of killing yourself."

I yanked myself away from her, forcefully extricating myself from her hug. "It's not like that. I'm not dreaming stuff that comes true or anything. I'm dreaming about stuff that already happened. Like, a super long time ago, way before I was born. Did—did my dad ever have dreams like that?"

"No," my mom said. "It was always about the immediate future, something that would happen in the next day or two. He'd dream it, and then we'd read it in the paper. Or we wouldn't hear about it at all. That was almost worse."

"This isn't like that," I said. "It's more like . . . a really vivid memory. But scary."

"Do you want to talk about it?" My mom asked, squeezing my hand. I suddenly had a flash of her asking my father that same futile question, night after night, as he wrestled with his terrifying dreams, and I sensed a surge of protective white energy radiating in my direction.

"No," I said, deflecting it, sending the energy right back in her face. I could see her recoil, and I didn't even feel bad about it. "You should have told me about my dad."

"I'm sorry, Daisy, it's not easy for me to talk about."

She babies you. She can't even tell you the truth about your own father.

"By all means," I said, a cruel tone in my voice, "don't ever do anything that's not easy for you."

She was silent for a moment, and when she spoke next, her voice had the controlled edge of someone trying very hard not to cry. "You're right. I should have told you. I'm sorry."

"Is there anything else you need to tell me?" I asked, still hugging the pillow to my chest. "Anything else you've been holding back?"

She shook her head.

"Then can you go?" I turned over so that my back was facing her, and I felt the hot, angry tears slide sideways down my face.

I heard her sigh as she stood up. "You know, it's almost 5:30 in the morning. I don't think I'm going back to sleep. I'll make us an early breakfast if you want."

I sensed her waiting for me to respond, but I wouldn't give her the satisfaction. When I was sure she'd given up, after I'd heard her close the door behind her as she walked away, I sat up in bed again. The dream terror still raced around me, competing with my own anger and confusion about everything my mom had just said. I felt a coldness prickle my skin as the hairs on my arms raised. I couldn't see anything ghostly in front of me, but I heard his voice.

What did I tell you?

"You were right," I said out loud, no longer caring who heard. "You were totally right."

I felt a lightness inside me, his lightness, the limitless fog coming back to me.

"But how did you know?" I asked, trying to interrupt it. "Did you actually . . . talk to my father?"

No, he said.

"I don't understand. Aren't you both dead? Can't everyone who's dead talk to each other?"

The room began to glow, and I sensed his impatience.

Being dead is not some kind of prolonged social affair. And in fact where I am is a very particular brand of solitary confinement. But I am able to sense your mother's thoughts—although not as clearly as I feel yours—and so it wasn't difficult at all to pick up on the reasons for her sadness.

"But did you know about the dreams? My father's dreams, his gift?" I felt him whisk the question away, dismissing it with a feathery wave of energy. What had it been like for my dad? How unimaginably difficult must it have been for him to be tortured by the knowledge of things he couldn't control?

I know nothing of dreams. Dreams are not my domain.

I moved in my bed, stretching my arms and legs against the fog that threatened to surround me again.

"You don't know anything about dreams? Not even my dreams? The dreams we've all been having?"

A pulsing icy blue enveloped the corner of my bed.

No.

"But the nightmare—"

I cannot control what anyone dreams. And I cannot control what anyone thinks. I merely make . . . suggestions.

I shivered.

Besides, your dreams are not my concern. This is, I felt him say as I flooded with energy. *This energy, this power—all of it is yours. So what do you say you forget about your silly nightmares and stop holding yourself back?*

thirty-nine

I left without breakfast. Actually, I left without even saying good-bye. I got myself dressed and ready for school, then waited until my mom was taking a shower and got the hell out.

It felt good to not hold back.

I felt my energy flaring, angry and wild, as I sat in first period. As class wore on and the French teacher droned at the front of the room, I decided to test my limits. Things didn't seem so bad when I was merely letting myself relax my vigilance; what would it be like if I actively tried to make things crazy?

I looked at the clock on the classroom wall, looming above Mrs. Benet's head. Fixing my gaze, I concentrated. I didn't even focus that hard; I just pointed my energy in the general direction of the clock. Within seconds the alarm bell went off, signaling the end of class. The students around me looked confused—weren't there at least twenty minutes left until the end of the period? Some people reflexively gathered their books and started getting ready to leave.

Mrs. Benet seemed more annoyed than concerned. *"Mes amis,"* she warned over the blaring bell that seemingly wouldn't stop, over the students' general noise and conversation. "Something is wrong with the bell. If you have to talk, please do it in French!"

She poked her head out into the hall to investigate.

"It's definitely just this classroom," she said. "I don't hear any other class bells ringing."

Oh really, I thought. We'll see about that.

I smiled and closed my eyes, imagining the energy I'd directed toward the clock in our classroom now expanding to include the classroom next door, and the one across the hall, and the one on the other side of the building. Oh, what the hell, I thought, opening my eyes and looking at the fire alarm on the east wall of the room. *Flip!* went a switch in my brain, and just like that the fire alarm added its slightly higher, shriller tone to the general cacophony.

"Okay, people, there's obviously some kind of malfunction happening here. But now it's the fire alarm, and even if it's a false alarm, we have to exit the classroom," said Mrs. Benet. "Come on, just like we practiced in the fire drill."

None of the students reacted with any urgency whatsoever. They merely grabbed their stuff and left the room like they'd been sent upstairs without any dinner, like it was just some huge stupid inconvenience rather than a serious emergency.

I followed their lead, looking vaguely perplexed and concerned, but not too noticeably perplexed or concerned, murmuring along with everybody else who wondered out loud what the heck was going on. The fire drill plan was to exit the building and go directly to the big lawn, waiting there until an indefinite amount of time had passed, at which point the building was deemed safe to return to. We all congregated there, and for most of the students it was merely a handy get-out-of-class-free card. A kind of party on the big lawn. I saw Danielle and Vivi emerge from the 200 and 300 buildings, and I waved them over. They headed my way, Danielle looking overjoyed to be out of class, and Vivi looking distracted, as usual.

"What's up with the bells?" Danielle said as she got close. "It's like they're possessed."

"Huh," I said, trying to keep my face neutral.

Vivi stood next to us. "What is this all about?"

"I don't know," I said, unable to stop myself from smiling just a little. "Some kind of alarm-bell fire-drill weirdness, I guess."

Danielle looked at me closely. "You're seeming suspiciously okay with this turn of events. Might this have anything to do with you?"

"With me?" I asked, a hand to my chest, the picture of innocence. "You know I only use my powers for good."

"Mm-hmm," she said, looking at me with a grin. Her smile faded quickly as she stepped closer to me, speaking low. "So there was another dream, right? A nightmare?"

"Yep, major one," I said. I couldn't put my finger on exactly why, but I felt irritated by her too-casual question. "Wait, how did you know?"

She made a face. "Just a hunch. But you don't seem all that freaked out by it."

I shrugged. "Oh, I was, believe me. But then I decided to stop being so afraid."

"Uh-huh. And how's that working out for you?"

I gestured around us, indicating the landscape of confusion, students milling, administrators running, general chaos. "Pretty great, actually. Come on, let's get out of here."

Vivi looked concerned. "Out of school?"

"No," I said. "Unless you want to. In which case, sure. But why should we stand around waiting out here? Let's go to the caf or someplace, at least."

I led the way to the cafeteria, which was empty. Most students stood around the big lawn or ambled the hallways aimlessly over the ringing bells, waiting for teachers to take charge or for an announcement to echo over the PA system. The three of us sat at one of the tables and watched as people wandered past, poking their heads in, looking for someplace to be.

"I'm hungry," I announced. "Who wants a snack?"

"It's only like eight thirty," Danielle said. "The vending machines aren't turned on till nutrition break. Which isn't for a million hours."

Ordinarily, that might have stopped me. But not today.

"I don't think that'll be a problem," I said. I walked over to the bank of machines and put my hand on the thick plastic display spanning the first array of snacks. It took nothing to zap it to life, and little more than that to send a rain of Snickers bars and a half-dozen bags of Fritos into the pit below, where I claimed them.

I felt completely exhilarated. Patrick was right—what had I been waiting for? Why had I been holding myself back? This was incredible, this feeling of . . . what was it?

Power.

"Vivi? Do you want anything?"

She shook her head no. She sat primly at the table, hands folded in her lap like she was about to say grace at someone's fancy dinner rather than eat snacks from a bag at the stained, plastic table of some dingy school cafeteria.

"Whoa," Danielle said. "I thought that was, like, against your code or something."

"You're the one who said I needed to relax. I'm relaxing." I turned back to the machines, trying to decide what to get next.

"Oh, hey, there you are," Kevin said as he pushed open the double doors of the south entrance.

"Look alive," I said, tossing him a Three Musketeers.

"Uh, thanks?" He looked at me strangely.

"What, I'm just getting us snacks," I said. "It's not like there's anything else to do."

"Yeah, well, I'm not so sure about that." He dropped his stuff on the table and came closer to me. "Are you . . . all right?"

"I'm fine. What is the big deal? We're hungry. I'm solving the problem."

I felt a flare of energy spike around me, my irritation literally palpable, and he stepped back.

"I just thought—"

"Well, you thought wrong," I said, plucking a Diet Coke from the rectangular receptacle at the bottom of the machine. "Hacking the vending machines isn't 'against my code,'" I said, looking pointedly at Danielle, "and I'm fine. I'm better than fine. I'm feeling better than I have in, like, a really long time, so you guys can just deal with it, okay?"

Danielle shook her head and looked away from me, an irritated expression on her face. Kevin, however, looked shocked.

They don't like seeing you in your full powers, I thought I heard Patrick say. *They can't handle it when you are outside of their control.*

"You just . . . don't seem like yourself is all," Kevin said. I watched as comprehension dawned on his face. "Wait, this whole thing is you, isn't it? The fire alarms? The crazy bells they can't fix? All of this?"

"So what if it is?" I said. "Would that be so terrible?"

"Yeah, it would be. Especially if you had anything to do with what's really going on right now." He seemed angry, and for a moment I felt like I could no longer connect with his energy, which only made me more irritated.

"What, it's so terrible that we're getting free snacks while we wait for all the grown-ups to figure out what to do to make the loud sounds stop?" I said. I felt sarcastic and condescending, but I couldn't stop myself.

He looked at me like I was insane. "No, it's terrible what's happening to Mr. Terry."

"What are you talking about?" Danielle asked, her voice suddenly tight and anxious. I looked at Vivi, who still sat, hands folded, eyes focused ahead.

"He's been suspended," Kevin said. "Pending an investigation into allegations of impropriety. With a student."

forty

"I had nothing to do with that," I said as Kevin took me outside, presumably to tell me more about what he knew about the Mr. Terry situation out of earshot from Vivi, who seemed to be in shock, and Danielle, who seemed to be freaking out.

"Well, someone did. Someone brought it to the school's attention. I know it wasn't me, and I'm pretty sure it wasn't Vivi. That just leaves you—and Danielle."

"Or Danielle's mom," I pointed out.

The incessant blaring of the still-ringing alarm bells filled the air, thanks to me.

"Can you make that stop?" he asked.

"Eventually," I said, shrugging a shoulder.

"What is up with you today? I got your whole speech in there about how you're fine and awesome and never been better and everything, but seriously. What is going on?"

He sounded so exasperated with me, and a part of me knew I wasn't being fair to him. For just a moment I allowed myself to let go of the Patrick-inspired energy that was making me feel so powerful and yet so hostile.

"I had another dream last night. A nightmare. A bad one."

He nodded, his face serious.

"And—my mom finally told me the truth about my dad. Evidently he had dreams and stuff, too. Prophetic dreams. The kind that come true."

217

"So you think it's some kind of family legacy then? Like, in reverse? He dreamed about the future and you dream about the past?"

"Maybe. I don't know." I felt myself becoming irritated again by his questions, and I let myself power up again. "Anyway, he killed himself because of it."

"Oh, Daisy," Kevin said, stepping toward me.

"Whatever," I said quickly, waving him away and taking a step back myself. "He's been dead my whole life. I just didn't know why. Or how. But now I do. And now I know I'm not the only freak in my family. So. That's it. That's what's going on."

"That's all?" he asked.

"That isn't enough for you?"

"No, I just meant—you haven't been, you know, talking to Patrick, have you? The ghost?"

"No," I lied. I felt full—filled up with energy—as though the lie made me stronger.

"Okay. Well, good. Because I've been doing some more research about the house from the dream and the Stone family and everything, and, well, you know, the son? Jameson Stone?"

"Yeah?"

"Guess what his middle name was?"

"I don't know." I did my best to make it sound like *I don't care.*

He gave me an exasperated look. "Patrick. His middle name was Patrick. Jameson Patrick Stone."

I felt a cold air envelop me, and my skin prickled everywhere with goose bumps.

"Why are you telling me this?"

"I'm saying, I think Vivi's ghost—our ghost—could be that guy. Jameson Patrick Stone."

I shook my head. "But . . . that doesn't make any sense. Patrick doesn't know about the dreams—he said he isn't the one sending them, so—"

"Wait, so you *have* been talking to him?"

I rolled my eyes. "Duh."

"So, you just lied to me?"

"Duh!"

Kevin grabbed my wrist, holding it hard. "Daisy, seriously. Has he been communicating with you? Have you actually been talking to him?"

I shook his hand off angrily and rubbed my wrist with my other hand. "It's not a big deal. I told you guys before, he showed up. And he's just been around for me like the way he's around for Vivi. I can hear him and stuff. But I don't see what the big deal is. He's been, I don't know, helping me. With my 'gift' or whatever."

Kevin stepped back. "Helping. That's what you call it."

"Yeah, that's what I call it."

"Shutting the school down for a day? Breaking into the vending machines? That's helping? What, are you planning to knock over a few ATMs on your way home?"

"What's your problem?"

He turned to me. "My problem is, this isn't like you. At least it kind of makes sense now, that you didn't just start going out of control for no reason."

"Out of control? You think I'm out of control? Do you really want to see out of control?" I felt a well open up inside me, and a flare shot out, invisible shockwaves emanating from somewhere deep within me. All around us people dropped their cell phones, moved away from their netbooks and laptops like they were on fire, yanked the earbuds from their heads. At the last minute, feeling guilty, I reflexively diverted the energy away from Kevin, so he wouldn't be hurt.

I felt a swirling chill around me and heard Patrick's mocking voice. *What's this? A little trouble in paradise?*

Kevin stood calmly, eyes closed, breathing steady until it passed. Then he opened his eyes.

"Can't you see what's happening?"

I crossed my arms, ignoring him.

"He's doing to you what he did to Vivi—he's showing up for you in the way that makes him most appealing. He's distracting you.

He's tricking you. He's messing with you."

"You don't know what you're talking about."

Kevin took my hands again, this time gently, urgently, ignoring the zap emanating from my fingertips. "What if I do?"

I tried to avoid his gaze.

"Is he here right now? Tell me." He squeezed my hands, looking the way my mom had looked when she'd told me about my dad. "You have to tell me."

"Yes," I snapped.

"Can you make him go away?"

I stared at him.

"Just—can you? Or not?"

I flashed back to the night when Kevin and Danielle had stayed over, when Patrick talked to me about my powers. *You have a choice,* he'd said, and I'd exercised that choice by shutting him out, sending him away.

"I can . . . create a force field," I admitted.

"A force field," he repeated. "Like, he won't be able to hear your thoughts or what we're saying?"

I nodded. "If I can make it strong enough, and put it around both of us."

"Do it."

"What?"

"Do it," he commanded, still gripping my hands.

I weighed for a moment the option of ignoring him, walking away, continuing to ride high on this surfer's paradise wave of energy, but I saw the worry and intensity in his eyes, and I decided to stay. I closed my eyes and tried to focus my energy, channeling it into a white ball in the middle of my chest. Then I drew it out, expanding it until it surrounded both of us. When I opened my eyes, it appeared to me as though we were enveloped in a cottony haze, a white glowing sphere that pulsed with my heartbeat.

"Is it done?" Kevin asked.

"Can't you see it?"

He shook his head.

"Well, then you'll just have to trust me," I said.

"Trust you. Even though you just lied to me about not talking to Patrick?"

"What is the big deal?"

"The big deal is—look, I just think, if Patrick really is the guy from the dream, isn't it just a little bit strange that he wouldn't come out and tell you guys that? Don't you think it's odd that whenever you get close to learning more information about the house or the dreams, he shows up and distracts you somehow? I mean, think about it: We're at Danielle's, looking at the info about the house, and what happens? Ghost incident with you and Vivi. Then you have another dream about that stuff, and, bam, there he is again. It's like there's something from that time he doesn't want you to find out. And that makes me worried. Because if Patrick is really the ghost or whatever of this Jameson guy, and if what you've been dreaming is true . . ."

I felt very still inside. Very still and suddenly chilled to the bone. "Then I killed him."

"What?" Now Kevin was still.

"That was the dream I had last night. Jane killed him. I killed him. I stabbed him with a piece of that wooden box, and left him to die in the fire."

He gripped my hands tighter.

"This may not even be about Vivi at all," he said, sounding like he was thinking out loud. "I mean, yes, he may have started out haunting her. But if you're the one who killed him . . . it may be that he's here—that you're having these dreams, that all of this is happening—because he has unfinished business. With you."

I dropped the force field abruptly, at the same time that I dropped his hands.

"So, this is all my fault, basically," I said. I was overwhelmed with prickly, angry energy that made me want to jump out of my own skin. "We're all being haunted by a ghost because I did something in a past life—which, by the way, you said only last week was totally all just imaginary."

"No, of course not, I just think—"

"*You* just think about a lot of things."

I started to walk back toward the cafeteria again. He followed me, walking faster than I did so that he got to the door before me. "Listen, I get it, there's something going on here with you and your energy or whatever, but—"

"You know what's interesting to me?" I said, and I felt the cruel rush of powerful energy bolster my words. "It's interesting that of all the four of us, you're the only who's not really in the dreams. I mean, I'm Jane, Danielle is Veronica, Vivi is Lily—the only person not in there is you. And yet you have such interest in them."

"So?"

"Vivi tried to tell me before that Patrick's a force for good. And you know, after communicating with him for a while, I totally see it. He helped me start accessing my full powers—no more holding back, no more being afraid I might do something I can't undo or be more powerful than I can control. And let me tell you, it feels amazing. But here you are, trying to tell me that Patrick is a bad guy. That he's the dude from the dream. Wouldn't it make more sense—wouldn't it be a sounder *theory,* and I know how you love theories—that the dude in the dream is you? That *you're* the bad guy?"

"What?" he stammered. I could barely hear him over the still-ringing alarm bells. "Daisy, I'm not the bad guy here. *Or* in the dreams. I'm trying to *protect* you! Or at least help you protect yourself!"

"If it was up to you, I'd just put up a force field all the time, right? Be living in a permanent force field so my powers can't affect anybody? You're just like my mom. Everyone wants me to hold back all the time. Nobody wants me to be who I really am."

"That's not true," he said.

I let my energy flare, and he backed away from me, wincing.

"Daisy!" he said. But I walked past him and went into the cafeteria. Vivi and Danielle sat at the table where we'd left them, and I could tell the atmosphere between them was supercharged with tension. So much that they didn't even notice the tension between me and Kevin when he followed me in.

"What," I said, and Danielle shrugged in Vivi's direction.

"She's upset."

"Of course I'm upset," Vivi said. "Mr. Terry's in trouble, and now I have no place to go."

"You could stay with me," I said, sitting down next to her.

"Really?" Vivi said, wiping her eyes.

"Sure. I mean, it'll be fun, right? You, me, Patrick, all hanging out . . ." She looked at me sharply and I laughed. "Oh, come on, just a little ghost joke there. No, seriously, come on. You can totally stay with me. We could leave right now."

Danielle looked up at the large wall clock over the bank of vending machines. "Uh, it's like nine fifteen at this point."

"Whatever. It's not like school is actually happening."

"Yeah, thanks to you," Kevin said under his breath.

"Okay, fine, whatever," I said. "What do you want me to do?"

"How about stopping the alarms, for starters," he said.

I sighed. I screwed my eyes shut and sent out what I hoped was a bomb-size blast of energy. Sure enough, the noise stopped. The vending machines also rained down snacks, and sodas rolled out onto the floor.

"Oops, collateral damage," I said, leaning down to pick up a few Sprites as they rolled my way.

When I sat up, I saw Kevin holding his head, looking pale. All of my angry, annoyed bravado dissipated as I realized with a start what I had inadvertently done to him with my show-offy "not holding back" powers.

I started to go to him, but he waved me away, pushing my hands away before I could touch him, and turning his back on me as he sat down at the next table.

"Kevin," I said.

"Just wait," he snapped.

"I can help you."

"I don't want your help." He spoke through clenched teeth, and I could tell he was trying to stave off whatever was happening to him, so I tried to help him anyway.

I put my hands on either side of his head, touching his temples gently, and I felt him tense for a moment and then relax. He laid his head on the table, and I sat down next to him.

"I'm sorry," I said in a whisper. "I didn't mean to."

"But you did," he said, his eyes sleepy, his breathing shallow.

"But then I fixed it."

He closed his eyes. "But you shouldn't have broken it in the first place. I know you didn't mean to. But you have to be careful. Sometimes you actually really do have to hold back."

I was instantly annoyed again. "I'll keep that in mind," I said, trying to keep my voice even.

Curious how invested everyone else is in your holding back, I heard Patrick say.

Vivi suddenly stood up. "Let's get out of here," she said.

"Fine by me," said Danielle.

"Let's go to the principal's office," Vivi said. "I want to tell them it's not true about Mr. Terry. That there was no impropriety."

"Uh, okay," Danielle said, looking really uncomfortable. "Why don't you do that, and I'm just going to head to class. If there *is* class after all this."

"I'll go with you, Vivi," Kevin volunteered. "Just give me a second and I'll go."

"Are you sure you're okay?" I asked him.

"Totally sure," he said. He didn't look at me.

We all stood up and gathered our things. The floor was littered with chocolate bars and bags of snacks, and we kicked them out of our way as we made our way out.

Kevin and Vivi started to walk toward the 100 building, where the principal's office was.

"Kevin," I started to say.

"Don't worry about it," he said, but he still wasn't looking me in the eye. "Just think about what I said. About protecting yourself."

I nodded.

"What's up with that?" Danielle asked. Now that Vivi was farther away, she seemed less nervous.

"I don't know," I shrugged.

"Well, I guess it's always a good idea to use protection." She wiggled her eyebrows. "I hope Mr. Terry did."

"Ew, God, Danielle, you are so inappropriate."

forty-one

My mom had been surprisingly receptive to the idea of hosting Vivi when I'd called to tell her what was going on. I had expected more resistance from her, but she seemed easy to convince. Of course, I'd tried to present the situation as sympathetically as possible—not in excruciating detail, but enough to deflect her mom-radar for hinky situations. And she was eager to appease me anyway, after our fight. In any case, she had said yes, and that she looked forward to meeting Vivi in the morning, when she was home from her shift.

"Thanks again for letting me crash here," Vivi said.

"No problem." I took our dinner dishes over to the sink and rinsed them off. "I mean, it's not luxury accommodations or anything, but you're welcome to stay as long as you need to."

She nodded and sat on the couch, legs folded under her, as though she were trying to make herself smaller, less noticeable.

"The couch doesn't turn into a bed," I told her. "But you could sleep there if you want. Or camp out on the floor of my room. Or actually we could take turns, you know, I have the bed one night while you're on the couch, you have the bed the next night while I'm on the couch. My point is, we can figure it out."

She nodded again and I could see that she was fighting back tears.

"Nothing happened, you know?" she said. "It wasn't like that, it wasn't like anything. Mr. Terry just let me stay there. It was just going to be for a few weeks."

"I know," I said, sitting next to her. "Don't feel bad. This isn't your fault."

"Why would Danielle do this to me?"

"What do you mean?"

"Why would she report Mr. Terry or whatever?"

"Whoa," I said. "We don't know for sure she's the one who said anything."

Vivi looked at me, her eyes ringed with purple, as though she hadn't slept in weeks. "Of course she did."

"How do you know?"

Vivi crossed her arms defensively. "Patrick."

"No. I refuse to believe she'd turn on someone like that."

"He said she did, and I believe him."

"Why? What reason would she have for doing it? Did you even ask her? Did you confront her about it?"

She turned away, her jaw muscle working.

The phone rang, and I jumped up to get it. I felt free-range angry energy boiling up inside me, propelling me forward. I was mad that Vivi could make such an accusation—but I was also mad because on some level I knew she was probably right.

"Hello?" I said, stacking the dishes in the sink purely for the satisfaction of the sharp sound they made as I carelessly slammed them on top of one another.

"Whoa, irritated much?" It was Danielle.

"Actually, yeah," I said. "You don't even want to know."

"How is she doing? Is she okay?"

I hesitated. "I guess. Pretty much."

"Well." Now it was Danielle's turn to hesitate. "Aw, crap, I don't know how to say this. I feel bad."

"Why?"

"Because . . . well . . . this whole Mr. Terry thing. It's all kind of my fault."

"What!"

"Please don't freak out, okay? Please don't freak out."

"How the hell am I not supposed to freak out when you admit something like that?" I hissed into the phone, my back to Vivi so she wouldn't hear me. I yanked on the long phone cord, untangling it as I walked down the hallway toward my room. I made it as far as the bathroom before it pulled taut. "I'm just going to be a minute," I called to Vivi as I maneuvered myself and the phone line behind the door. Then I spoke to Danielle, my voice a harsh whisper.

"How could you do this? Seriously, how? I was just defending you to her, I was just—"

"What, she knows?"

"She guessed."

I heard Danielle sigh. "I feel terrible."

"Yeah, you kinda should feel terrible."

"I didn't mean for it to happen," she said. "You have to understand—weird stuff has been going on, okay? I mean, I don't want to say I've gone Vivi, but . . . I don't know. I can't explain it. I just— sometimes I feel like I'm doing stuff and saying stuff, and it's not really me. Or it is me, but what I'm doing wasn't my idea. Or like— oh, what the hell, okay, I'll just say it: I feel like I'm being mind-controlled by Vivi's ghost."

I closed my eyes and took in a deep breath.

"Hello? Are you even there?" Danielle said. "Okay, forget it, I know it sounds crazy, I just don't have any other explanation for being such a jerk."

"Really," I said, my voice flat.

"I don't know, I just . . . I was talking with my mom about it— okay, well, she was talking to me about it, because she just couldn't let it die, that conversation she had with Vivi in the car, when Vivi was all 'Look at me, I'm living with my teacher!' like that wouldn't be totally alarming or something. Anyway, she kept saying that she was concerned, and so worried, and blah blah blah, and she wanted to call the principal or the school board. So I begged her not to, and I told her I'd handle it."

"And then you just called the school board yourself?"

gift

"No!" she said, insulted. "No, not at all. I just got her to back off. And then that night—I don't know—I slept so deeply, it was like I was drugged or something. And when I woke up, it was like I heard a voice talking to me, telling me I needed to do the right thing. And when I woke up I was like, wow, that was a creepy dream, but then when I got to school, I found myself going to the principal's office and just—I don't know."

"What. Happened."

"I just went in there and like breezed past the secretary and everything like I was some kind of big shot—I don't even know what I was doing. I felt like compelled, you know?"

She paused, waiting for me to commiserate, but I didn't.

"Well, maybe you don't know. But I just went in there like I was on a mission. And I sat down and it was like someone else sat me down instead, and I was talking but I was like a puppet, because I hadn't planned to say any of the things I said."

"And what did you say, exactly?"

Danielle sighed. "I said I was concerned because it had come to my attention that one of the students was cohabiting with a teacher."

"You said that?" I nearly shouted, then tried to bring my voice back under control so Vivi wouldn't hear. "What the hell were you thinking? 'Cohabiting'?"

"I know, I know," she said. "I'm telling you, it wasn't me. I mean, I didn't plan to do any of it. I certainly didn't plan to say cohabiting. Heck, I don't even think I even knew that word before I said it. Anyway, then Mrs. McCordy was all 'Thank you for bringing this to my attention,' 'serious allegations,' et cetera, et cetera. And then I was out of the office, and suddenly I felt like myself again. I barely even remembered what happened. I mean, I do now, obviously."

I slumped against the vanity and the phone cord stretched even straighter. I wondered if it would ever curl back into its original tightly wound shape after this conversation was over.

"So, that's it. *Mea culpa*. I'm really sorry," she said, and I could hear her waiting for my forgiveness. But I couldn't grant it.

"I don't buy it," I said, standing up, looking at myself in the mirror. My eyes were on fire, electrified with a sudden certainty I hadn't anticipated until I spoke.

"What?"

"I mean, I buy that you're sorry now that everything's turned out awful. But I don't buy that you didn't mean to do it."

"What are you talking about?" she stammered.

"You've never really been nice to Vivi. Right from the beginning, you were sarcastic and mean about everything she told us. She never did anything to you except be totally honest about her freaky situation, and all along you had to make her feel crappy about it."

I felt the way I'd felt when I'd kissed Kevin for real, the way I'd felt in French class when I'd taken a deep breath for the first time in years and let the chaos happen around me. I felt free, powerful—alive.

"I think you wanted to get her in trouble, and I think you wanted to get Mr. Terry in trouble, too."

"I don't know where this is coming from, but you're way off-base." I couldn't be sure, but I thought her voice sounded shaky. A part of me swelled with satisfaction, and I could have sworn I heard Patrick's voice whisper, *Good.*

"And now you want to try to blame it all on Vivi somehow, by suddenly jumping on the ghost bandwagon and pleading mind control? Sorry. I just don't buy it."

I heard her breath, ragged, on the end of the line. "You don't have to buy it. You just have to believe me. I'm your friend. Why would I make up something like this?"

"I don't know," I said. "And I don't care. All I know is that now I have a new semi-permanent houseguest, and my favorite teacher is banned from school. And it's all your fault."

"Daisy," she said, and then there was silence. After a long moment she spoke again, and her voice was stronger this time. "Just answer me this. Can you say, honestly, that you haven't been having weird things happen with you lately? That you haven't been acting out of control? Can you sit there and tell me, without lying, that you've been totally normal lately—or whatever normal is for you? You can't, can you? You can't. Because you've been having the same thing happen. He's been talking to you, too, I know it—"

"You're wrong," I said, looking at myself in the mirror as I lied to my best friend. "I haven't been having weird things happen lately. I haven't been acting out of control. The only thing you're right about is that I haven't been normal. I've been better than normal. For the first time in my whole life. And if you can't handle that, that's your problem. Now, if you don't mind, I have to go deal with Vivi, who, if you remember correctly, is now my problem precisely because of you."

And with that I hung up the phone.

Had I ever hung up on Danielle before? Come to think of it, had I ever hung up on anyone before? It felt good to press the disconnect button. The only thing that would have felt better was if I could have slammed the receiver into its cradle for that extra crash of finality. I'd do it when I brought the phone back to the kitchen, I decided, bang it down like I'd just hung up.

But when I opened the door to head back there, I found Vivi standing in front of me.

"I don't mean to be a problem," she said.

I shook my head. "You're not—I totally didn't mean to say it that way. I was just mad at Danielle, and—"

"It was her, wasn't it? I was right? She's the one who got Mr. Terry in trouble?"

"I didn't want to believe you, but yeah. It was her." For just a moment, I felt the triumph drain from my body. "For what it's worth, she said she's sorry. And she seemed to feel really bad about it."

"Well, that won't get Mr. Terry his job back," she said. I walked the phone back to its cradle in the kitchen. Somehow the idea of slamming it down no longer seemed as satisfying. I placed the receiver back on the wall and watched the cord slowly spiral back into itself.

I dug through the closet until I found my sleeping bag and laid it out on the floor like a thin nylon mattress for Vivi. For a moment, as I bent over to straighten it out, I felt a little dizzy. I wasn't sure whether that was due to the head-spinning events of that day, or the dizzying new heights of my energy that still needed some getting used to. I stood up slowly, to avoid being light-headed.

"Maybe we could stuff it with pillows, or some extra blankets?" I said, but Vivi shook her head.

"I'm so tired, I could sleep on a bed of nails," she said. "Really, this is fine."

"Okay, well, here's a pillow and a sheet and blanket. . . . Is there anything else you need?"

"No," she said. And then, for the first time in weeks, she smiled. When Vivi smiled, it was an amazing thing: It was impossible to see her looking so happy without smiling yourself in response. My heart ached for her as it struck me how long it had been since I saw her even so much as grin. She stepped forward and embraced me. "Thank you. You're a good friend. This means a lot to me."

I shrugged out of her hug, feeling suddenly embarrassed. "Please. It's the least I can do."

She looked at me with concern. "Are you feeling okay?"

"Yeah," I said, and I started to feel that creeping annoyance coming back. Why did everyone seem to think I wasn't okay? "Why do you ask?"

"You just feel really . . . warm." She rested the back of her hand lightly on my forehead, a cool surprise. "Yeah. I hope you're not coming down with something."

"Huh," I said, feeling my forehead with my own hand. "I felt a little dizzy before, but . . ."

She shrugged as she took the blanket and sheet and plopped them on the sleeping bag. "Maybe you just need some sleep. We both do."

"Yeah, I guess," I said. Now that she'd mentioned it, I felt a painful tenderness on either side of my jaw, the tightness of swollen glands. I hoped it was just the power of suggestion. Being sick was the last thing I needed.

I took some preemptive Advil while Vivi got ready for bed, and I took my temperature with our old-fashioned mercury thermometer: 100.3. Barely a fever. Practically normal—for me, anyway. Hopefully the Advil would help. On my way past the kitchen, the phone caught my eye. Should I call Danielle again? Should I call Kevin, let him know about what Danielle had told me? Would he even want to talk to me?

I shivered as a chill passed over me. *I should just go to sleep,* I thought. *I can talk to them in the morning. If they're still on speaking terms with me.*

As I walked back to my room, the chills continued. Perhaps the Advil hadn't been preemptive enough. I stuck the thermometer back in my mouth and paused for a moment in the hallway as I waited for a temperature to register. 101.9. Ugh.

"Vivi?" I called as I opened the door to my room. My throat hurt now, too. "I think you're right, I have a fever and stuff. Why don't you take the bed and I'll just sleep on the couch out here. I don't want to get you sick."

But Vivi was already asleep, passed out on the floor in my sleeping bag, and I didn't have the heart—or the energy—to wake her up. In fact, I didn't even have the energy to grab my blanket off the bed and head back to the living room. I felt shimmery all over, radiating fever, and as I stood in the doorway and closed my eyes for a moment, I began to start trying to justify the idea of sleeping right there, standing up, leaning against the door. It all seemed so logical, so possible: Yes, I could sleep here, that would be fine, of course it could work. Eventually, after lifetimes, centuries, eons of standing there, I opened my eyes in a fevery haze and made it to my bed, fully intending to pull off my blanket and get myself back to the couch somehow. But instead I lay down, and I felt as though I could sense every molecule of air hitting my body as I sprawled there. Moving seemed not only unlikely but actually unthinkable. Chills gave way to burning waves that left me sweaty and clammy; my eyelids felt weighted. I heard the thermometer make a quiet plinking onto the carpet as it fell out of my hand. And then, before I knew it, I was out.

forty-two

For the first time in weeks, I had a totally dreamless sleep. Perhaps I was so feverish my dreaming brain just shut down, shunted all its energy toward respiration and fever-fighting. It was just pure blankness, as though I were in a darkened room, or as though I was the room itself, dark and empty, no "I" there at all. This wasn't the sleep I'd slept before, when I charged like a battery as Patrick plugged in, recycling my energy, strengthening it. This was deeper than that. This was what I imagined it might be like to be dead: utterly absent, no consciousness to care about the absence, to ponder what it meant to be gone.

I opened my eyes only because I felt something cool and damp on my forehead, a gentle hand smoothing my hair back, a person hovering over me. It was my mother, wielding a washcloth and a look of concern.

"Shh," she said. "You're burning up."

It took me a moment to remember where I was, *who* I was. Something was off. I felt really wrong. Drained, not charged. I struggled to sit up.

"Uh-uh," my mom said, a gentle hand forcing me back down. It didn't take much; I could barely move. "You are staying in bed. Here." She shook the thermometer and stuck it in my mouth. "Indulge me."

I didn't have much of a choice. I felt those alternating chills and heat waves from the night before, and it took superhuman strength just to squint my eyes open. I tasted the thermometer in my mouth, a glassy straw.

"Okay, I'm taking you in," my mom said as she took the thermometer out from under my tongue. I somehow managed to fully open my eyes and make my mouth work to form sounds of protest. "Daisy, it's over 102!"

"Mom, please," I said, trying to make sense. "Advil?"

She considered it. "If that fever doesn't budge in another half hour, I'm bringing you to Urgent Care." She placed the washcloth on my forehead and stood up to leave the room. As she stepped over the sleeping bag on the floor, she asked, "Where's your friend?"

"What?"

"Your friend." She pointed to the sleeping bag, and as I slid my glance toward that side of my bed, I saw it, crumpled up as though someone had thrown it aside upon waking. "Wasn't she going to stay here last night? Or was it supposed to be tonight?"

Even in my delirious state I could tell this called for some diplomacy, so I closed my eyes and turned my head back to center. "Tonight, yeah," I managed.

"Well, we'll have to see about that," she said, heading out the door to the hallway, her voice trailing off as she walked toward the kitchen. "If you're not feeling any better by this afternoon, it might be best for her to find another place to stay. Wouldn't want her to catch whatever you've got going on here."

I opened my eyes again and eased myself up to sitting, the washcloth, now tepid instead of cool, falling into my lap. The room shifted sideways for a moment, and I closed my eyes to make things steady again. The fever settled on me like a fog, obscuring everything, but when I eventually opened my eyes again and looked over to the floor, I could clearly see no evidence of Vivi. No clothes, no backpack, no sign of her. Had she left a note? I moved my gaze to my desk, my bedside table, the other side of my bed. No note. Why had she taken off so early? Where had she gone?

Beneath the heavy blanket of fever and confusion, I felt a worrisome sensation of panic. Something bad was happening, I was sure of it. And not just with Vivi's disappearance—something felt majorly off with me. I heard my mom rummaging in the kitchen, the clinking of glass and running water telling me she was in the process of bringing me a drink to take the medicine with, and I knew I had only a moment until she was back. I tried to focus on the lamp on my bedside table, channel my energy into it to make it turn on—but nothing happened. Panic rising, I tried it again. Still nothing. Maybe the bulb was out? I leaned over, my arm feeling so strange and not-mine that reaching for the switch seemed like something someone else's arm was doing. The light blazed on, assaulting my eyes, and I recoiled as though I'd stared at the sun.

My mom came in and placed the water and the pills on the bedside table. She sat down on the bed again and pressed the washcloth, now warm, against my forehead. "I'll run this under some cold water," she said. "In the meantime, take the Advil and let's see if it makes a dent in your fever."

"Mom?"

"What is it?"

"I don't know—something's wrong with me," I said.

"You have a really high fever," she said, smoothing my hair back from my face again.

"No, I mean—something's *really* wrong. I can't—I tried, but—I just don't have any . . ." My voice trailed off and she looked at me with confusion. I took her hand, trying to grab it tight but only managing a weak hold. "Do you feel how it's nothing? There's no . . . electricity."

"Daisy, you're sick," she said, squeezing my hand. "You're going to feel better soon."

"But you don't understand, I can't—I couldn't even turn the light on."

She laughed. "Well, it was on when I came in here, so it looks like you managed."

"I had to do it the regular way. I just don't—I don't know what's wrong with me."

My mom put the washcloth on my bedside table so she could use both of her hands to hold mine, to ground me. "You have a very high fever. That's probably interfering with things. What you need to do now is take the medicine and wait for the fever to come down. Most likely, it will, and then you'll start feeling normal again." She smiled. "Well, you know what I mean."

"What if I don't?"

She stopped smiling, just for a moment, and gave me one last squeeze before she picked up the glass of water to give to me. "You're going to be fine. Okay? Just take the meds and try to sleep for now, and I'll check in on you again in about twenty minutes."

I took the water from her and placed the pills on my tongue. Swallowing seemed endlessly complicated, but I managed some-how, and then my eyes closed and I couldn't make sense of any-thing anymore. I felt a lightness as my mom took the glass from my hand and then a darkness as she turned off the light, and then everything was as silent as a dream.

"I'm still debating about whether to take her in," I heard my mother's voice say. It sounded as though everything was underwa-ter. For a moment the scene swam in my head like a cartoon sea movie, a maternal angelfish voicing my mother's lines.

"Is her fever still really bad?"

This voice was lower, and the water was murky. I couldn't tell who was speaking. Then it was my mom again.

"Well, it's down a little, but still higher than I'd like—she's been pretty much holding steady at just around 102 for the last few hours."

I swam my way up to the surface of consciousness. My body felt heavy, waterlogged, my right ear crumpled from the way I'd slept on my pillow, my neck protesting as I moved it back to a more reasonable angle. I felt my fingers and toes tingling as wakefulness echoed throughout my body.

"Daisy?" my mom said, and then the taste of thermometer was in my mouth, and her hand was firm and sure on my forehead as she assessed my temp the maternal way. "She feels a bit cooler," I heard, and then felt the thermometer sliding out from beneath my tongue. "101.5—that's an improvement."

I opened my eyes, barely, everything blurry and too bright.

"Good morning, sleepyhead," my mom smiled at me. "Or should I say afternoon? You've slept the day away. But that's good, you needed it. And your fever's down a little."

I nodded. It seemed to take forever to move my head. But now that I was waking up, I didn't feel as terrible as I did before. The fog was clearing a bit, I didn't have the fevery hypersensitivity to sound and touch, and pushing myself up to a sitting position didn't seem to require superhuman strength. Then I saw a movement in the doorway, behind my mom, who sat on the edge of my bed, and I realized someone else was in the room with us. My mom tracked my gaze and stood up.

"If you're up to it, uh, Kevin's stopped by to drop off your home-work and catch you up on what you missed today."

He stood in the doorway, looking a bit embarrassed as he smiled and made a kind of hello salute.

"I'll just go get you another glass of water and grab some Advil for you to take," my mom said. "I want to keep that fever down. So, you two . . . catch up . . . and I'll be back in a bit. Don't let her wear herself out, she's still not a hundred percent. She's not even fifty percent."

"Oh, I won't," Kevin assured her. "I'll do all the talking."

My mom gave him a look as she exited the room. "Ten minutes," she said.

Kevin sat next to me on the bed. He seemed a bit nervous, but whether that was because of the way we'd left things, or because he'd just run the gauntlet of my mom, or because I was sick, I wasn't sure.

"Hey," he said, putting his hand on my arm tentatively.

"Hey."

"You really *are* hot—I mean, warm. Feverish." He smiled. "Well, and also hot."

I rolled my eyes. "I am sweaty and disgusting, and I can't remember the last eighteen hours of my life. What are you doing here?" Words felt strange in my mouth after going for so long without talking.

"*Shh*, you're not supposed to be saying anything. Mom's orders."

"You brought me homework?" I asked.

He shook his head. "Nah. Not really. I mean, I can tell you what you missed in English if you want, but for the rest . . . Danielle will have to fill you in. I just wanted to make sure you were okay."

"I don't think Danielle wants to talk to me ever again. We kind of had a fight last night." Last night? Was it only last night I'd slammed down the phone in anger, furious on Vivi's behalf? Vivi. It all came rushing back, and I sat up in bed, preparing to—what? Get out and get dressed to go looking for her? I slumped back against my pillow again. I didn't have the energy. It all just seemed too much.

"Seems like yesterday was a fighty day all around," Kevin said, and I closed my eyes again, remembering our argument.

"I'm really sorry," I said. "I didn't mean to say all that stuff to you. I know you're not the bad guy."

He squeezed my hand. "It's okay. Obviously you weren't feeling like yourself."

"I guess," I said.

"Seriously, we're good. Don't worry." He glanced toward the doorway. "But we don't have a whole lot of time here, and we need to talk. Danielle said Vivi was here last night, with you?"

I nodded. "But when I woke up she was gone."

"She wasn't at school today, either. Nobody seems to know where she is. When did your fever start?"

"When Vivi was here. Last night. Before bed."

"And was there anything else, any other symptoms?"

"I don't know, just fever stuff, I guess. Although . . ." I hesitated. I didn't know if what had happened before—or hadn't happened—with my electrical powers was still relevant, or still happening. And I wasn't all that sure I wanted to tell him about it, especially since after our argument he'd likely consider my newfound inability to be a good thing.

"What?" he said. "Anything you remember, anything. It could be important."

"I don't know if this is just because of the fever or what, but . . . this morning I seemed to have—I don't know. It was like I lost my powers."

He sat back and for a moment looked quite serious. "Is it still like that?"

"I've been too nervous to test it out again. But I guess I still feel kind of . . . off. Like, no electricity whatsoever."

"Okay, good," he said.

"Good?" I glared at him, ready to protest, but then I saw the grin on his face.

"Yeah, because we can do this." He leaned in and gave me a kiss. I felt no crazy current, no sizzling spark—only the racing of my heart and a feeling of happiness that shivered throughout my body. He traced his finger down the side of my face and smiled. "There may be an upside to this after all."

I smiled, too. But then I stopped. "No, there isn't. First of all, I've lost my powers. Which you're probably happy about. And second, you're going to get yourself sick—you're going to catch what I have."

"Actually, no to everything you just said. You haven't lost your powers, and I don't want you to. And if I'm right about things, which I think I am, in a few hours you're going to feel totally back to normal—Daisy normal, anyway."

"I don't understand."

"Okay. This is a bit weird, but I think I have a theory about what's going on." He gave me a smirk. "You know how I like theories."

"I'm sorry, I'm sorry, I'm sorry," I said.

241

"Okay. Well. You know how I told you my mom is all New Age and chakra-healing and stuff, right? Well, she has quite the collection of random books—and not just hippie stuff, but spooky books about past lives, and dream interpretation, and spirit worlds, all kinds of stuff like that. Anyway, so last night I did some light reading about possession."

"You mean, like—scary, demonic possession?"

"Yeah, sort of. I guess now that you mention it, there aren't really any *non*-scary kinds of possession."

"Why would you read about that?"

"Because that's what we were just talking about, right? Patrick's unfinished business? Him possibly coming back for revenge?"

"What does that have to do with possession?"

He shifted on the bed. "Coming *back* for revenge. *Back*? Like, to the human world? As a human?"

"How would he even do that?"

"Well, how do you think a ghost becomes human? He can't materialize out of thin air—he can't *make* himself human."

"He has to take someone over," I said. "He has to possess someone." I felt a ripple of goose bumps on my arms and legs.

"Bingo."

"But how? And who?"

"Well, see, one book said that sometimes poltergeists—super angry ghosts, basically—channel the energies of out-of-control teenagers and kind of use that to manifest their own energy in the physical world. Your classic vase-falls-off-the-mantel or books-fly-off-the-shelves scenario." He held up his hand to stop me from saying anything. "I'm not saying that Patrick is a poltergeist or that you are out of control. But I am saying that I think Patrick has been tapping into your energy to make himself stronger."

I felt myself blush as I remembered the glowing green nights of charging like a battery: Patrick's energy feeding off mine.

"But what kinda freaked me out is that I also read that sometimes a ghost or spirit or demon or whatever who's trying to possess someone can use another person's energy as a wedge to get into the person they're actually trying to possess. Sometimes that can take the form of a sudden fever or unexplained illness that weakens the stronger person as the ghost sucks up their energy. Then the ghost is able to use that energy to possess the person who's weak enough to be entered."

It took me a moment to put it all together.

"So I could be having this fever . . . because of him?"

"Maybe. It could be that last night, he was able to tap into your energy big-time, send you into overdrive, and ride that wave of energy straight into . . . well, being able to possess someone."

"Wait—am I possessed? Is that what you're saying?"

He laughed. "No. You're not possessed. Your energy was churned up and you have a fever. But you're not the one who's possessed. You're too strong. He can only possess someone weaker."

"Oh," I said, realizing finally. "Vivi."

"Yes. Vivi."

We both sat for a moment, serious.

"This is crazy," I said. "What makes you think any of this is really happening? I thought you said before this was all some group hallucination—that maybe none of this was really real."

"Yeah, I did. But after yesterday, and after everything that's been going on with you energy-wise lately—and then after I read that stuff, and then when you and Vivi were both absent today—I just had a really bad feeling. And so I came here straight from school to make sure you were okay."

"But why not me, then?"

"I just said I came to see you," he grinned.

"No, I mean, you said the ghost gathers energy and then possesses the person who is weakest. So if Patrick 'fried' me by making me sick and used all my energy, wasn't I the weakest? Why didn't he just possess me?"

"He probably wanted to—but I bet even in your feverish state you were too strong for him to take over. Vivi, however . . ."

"She's fragile," I said. "And he's been wearing her down for years. She would probably welcome it."

"Probably. Though I think there's a part of her that wants to fight it. I think that's what the dreams are about. I think you were right: They're not coming from Patrick. They're coming from her. Not consciously—I think it's more like she's . . . channeling them. Like they're memories from before that she can't face. So my theory is that they psychically got shunted to you." He grinned. "Since you're like a magnet for supernatural wackness."

I remembered the intensity of the last dreams, and I closed my eyes, trying to make sense of it all. "So, what do we do?"

"Well, for one thing, we have to get you better. You need your energy. Literally. I think we're going to need you strong and zappy."

"And we need to find Vivi," I said.

"And we need to talk with Danielle. I know you're not Danielle's biggest fan right now, but I think we could use her help."

"You know why we were fighting, right? She was the one who ratted out Mr. Terry!" I said, sitting up straighter in bed. I could tell that I was feeling better by how animated I felt when I spoke now. No more underwater slogging, above-water fogginess; I was feeling more like myself by the minute. My fever must be inching back toward normal.

He held up his hand. "I know what she did. And I think I know why, too."

"Oh, she told you her bogus, 'the ghost made me do it' explanation?" I said, my arms crossed against my chest.

"Look, I'm not happy about what she did, but yeah, she explained herself to me, and on some level, I guess I believe her. We kind of have to. Because if Vivi's really in trouble, we're all going to need to be on the same side."

I closed my eyes for a moment and tried to make sense of it all.

"Okay," I said. "So, let me get this straight. Your theory as of now is that A, the dreams we've all been having are past-life memories that are totally real, which means B, the man I killed in that past life is this ghost who's been haunting all of us and C, he has now taken on the human form of Vivi, who has gone missing."

"You forgot D."

"Which is?"

"That he's angry and coming after you for revenge." He saw the look on my face and backpedaled. "Or, you know, E, nothing happened except that you got sick last night and Vivi took off early this morning, and all of this other stuff is just . . . ghost stories."

"I'll take E," I said.

The knock at the door made us both jump as my mom came back in.

"All right, sorry to break it up, but visiting hours are over." Then: "Everything okay in here? You guys look serious."

"Oh, yeah, totally okay," I said. "I'm actually feeling much better. Really. Go ahead, take my temperature."

"That was the plan," my mom said, handing me the thermometer. She stood for a moment, looking back and forth between me and Kevin as she waited for my temperature to register. Then I saw her turn toward Kevin and open her mouth to speak, and I quickly removed the thermometer from my mouth to head off a mom-interrogation.

"Look, 99.9," I said. "That's practically normal."

"Not really," she said, "but it is an improvement. Still—time to say good-bye to your guest, and time to get some food into you. Unless—" she looked at Kevin, "would you like to stick around for dinner?"

He stood up. "Oh, no, that's okay. I should probably get home—but thanks. Some other time, though, definitely, that would be great."

I grinned. Was he actually a little nervous around her?

"Anytime," my mom said.

"So, Daisy," he said, turning toward me. "I'll talk to Danielle to see if she's been in touch with Vivi."

"Oh, right," I said.

"And then I'll call you later on to see how you're doing." He looked at me to make sure I understood what he was really talking about.

"All right, all right, I'll give you a minute to say your good-byes," my mom said, and left the room.

Kevin leaned in close. "I'll let you know what Danielle says. And if there's any chance that Patrick-slash-Vivi's coming here, I'll come right back, no matter what your mom has to say about visiting hours." He put a hand on my shoulder. "Don't worry—if Patrick really did take over Vivi last night, it's likely he's still . . . processing what's happening. He won't fully be in control for a while yet."

He kissed me on my forehead and then on my lips, and again I felt my heart race—and this time, a small zap to our lips as well.

"Okay, you're coming back," he said.

"Sorry."

"No, it's good," he said. He kissed me again, lightly this time. "I want you to be well. We need you to be full force for the plan to work."

"What plan?"

"The one I don't have yet." He smiled. "I'll call you later. Feel better."

I leaned back onto my pillow and stretched, feeling the muscles in my arms and legs expand and contract, and a familiar current chug to life in my body. I saw the lamp on my bedside table begin to glow, and I realized he was right: I was coming back.

part four

forty-three

Kevin had been right. Just as he had predicted, by dinnertime a few hours later I was feeling much better. My fever was gone, and my power was slowly coming back. I could sense its gradual return, the way my focus sharpened, the way every sensation was heightened as the energy flowed back into me little by little. The steadiness of its increase gave me confidence as well: I felt more in charge of things, less like I was trying to keep a lid on a volatile pan of popcorn, popping out of control.

Control.

I had been so reckless earlier, I realized. Under Patrick's spell, at his suggestion, my power trip had been not only self-indulgent but dangerous. I had sent the school into chaos, disrupted things for everyone, risked getting myself in trouble—risked actually hurting people. I flinched as I thought about how I had nearly triggered a seizure for Kevin. What had I been thinking?

But I knew what I'd been thinking. I'd liked how it felt, breathing deeply and not hiding who I was. There had to be a way to do that but still keep myself—and those around me—safe.

My mom continued to check my temperature, even after it leveled off around normal, and tolerated only one phone call from Kevin before I went to sleep for the night. I tried to sound like we were talking about homework, for my mom's benefit, as he gave me the update: Vivi was still missing, as far as anyone could tell, and neither he nor Danielle had had any luck in finding her. But, he said, he was working on a plan, and tomorrow the three of us would meet up at lunch, and hopefully brainstorm a way to save Vivi and banish this ghost once and for all.

There was only one thing standing in the way of that.

My mom.

"There is no way you are going to school tomorrow."

"But I don't have a fever anymore! I'm totally back to normal."

She fixed me with a look I was sure she'd used on unruly patients before. "I will be the judge of that."

"I am—I've been fever-free for hours now. Since dinner at least. I'm fine, I swear."

She sighed with exasperation. "Since when is it so important that you go to school? Normally I'd expect you to be trying to convince me to let you stay home."

I put on my best pleading face. "I don't want to miss any more— I don't want to get too far behind on my homework."

"Oh, it's about homework, huh?" she said, and then a knowing smile crossed her face. "Ohhh, it's about *homework*!"

"What?"

"You want to get back to school so you can hang out with Kevin, the kid who brought you your 'homework,'" she said, resorting to air quotes.

"Mom!" I blushed, but I didn't try to dissuade her. Letting her think it was all about a high-school crush was a pretty safe way to get what I wanted from her—much more effective than telling her I needed to get back to school so that I could exorcise a ghost.

I could see her teetering toward saying yes and allowing me to go, and just on the off chance it would help tip the scales, I summoned my newly returning energy into gentle pulses of calm blue positivity radiating in her direction.

"Well," she said, giving me a hug goodnight and kissing me on the forehead just to double-check my temp. "I guess it must have been some kind of virus. If you're fever-free by the morning—and I mean fever-FREE—you can go to school."

"Yes!" I said, giving her another hug, my excitement making my energy surge.

"Ouch!" She jumped back. "You haven't zapped me like that in a while. I guess things are starting to work again."

I smiled my best "see, I'm okay" smile. "Probably because I'm feeling so much better—in the sense that I am fever-free and totally back to normal and ready to go back to school because I'm all better."

She rolled her eyes. "Okay, okay, you're better. I'm glad you're better. Now good night. I'll check your temp in the morning."

Romeo curled up next to me in the bed, purring louder than I'd ever heard him. He kneaded his paws on my arms and nudged my chin, snuggling in for the night. Once I zapped off the light, I fell asleep almost immediately. My dreams were fleeting and fragmentary: Kevin and I walking on a beach that suddenly became a shopping mall; me sitting in class about to take a test I hadn't studied for.

In other words, for the first time in a long time, normal.

forty-four

Kevin and Danielle and I met on the big lawn after the first-period bell rang. If anyone asked, Kevin would say that we were doing some kind of extra-credit project under his guidance. But luckily, the place was empty, no Mr. Avila on the prowl for ditchers. Devoid of students, the big lawn didn't seem as intimidating to me. Now that we were the only ones there, it was just a grassy expanse between buildings, not the charmed and dangerous lair of upper-classmen. It had lost all its power.

"So, are we talking exorcism here?" Danielle said once we were all sitting down. She was speaking even more quickly than usual, and I couldn't get a handle on her energy. Actually, I couldn't sense it at all. I took that to mean that she was as nervous as I was. "I mean, is that the plan? Vivi shows up and her head spins around and then we—what—grab a priest and get down to business? Does one of us need to get ordained over the Internet?"

Kevin shook his head. "Nope, not the plan."

"Okay, what is the plan, then?"

"Well," he said. He looked from me to Danielle and back to me again, the tension building as we waited. "We're going to go to the underworld."

There was a moment of stunned silence before Danielle burst out laughing. "That's your plan. Really. We just go to the under-world. Just *go*—to the *underworld*. Sure, why not? I'm sure it'll be totally easy to somehow, magically, get to some mythical place that doesn't really exist, and then Vivi will just be randomly waiting for us, like, at an underworld bus stop or something!"

"Kind of a metaphor here," he said.

"Uh, no offense, but we don't need metaphors, we need action," Danielle said.

Kevin turned to me, ignoring Danielle.

"Do you remember what I said when you first told me about what was going on with Vivi without really telling me what was going on? When you said it was just a story about a girl in love with a ghost?"

"Yeah," I said. "You said it was like a reverse-Orpheus situation."

"Right. But now it's pretty clear this isn't really a love story— Patrick hasn't been trying to come here so that he and Vivi can live happily ever after. He's got other reasons."

I nodded. I remembered everything now. The final dream I'd had, my last dream of my life as Jane, was like placing the last pieces of the puzzle, finally enabling me to see the whole picture. Patrick—James— was a killer. And he'd had everyone fooled. This time, it would be different. We were on to him. He hadn't killed anyone else. *Yet.*

"So where does the underworld come in?" I asked.

"If Vivi's been possessed by Patrick, then he's taken over her physical form, traded his consciousness for hers. And so the question is—*if* Patrick really did take over—what happened to Vivi's . . . Vivi-ness? What happened to her soul? Consciousness just doesn't go dormant. Even when you're asleep and dreaming, you're still *you.* So she—Vivi, the part of her that makes her really her—has to have gone somewhere."

The chill rippled up my arms.

"You think they've traded places," I said. "Patrick's here now, walking around as Vivi, and she's . . . in hell?"

"I think his consciousness is here, and hers is in the place where *his* has been for all these years—the underworld. The ghost realm," Kevin said.

"This just gets better and better," Danielle said, rolling her eyes. "I think we'd be fine just getting a priest and a crucifix and yelling at her until the demons are gone or whatever."

Kevin gave her an exasperated look. "Listen. In the story, Orpheus went to the underworld by himself, and he was able to convince the gods to give up his wife purely through sweet-talking them into it. But there's three of us here—two of us who are pretty good at talking, and one of us who has mad electricity skills. Between the three of us, we should be able to pull off our own reverse Orpheus with a twist."

"And that means what exactly?" Danielle asked, sounding bored.

"Orpheus ruined the whole deal by looking back. The gods told him not to, but he did it anyway, and he lost Eurydice forever."

"So . . . we just make sure we don't look back?" I said.

He shook his head. "No. You're not getting this. We're not Orpheus in this scenario. We're the gods."

"Well, that may be overstating things," Danielle said dryly.

"No, I get what he's saying," I said. "Patrick's the one asking for something, or, in his case, taking something. We're the ones who have the power to stop him. We just have to trick him into giving up Vivi somehow. Offer him something he can't refuse. Or can't resist. But what?"

"Well. That's where you come in." He turned toward me and lowered his voice, even though we were still the only ones on the big lawn. "Is your energy back, full force and everything?"

"Yeah, I think so." I shivered, my teeth chattering again. "I'm just so cold. I think Vivi—I mean, Patrick—must be around here somewhere. I always feel so cold when he's near, and right now it's just unbearable."

"If and when Vivi does show up here, we're going to need to stay calm and treat her like we don't know that anything's wrong," he said. "She could come storming in here as Patrick, angry and out of control or whatever—but it's also possible she could show up and seem totally normal. It all kind of depends on how fully Patrick's taken over and how well integrated he is."

"Okay, so blah blah blah, we act like everything's normal," Danielle said. "Then what?"

"Then we try to get her someplace where we can talk in private," Kevin said. "Hopefully we can just use Mr. Terry's room, but depending on when she shows up, we may have to go elsewhere—some other empty classroom, where we can talk. The whole time, Daisy, you need to be focusing on gathering your energy."

"Because . . . ?" I prompted.

"Because while Danielle and I are using our sweet-talking skills to talk him down, we're going to need you to make a force field."

"A force field," Danielle said flatly.

"Yeah," he said. "Make a force field around us. Like you did before."

"And what good would that do?" Danielle asked.

"It's going to protect us all when we offer him the chance to 'look back'—to forget about Vivi . . . and take over Daisy instead." Kevin looked at me, his eyes wide and serious.

"Me!" I couldn't help the energy surge around us as I panicked just a little at what Kevin had just said.

"Think about it," he said, holding my hand even though I could feel it buzzing. "He wants revenge on you. What could be better revenge than possessing you and taking your powers? He could be more than human—he could be *super*human."

"I wouldn't go *that* far," Danielle said. "Freak of nature, yes; electrically challenged, sure. But superhuman? She's not a comic book."

Now I battled irritation. "You're not suggesting I actually become possessed, are you? Because I don't think I like this scenario."

"No, of course not," he said. "I'm suggesting that you let him *think* you'll let yourself become possessed. If we offer you to him in exchange for Vivi, there's no way he'll turn that down, because that would mean he'd have your power. And that's exactly what he wants—power. So we'll do a kind of bait and switch."

"And I'm the bait," I said.

"You're forgetting about the 'switch' part. Bait and *switch*," he said. "At the last minute, when he's leaving Vivi and coming to you, you can put up that force field around all of us—you, me, Danielle, Vivi—and then he'll be stuck outside of it. He'll be out of Vivi, and he won't be able to get to you, or tap into your energy, because the force field will be protecting us and repelling him at the same time. So he won't be able to overtake you or anyone else. He'll be shut out, and he'll become steadily weaker. And if your energy is strong enough, Daisy, it might be enough to send him back to the ghost realm. Forever."

"Brilliant plan," Danielle said, and her tone was so icy I couldn't tell if she was being sarcastic or not. "Thank you *so* much for sharing it with us."

"And just in time, too," I heard Kevin say quietly as he looked past us. I followed his gaze to see Vivi on the edge of the field, making her way to where we sat on the big lawn.

forty-five

"How *could* you?" she cried as she strode toward us. I had never seen Vivi move so quickly before. I realized I had also never seen her so angry before, either. Or so, for lack of a better word, messy. Her hair was tangled as though she'd just woken up, her makeup smudged and caked as if it was days old. And could those be the same clothes she had been wearing at my house the other night? I glanced at Kevin, trying to gauge how scared I should be. He gave me a subtle nod and then stood up to intercept her, trying to sustain his usual reassuring demeanor.

Danielle stood up, too, and began walking quickly toward Vivi. "What are *you* doing here?" she demanded.

"Hey," Kevin whispered sharply, pulling her back. "Remember? We're trying to keep things calm? Normal?"

"Hey, Vivi," I said. "We were worried about you."

She stopped abruptly, looking confused to see me. The chill I'd been feeling before was back, even stronger now, making my extremities feel numb. I remembered what Kevin said, about needing me to create a force field, and I tried to concentrate on circulating my energy, sending it spiraling around me to warm myself up, trying to generate some power now so I would be able to use it when the time came.

"What are you doing with *her*?" she said, gesturing shakily to Danielle, who stood next to Kevin. I began to stand up as well. "After what she's done to me?"

257

"Vivi, it's okay," Kevin said, stepping in front of Danielle protectively. But Vivi pushed him aside, and I watched him yield as she stormed up to Danielle.

"How *could* you? How could you *betray* me like that?" Vivi's voice was hoarse with tears. "You have no idea," she said, turning to us, "*no idea* what she's capable of!"

"Vivi," Kevin said, trying to get her to maintain eye contact with him. "It's okay. We know what she did. She's going to make it right with Mr. Terry. She's already made an appointment to speak with the school board and the principal to explain how she was wrong about her accusation."

"Accusation?" she yelled. She looked at us with wild eyes. "Is that what you think this is about?"

"I don't know what it's about," Kevin said calmly. "But I know we can work things out. Let's just find a place where we can sit and talk. All right?"

He looked at Danielle and me, as if reminding us of the plan. We needed to get Vivi to a safe, enclosed place. Someplace we could talk, and someplace we could contain her should things get intense. The bell rang, signaling the end of first period, and almost immediately students began streaming from the buildings around us, filling the hallways and crossing the lawn on their way to class.

"All right, Vivi?" he repeated.

"Let's take her to the computer lab." Danielle stepped forward and clutched Vivi's arm, a little tightly from my perspective. I watched as Vivi deflated, all the fight draining from her, at Danielle's touch.

"The computer lab?" I frowned.

"Yeah, the computer lab," Danielle said. "It's totally empty second and third periods. Plus, it's in the temporary classroom now, the trailer near the 600 building, toward the parking lot. Totally deserted. It'll be perfect."

I looked at Kevin, who nodded. "Sounds good. Vivi?"

But Vivi just stared ahead, tears staining her cheeks, looking utterly spent. Danielle tightened her grip on Vivi's arm and said, "It's all good. Let's go, before we make a scene."

We walked to the southwest corner of the big lawn and into the covered outdoor hallway straddling the entrances to the 200 and 300 buildings, swimming our way upstream, past the cafeteria, past the student government outpost on the edge of the 400 building, past the 500 building where Mr. Terry should be teaching. Finally we reached the 600 building and the set of classroom trailers beside it.

The original computer lab was housed in the 100 building. But sometime during first semester a water leak had been discovered, affecting the lab and the art classroom next door. The school administrators took the opportunity to do a complete overhaul, which had dragged on for months. In the meantime, the classrooms were moved here, to a set of air-conditioned trailers large enough to accommodate two reasonably sized classes.

Kevin loped up the stairs to the doorway and peeked in.

"Coast is clear," he said.

He held the door open for us as Danielle walked Vivi in and I followed. It was cool inside. The fluorescent lights flickered on, and I could see the room was essentially bordered by long tables holding somewhat outdated computer equipment. Flat screens sat alongside heavy massive monitors, flanked by CD-ROM drives, external hard drives, and grimy computer towers. Mice proliferated on the tables, their wires tangling like veins as they snaked around keyboards and speakers. The center of the room was empty. Danielle was right; this would be a good place to talk.

"Why does she seem so weak?" I whispered to Kevin, watching how limp and pliable Vivi seemed as Danielle sat her in a chair near one of the computer tables. I turned back to him as he closed the door behind us. "She was so agitated before, but now she's out of it. It doesn't seem like she's possessed or anything."

"I don't know," he said, keeping his voice low. "It could be that Patrick hasn't fully taken over. Maybe he's not totally in control yet."

"Oh, but I am."

The hairs rose on the back of my neck, and both of us turned away from the door to see Vivi slumped in her chair and Danielle walking toward us.

"I wasn't sure exactly when to break it to you," she said, her voice deep and strong and utterly unlike her. "But I suppose now is as good a time as ever. Besides, you *were* considerate enough to tell me your entire plan. And now I know exactly what to expect. Sadly, I don't believe I'll be playing along."

forty-six

"Danielle," Kevin said, putting up both hands as if that could protect us.

"Are you dense? I am not Danielle. This may be her body, but I have taken over. Danielle no longer exists."

"Patrick," I whispered.

"Clever girl. You're catching on," he said, looking at me cruelly through Danielle's eyes.

"I thought—Vivi . . ." I stammered. I felt panic racing through me, and I tried to summon my energy, control it somehow, despite the cold and the fear. I could feel Patrick's energy charging the room. I tried to piggyback on it, ride the wave of it the way he had charged from me before.

Danielle waved her hand and walked toward us, forcing us to back up. "Sit," she commanded, gesturing to the chairs near the computer tables. Kevin gripped my hand as we obeyed. Vivi appeared to be unconscious in the seat next to us.

"Yes, Vivi. Well, that was the idea. I had spent so long preparing her. But Danielle was an opportunity I couldn't pass up."

"What do you mean," I asked nervously.

"I mean," she said, whirling around to face me as she paced the floor. "Vivi was my point of entry. But she was *weak*. I could have become embodied through her, sure—and with your help, of course—but what good would that do me, to be human again in a shell so easily broken? Danielle, on the other hand . . . she was surprisingly willing. A few nighttime visitations, a few calculated, eerie messages from the great beyond—she practically offered herself to me, all just so that she could feel a part of what you and Vivi were experiencing. The lot of you, so easy to manipulate," she said, shaking her head.

"There's no way Danielle would have agreed to this," I said.

"And yet she did," Danielle-as-Patrick replied.

I thought back to the beginning, how resistant Danielle had been to the whole idea of ghosts and shared dreams and supernatural experiences, and yet how drawn in she had been, despite herself. *Can I be president?* I remembered her saying about our silly lunchtime club, just days after she'd fled from the bathroom and dismissed the notion of even discussing the subject. She'd made fun of it all, kept it at a distance. Was that because she'd secretly wanted to be a part of it? I had my gift, Vivi had her ghost. What did Danielle have?

"Of course, Danielle didn't know exactly what she was agreeing to," she continued. "You have to give me some credit. But by the time she realized what a mistake that was, it was already too late."

Vivi stirred in her chair.

"What have you done to Vivi?" Kevin demanded. "Why isn't she conscious?"

Danielle shrugged. "Oh, that? That's just a little mind control—plus residual effects from the medication."

"You drugged her?" I asked. Kevin tightened his grip on my hand.

"You needn't act so shocked," she laughed. "It's just a temporary measure."

"You're telling us that you took her from my house and drugged her?" I said.

"I didn't take her, my dear. She left of her own volition," Danielle said. "I merely called her—or, rather, had Danielle call her—early in the morning of your fever, when she was sleeping at your place. Told her I'd been communicating with Patrick, that he had an urgent message for her, that he was planning to come through but needed her help. I told her not to involve you—I claimed your energy was interfering with his abilities, and that in fact you had been thwarting his attempts to materialize for weeks. You may be surprised to know how willing she was to believe this. She left your house immediately and came to mine, so grateful for my help. She was quite trusting when I gave her the medication, telling her it was something that would help the process of getting Patrick from his realm into ours. Of course, I had already helped myself to your quite prodigious energy and used it to take over Danielle—so really what it helped with was buying me some time, allowing me to become fully in control. She was knocked out for a good long while . . . though I'll admit I was surprised to see her here quite so soon. I'd expected her to remain unconscious for a full forty-eight hours. So my plan, like yours, has been somewhat thwarted."

"What plan?" Kevin asked.

"What *plan?*" Danielle echoed incredulously. "To kill you, of course. Well, originally, it was just going to be Daisy. But one has to be flexible. And you *are* all right here. It's working out rather well, actually."

Kevin squeezed my hand so tightly I thought my circulation was going to be cut off. But instead I felt a jolt of energy from him, and I could have sworn I heard Kevin's voice inside my head.

Force.

I looked at him sharply, and he held my gaze, squeezing my hand again as I heard it.

Force field.

I glanced at Danielle, trying to gauge whether this message was actually coming from Patrick, or, if it wasn't, whether he had sensed its transmission; but Danielle-as-Patrick was pacing, caught up in her own rapidly cycling energy rush. I needed to act quickly. Patrick was strong, stronger than I'd sensed him before, and I didn't know if my own newly returning power would be enough to stave him off.

Even more concerning was the realization that if I wasn't careful he could hijack what energy I had left, debilitating me and making himself practically invulnerable.

I kept my eyes open, trying to stay under his radar, and began weaving a protective band of energy from the ground up, imagining invisible strands of color and light braiding together, a psychic rope that became thicker and stronger as it formed and wound around us, reinforcing itself. Kevin squeezed my hand again, and again I heard his thoughts in my head, faint but perceptible.

I . . . keep . . . talking.

You'll keep him talking, distract him, I zapped back and I saw him nod, just barely.

"Why?" he demanded, sitting forward in his chair, angling himself toward Danielle. I could feel the way Kevin's energy spiked and waned, and I hoped I would be able to put the force field in place before the sheer amount of electrical disturbance in the room became too much for him. I didn't know how long he could hold out before a seizure was inevitable. It struck me that this was something Patrick might be counting on as well.

"Why what?" Danielle laughed. "Why kill you?"

"Why any of it?" Kevin asked. "Why torment Vivi? Why kill Daisy? Why be human? I mean, speaking of plans that aren't thought through very well . . ."

"Oh, I've thought about this, believe me," she said, leaning down to him so they were at eye level. "I've thought about this for a long time."

"For a long time—because you had no choice, you had nothing else to do because you were banished to the spirit realm," Kevin said. "Because you were evil. Because you were being punished for being a sociopath in your last life as Jameson Stone. So, why not just serve out your sentence, then come back fresh, be born like a normal person, with a clean start? Why hijack someone?"

"Do you mean to tell me that with all your theories, all your researching and homework, you don't know?" she laughed, pacing again. "That's how banishment *works*. I was banished there, unable to return to this realm until I served my time, a hundred human years for every life I'd taken—unless some poor soul took pity and freed me."

Now she stood near me. I kept my energy steady and stealthy, focusing on continuing to build the force field that could protect us. I had to do it slowly so as to escape Patrick's notice, and it took much more concentration than just summoning it in a burst. This was fine, careful work, made all the more challenging by the proximity of someone who could easily and instantly destroy it.

"Lily—Vivi—was *weak*. Porous. Barely living. She was my way in. I prepared her for years—years!—to grant me access, to gladly give up her soul for mine. And then imagine my delight to discover that this life, *this miserable, uneventful life,* was the one in which you, Jane, were once again connected to her. That day when you found her in the bathroom, I had finally convinced her to kill herself. I'd spent her whole life making her think I was some sort of ghostly soulmate, and I'd finally convinced her that we could be together forever if she just took enough pills. When you walked in, she was nearly weak enough for me to slide in and take over—perhaps not fully, but it could have been enough. And then there you were, standing over her, and I realized it was just too perfect."

"What do you mean?" I asked, shaken out of my stealth work by that statement. Kevin shook his head at me, and again I heard his voice in my head: *Don't . . . attention . . . yourself.*

"What do you *think* I mean?" she said. "You've had the dreams, I know you know what happened. *You* are the one who trapped me there in that torturous realm. *You* are the one who killed me. I had merely planned to be alive again, to take over the body of that crippled soul and live until I died—of natural causes, this time— and then be officially freed from that realm, never to return. But when you found Vivi that day and I realized who you were, it made me see that simply being alive again was only the beginning. It wouldn't only free me from the ghost realm. It meant that I would be embodied. Human. True, a ghost can torment people. Influence their behavior, perhaps drive them mad. But a *human* can kill. So you see what I mean by 'perfect.' I get to be alive, and I get to kill you, the way I should have killed you a lifetime ago."

The force field I was creating now enveloped us from the ground to our knees, and I struggled to keep going with it as she leaned in closer to me.

"I have so missed the pleasure of killing for real," she whispered.

Then she stood up abruptly, gesturing to our surroundings. She seemed to shimmer with vitality.

"It's a bit poetic, don't you think, Daisy? This setting? I don't imagine anyone will be surprised. With your track record, not to mention your recent out-of-control behavior, this will all seem tragic but inevitable to anyone who cares to analyze it."

"What are you talking about?" Kevin jumped in before I could speak, and again tightened his grip on my hand, silently urging me to continue creating the force field. I could feel the energy stream continuing to build, Patrick's powerful force emanating from Danielle's physical body.

She gestured to the equipment around us. "The computer lab? Isn't this a most familiar setting for you, Daisy? Weren't you famously ejected from your last school due to an unfortunate incident in a classroom much like this one?"

I tried to gather my energy around me, even as I continued to build the force field, holding it steady to prevent Patrick from plugging in and stealing my current. But a frozen wind whipped through me and my teeth chattered.

"It won't take much to set it off, and when I do, you will simply be an unfortunate casualty of your own freakish nature." She smiled slyly. "It's all there in your file—your propensity for arson, for deliberate acts of malfeasance, for delinquency. What's the more likely explanation: that you got caught in the fire you deliberately set at school in the computer lab, or that you were killed by a ghost made human? Everyone will assume it was a tragic accident, a sad side-effect of your precious, so-called gift."

"And why is that poetic?" Kevin asked, sounding derisive, surely trying to provoke her, keep her talking so I could finish the force field.

"Because she'll die the way she left me to die, burned to death in a fire. And then I will be truly alive."

The cold wind stung my ears, and I felt my eyes tearing from the swirling, freezing vortex that was beginning to envelop us.

"Now, this is the part of the plan where you put up your little force field," Danielle said mockingly, "and then banish me away."

"You forgot something," I said. Kevin gripped my hand intensely, a warning, but I kept my voice steady and continued.

"And what's that?"

"The trade."

She stopped, crossing her arms like a stern, disappointed teacher. "The trade. Oh, yes, the bait and switch, where you offer yourself in exchange for your friend. Do you really think I'd fall for that? Do you really think this pathetic excuse for an energy field you're assembling will protect you?"

I felt my face flush and my energy waver. She flicked her wrist, and everything I'd assembled was dissipated, the force field instantly destroyed.

"And besides, this isn't helpless, sad Vivi you're trying to save now. It's Danielle, your lying best friend, who's been fooling you for far too long. You'd really sacrifice yourself for the friend who kept so many secrets? We'd both be stupid to believe you'd actually do that."

"I would," I said, struggling to maintain my energy, to resist and repel Patrick's. "Danielle didn't know what you were planning. You took advantage of her, the same way you took advantage of Vivi, the same way you tried to take advantage of me. She never would have consented to let you in if she'd known it meant that you would kill me, or that she'd be stuck taking your place in the ghost realm. None of this is her fault."

"And what if I *were* to take you over?" she mused, almost glowing now with Patrick's powerful force. I felt my energy draining as she spoke. "Do you think that would spare your friends? I'd still be killing them. I'd just have the added benefit of having your powers when I do it."

"Well, that's what you want, isn't it?" Kevin asked. "You want to kill Daisy—for some sort of ridiculous hundred-year-old revenge—and you want her powers. So why not just jump in? Take her over. What's the downside?"

I felt like I was going to pass out, but Kevin's strong grip propped me up.

"Good point." Danielle laughed. Then she stood with her arms outstretched, and I felt the familiar creep of electricity all over my body, the hairs on my arms rising, a prickling sensation across the top of my head. The air felt weighted with it, charged with something dangerous and uncontrollable. But this time it wasn't coming from me.

I watched as the computer screens flickered to life, the hard drives chugging as they powered up. Power strips sparked beneath the tables and mechanical beeps sounded all around us. Danielle stood in the middle of the room, her eyes closed as the chaos swirled around us, commanding it all. I felt Kevin's hand growing weaker in my grasp.

Hold on, I thought, hoping Kevin could hear me.

"Hold on? Yes. That is an excellent idea," Danielle-as-Patrick said, her eyes flying open. Then she thrust her arms forward, and a bright arc blasted in our direction, a bolt of electricity meant to strike the both of us. I tried to deflect it, but I felt the heat of the electrical discharge as it hit me, traveling through my body, tensing me for a moment as I absorbed the shock. I felt the jagged course of it as it moved through me and down my arms, realizing only too late where it would lead to. *Kevin.* My muscles were tensed with the electricity, and I couldn't release my hand from his; I couldn't move. Before I could gather the strength to reverse it, send it back to her, turn it in on itself and force it outward, I realized it was too late.

Kevin writhed in pain, his body contorting, arching backward as he seized, his eyes rolling to the back of his head.

"Please!" I yelled to Patrick, as Danielle continued to direct her considerable energy into Kevin. "Don't do this—this isn't about him. I'll do whatever you want!"

"Whatever I want," she said idly, as though she was contemplating dinner rather than torturing my boyfriend.

Suddenly Danielle's body fell to the floor, and an icy blue glow shrieked from her body, charging across the room toward me.

I closed my eyes and felt an energy surge unlike any other I'd experienced. It was as if I was literally opened up, split from head to toe, hollowed to the core by a brilliant white light that pierced me—pure, holy energy.

I felt myself floating, floating to the floor, but never landing, everything silent, blank, and white.

Pure.

Consciousness.

forty-seven

I felt myself falling. Though of course I wasn't literally falling. It was the sensation of falling, the kind of fall you experience in dreams, spinning out into space, spiraling downward, around and around, with no sense of where gravity might take you. I thought of Alice in Wonderland, tumbling down the rabbit hole, all manner of strange things passing her as she made her descent. And I thought of Orpheus, forcing his way into the underworld to save his poor, dead wife.

The underworld.

No longer was I transfused with light, I realized. Instead, I spun around in freezing darkness, completely disoriented. I had no idea which way was up or down, no concept of left or right, no awareness of my physical body in space or time. I felt only my mind, spinning and spinning as I continued to fall.

This is not the underworld, I heard him say.

Patrick was with me, whispering in my ear as I fell.

It was chaos, this swirling, falling sensation. I opened my eyes and saw only darkness, the blackest darkness I'd ever seen. I began to hear a screaming wind, the screeching chill of pure fear.

This is my realm, this is the place I inhabit. He laughed. *It can make a person mad.*

I felt a thought form in my brain, a wordless communication instantly existing in my mind and his.

—You were mad to begin with. And you are not a person. You are a ghost.

Mad or not, I will be a person and no longer a ghost once this transfer is complete. And then you shall take my place. You will dwell here, in the darkness, and I will walk the earth again. With your powers. The only question is, shall I destroy your friend here before or after?

I struggled to resist the falling, the spinning, the shrieking wind. I felt a sensation in my right hand and realized that somewhere, in some dimension of space and time, I was still holding on to Kevin, and I tried to draw some energy from that.

I stopped falling, and I felt myself suspended from a great height. I looked around me and saw what looked like the wall of a cave, water beneath me, a river. The underworld?

I heard Patrick laugh. *None of this is real. This is a mere projection, the thoughts of your flailing friend, who thinks he understands the fabled underworld. Here you see his feeble vision of what he's read in those silly myths—the River Styx, the banks of Erebus where unburied souls roam, the grass and flowers of the Elysian fields.*

—Where is he? What have you done with him?

I felt myself spinning again, falling through space, and then I was yanked to a halt. The vertiginous sensation lingered, and I saw that I was no longer suspended over the River Styx. Instead I was confronted with an entirely different scene.

It was as though my own memories were being projected on invisible screens all around me.

Look at this, he commanded. *There is no underworld. There is no afterworld. This is all your own creation. It's the inner landscape you construct for yourself in dreams, the backdrop of your own mind when you read books or think your worthless thoughts.*

I felt the strong sense that somewhere, in some other dimension, someone was gripping my hand, pulling at me, and I thought about where my arm might be if I wasn't this floating mind.

Around me I saw the scenery abruptly transform into a landscape. A huge house with a wraparound porch, a darkening, ominous field. I saw myself and Danielle, looking like Jane and Veronica, walking in the wind, passing Lily, arguing, Veronica running away into the field. Then me, standing at the window of the schoolhouse, watching James and Lily talk. Then looking out the window in the study, finding Veronica's diary, fighting with James, leaving him in the fire, running into the field away from the blazing house. Then it faded into shadow, as other scenes were superimposed upon it, scenes from my life: me finding Vivi in the bathroom, my mother tearfully telling me the truth about my father, Danielle laughing cruelly, Kevin seizing, all of it cycling over the scenes from the dreams. It played like a movie, in an endless loop.

You will be mired here, he whispered. *There is no escape. You cannot save your friend, and you cannot save yourself.*

I felt my throat clog with panic as the scenes before me descended into chilly darkness that threatened to envelop me once again.

Say good-bye to your powers, Daisy, he said. *Say good-bye to your friend here and his fragile mind. Say good-bye to your life. This is your fate.*

I felt myself being pulled into a vortex, the spiraling gravity sucking me down, pulling me in. If I couldn't hold on somehow, I would fall into the oblivion, be trapped there, swirling in a darkness of my own making for all eternity. But there was nothing to cling to. I was plummeting through a never-ending tunnel of darkness.

And then I heard Patrick thunder from somewhere: *You cannot stop this!*

I felt a rush of sensation, as though I had limbs again, and I felt the strong, sure grasp of someone's hand. A human hand. Kevin.

I'm here, I felt him say. *Hold tight, and don't let go. You know what you have to do.*

No, I heard Patrick shout.

I forced myself to shut Patrick out, to resist this spiraling darkness he wished to trap me in, and tried to channel my energy. I gripped Kevin's hand with all of my might and my whole world narrowed down in that moment to the feel of my fingers straining to hold on to his wrist.

A lightning bolt of current passed into my hand and traveled into my body, allowing me to feel my physical form, and I realized it was his energy, his electricity, his own faulty current sparking me back to life again. I opened my eyes to see the computer room bathed in brilliant, streaming light—pure energy.

My energy.

I was full of light, pouring out of my eyes like headlights, emanating from my skin, shimmering around me like a million laser beams, the most powerful, blinding light I'd ever seen, and I felt Patrick recoil as the light transfigured my entire body. It extended from my head up to the ceiling and beyond, from my hands out into Kevin's body, from my feet through the floor, and outward all around me, radiating from me, shining.

I was manifesting the energy, channeling the energy, all of it, directing it toward Patrick.

The power strips along the floor began to smolder, and the walls grew thick with heat and smoke. The smell of burning plastic filled the air, and in the distance, a smoke alarm sounded.

Danielle and Vivi both lay on the floor, unconscious, but Kevin stood beside me, still gripping my hand, shielding his eyes with his other hand, warding away the light and flames. I could sense Patrick's presence nearly upon me, his icy blue shapeless form fighting through the blazing force field of light, trying to penetrate and pull me back down.

"Run," I shouted to Kevin, this time able to use my voice. "Get them out of here before it's too late!"

He released my hand and moved quickly toward Vivi, dragging her to the door, forcing it open and getting her to safety, then returning for Danielle. I kept my energy churning, recirculating, an incredible fire of its own pushing back against Patrick's force. Through the smoke and haze I saw the door open as Kevin returned for me.

"No!" I yelled. "Run!"

Suddenly I felt the cold grip of paralysis as Patrick's voice slithered in my ear. In the split second of my distraction, he'd been able to slip in.

Welcome to your fate, he said.

"No," I said, summoning every last bit of my power. "Welcome to yours."

I squeezed my eyes shut and blasted forth an explosion of electric whiteness that was beyond all sensation. I felt it travel outward from me like a shock wave, with me at the center, untouched by its power. I heard the windows of the classroom trailer explode into shards of glass as they shattered, felt the flames around me leaping toward the ceiling, engulfing the room. And when I opened my eyes, I saw the painful, powerful white light devouring him. I heard him screaming in agony as the current grew stronger and stronger. I saw Patrick disintegrate before my eyes.

forty-eight

The flames surrounded me, and I dropped to the floor, those years of in-school fire drills suddenly coming in handy as I remembered: Heat rises. I crawled toward the door, reliving the memory of my dream—the night terror of Jane fighting off James, leaving him to the fire. I couldn't ignore the parallel. Once again, I had vanquished him with fire; once again I was barely escaping. This time, though, it was not a dream. I did not have the luxury of waking myself up. And I was so tired, I realized. The light was gone, my energy sapped as though I was back in the grips of fever again. I strained to breathe, and for a moment I became light-headed, unsure of where I was. I tried to open my eyes so that I could see, but I realized with a start that my eyes were already open, that a wall of black smoke surrounded me, and that I was trapped, as Patrick had planned all along, doomed to die the way I'd killed him.

Then, suddenly, there was a rush of air, sweet oxygen, and a sensation of coolness around me. Perhaps this was what it was like, surrendering to the underworld. I felt peaceful, ready. I could go, I thought; I'd done what I needed to do. And then a voice came to me.

"Daisy?"

And then I was lifted, my body cradled, and I could feel that I was still alive, not dead, not whisked away to the underworld, as I was carried out of the room and into the sunlight, the real light, where the air was clear and bright and filled with sounds of alarms and radio signals and the concerned voices of students and teachers.

"You're okay," Kevin said, and I realized he was the one holding me. "I've got you."

forty-nine

"It was actually pretty crazy," Kevin said as he sat on the edge of my hospital bed. My mom, speaking as both mom and floor nurse, had promised to have me sprung by morning after a day there, but in the meantime I was being treated for smoke inhalation—and, she'd said, a general work-up probably wouldn't be the worst idea ever, considering how sick I'd been just a day before.

He held my hand, careful not to aggravate the IV. "When you first powered up, or whatever, it totally jolted me out of the seizure. And then you were, like, just frozen."

"Frozen as in cold? Or like a statue?" I said, my voice hoarse and weak still from the smoke.

"Statue-esque," he said. "It was like you were catatonic. I was yelling, waving my hand in front of your face, shouting your name . . . But I couldn't get you to respond. I also couldn't get you to let go of my other hand. Still hurts, by the way."

"Sorry," I grinned.

"But then I realized what was probably happening—I saw that Danielle and Vivi were both out, so I figured Patrick was wrestling with you—and so I tried to focus in and get to you, you know, psychically."

"I know," I said. "I could have sworn I actually heard your thoughts a couple times."

He smiled his one-side-of-his-mouth smile again. "Maybe you're not the only one with a gift."

"Knock-knock," my mom said, poking her head around the door. "I have some visitors for you."

I sat up in the bed a little bit, which made me cough, and saw Danielle and Vivi walk in.

"Don't stay too long, girls," my mother warned. "She needs her rest."

She smiled at me and shut the door behind her on the way out.

"Hey," Danielle said, keeping her distance by the door.

But Vivi rushed up, embracing me gently around the tubes and wires.

"Kevin told us everything," she said. "You are amazing. What you did for us . . ."

"You would have done the same," I said.

Danielle sighed heavily. "I wouldn't have."

"Oh, come on," said Kevin.

"No, I mean that in a bad way about myself," she said. She came closer and sat on the other side of the bed, opposite Kevin. "Kevin explained what happened, and I don't even know what to say. I've been a terrible, terrible friend. I'm so sorry. I mean, there aren't even *words* to say how sorry I am. I can't believe I did that stuff, that I almost *killed* you—" she stopped, and I could hear her voice thick with tears.

"It wasn't you, Danielle. I know that," I said.

"Still. I could never forgive myself if anything had actually happened."

"But nothing did," Vivi said, then turned back to me. "You saved us."

Kevin squeezed my hand. "You are a total hero, you have to admit."

"I admit nothing," I blushed.

"Anyway, total penance here," Danielle continued, wiping her eyes. "Once I got the all-clear from the paramedics, I told them the fire was my fault."

278

"Oh, Danielle," I said.

"And then of course I had to tell the principal and everybody. And while I was at it, confessing to the school officials about being a firebug, I also told them I exaggerated all that stuff about Vivi and Mr. Terry. So now I have a disciplinary file about a mile thick, a hefty bill to pay for fire damage to the classroom trailer in exchange for them not pressing charges or whatever, an appointment with the school psychologist, and I'm, like, in permanent detention."

"Better than being in permanent underworld," Kevin pointed out.

"And, oh my God, don't even get me started on my mom," she said. She sighed again. "Anyway, it's the least I can do to make it up to you for what happened, and besides that, it's the truth. I really did those things. And I feel terrible. I've already apologized to Mr. Terry and written a letter the principal is keeping on file saying that all of my allegations are false, et cetera, et cetera."

"And Mr. Terry has been reinstated," Vivi said, beaming.

"Effective immediately," Kevin said.

Danielle stood up. "My mom is waiting out there to take me into mom-custody, so I have to go. I know it can't make up for everything, but I'm so, so sorry, Daisy. I truly am."

She came close and gave me a hug.

"Don't worry about it," I said. "Literally. Don't even spend a second thinking about it. I'm just glad we're all okay."

She squeezed my hands and blinked back tears. "Okay, well. Talk to you in about twenty years to life, depending on my mom's leniency at sentencing."

As Danielle left the room, Vivi remained at my bedside.

"What about you, Vivi? Are you okay?" I asked. "I mean, I know this all worked out and everything, but still—I mean, as Danielle might put it, I kind of killed your imaginary friend."

She ducked her head and sat down next to me.

"I'm sorry," I said. "I didn't mean to joke."

"No," she said, sitting up straight, her posture Vivi-perfect once again. "It's fine. Confusing, a little, but . . . I have to say, I feel like I had been living in a fog for so long I didn't remember what it was like to see the sun. And now that he's gone, now that you did what you did to banish him—it's like I'm alive. For real. For the first time since I don't know when. Since maybe forever."

She did look alive—her eyes danced with vitality, her cheeks were flushed, her face actually betraying emotion. If I concentrated very hard, I could feel a faint pulse of yellow energy radiating from her, a positivity and presence I'd never sensed from her before.

"Do you still need a place to stay?" I asked. "My mom had said before you could stay with us if you needed to."

She shook her head. "I talked to Mr. Terry this morning, and he's going to help me explain things to my mom." She smiled, and actually laughed out loud—a rarity for Vivi. "Well, not everything, obviously. But he's going to help me get back home."

There was a rap at the door, and my mom stuck her head in again. "Sorry, visitors, time's up."

Vivi stood up and gave me another hug before she left. "Feel better. I expect to see you out of here very soon."

"I will go into healing overdrive, I promise," I said.

Kevin began to stand up as well, but I clutched his hand, wincing a bit as the IV dug in.

"Can you stay a bit longer?" I asked. "Mom, can he stay just a few more minutes?"

My mom twisted her mouth as she considered the request.

"A *few* more minutes," she said. "A *very* few."

Once the door closed behind her, Kevin eased his way onto the bed so that he was laying down next to me.

"This really isn't big enough for more than one patient," he said.

"You know, visiting hours *are* technically over, so, you're free to leave if the accommodations aren't to your liking."

He turned over onto his side, propping his head on his fist. "Nah, this suits me just fine."

He looked around the bed, taking in all the electrical machinery

I was hooked up to. "So, I'm guessing you're still kind of energy-deficient at this point?"

I followed his gaze. "Yeah, pretty much. Otherwise all this stuff would be going haywire."

He smiled, a single eyebrow raised.

I smiled, too.

He leaned in and kissed me, his lips on mine soft and sweet, his hand on my hair a gentle caress. Slowly I felt a dull buzzing sensation where we touched, and then first one, then the other, and then the other of the machines began their frenzied beeping.

"You're back," he laughed.

"I'm back," I whispered, and I kissed him again.

More Gift

Kevin

By day, I'm Kevin, an ordinary high school senior.
By night . . . well, I'm still just an ordinary high
school senior! One of these days, though, I plan to be
a rock star. My favorite bands are Rush, Queen, Yes,
System of a Down, Dream Theater, and the Beatles.
In the meantime, check out a few of my recent songs
at http://www.youtube.com/user/KevinBeckProject.
Hope you like them!

~Kevin

Is It All Right?

Is it all right to tell you that I'm happy,
And is it all right to tell you that I care?
And is it all right to tell you that I miss you when you're
not there,
And that I think about running my fingers through your
hair—
Is it all right to tell you?

Is it all right to tell you that I'm smiling
Whenever I think of all the things you said,
Whenever I needed someone to make me happy or clear
my head?
And if the thought of you can really brighten up my day,
It must be okay to tell you.

But I don't know
How much you feel.
Is any of this real?
I need you to tell me.

Tell me,
Is it all right?

Is it all right to tell you that I want to
Tell you that what I'm feeling can't be wrong?
And is it all right to say I want to kiss you?
It's been so long.
And my heart is filled with so many things I wanna say
But how much is okay to tell you?

Because I just don't know
How much you feel.
Is any of this real?
I need you to tell me.
Tell me,
Is it all right?

Is it all right to tell you that I want to
Tell you that what I'm feeling can't be wrong?
And is it all right for me to be this happy?
It's been so long.
And I need someone to tell me,
If it's really true,
Is it all right
That I'm in love with you?

Don't Look Back

She takes my hand
and she leads me there—
don't know where—
I follow.

The path is dark,
but she pulls me through—
doesn't say where to—
I follow.

"Don't look back," she says,
and I won't.
"Don't look back," she says,
and I don't.

Because I know how the story ends:
the doubting thought that turns everything wrong.
Because all it takes is one backwards glance,
and then she's gone.

The one who looks
is the one who's lost.
Nevermind the cost,
I follow.

The one who doubts,
is the one who grieves,
and the one who leaves.
So I follow.

"Don't look back," she says,
and I won't.
"Don't look back," she says,
and I don't.

Because it's how all the stories end:
one twist of fate that turns everything wrong.
All it takes is one backwards glance,
and then she's gone.

So she walks ahead,
doesn't say a word,
but I've already heard.
I follow.

When we're finally there,
I can take her hand.
She will understand.
She'll follow.

Vivi

NOW THAT WE'VE ALL MADE IT THROUGH, I FINALLY KNOW THE WHOLE STORY.
BUT SOME THINGS ARE EASIER DRAWN THAN SAID.
SO HERE'S THE STORY I COULDN'T TELL UNTIL NOW.
THE STORY OF A GHOST WHO ALMOST TOOK OUR LIVES,
AND HOW WE GOT THEM BACK.

—VIVI

THE STORY BEGINS IN THE PAST, AT THE STONE HOUSE, WHERE OUR LIVES FIRST INTERSECTED . . .

SHORTLY BEFORE THE ANNUAL SPRING PARTY HOSTED BY VERONICA'S FATHER, THERE WAS A SHOCKING ATTACK. LILY, WHO WORKED FOR THE FAMILY, WAS BADLY HURT, BUT SHE MANAGED TO ESCAPE WITH HER LIFE.

THE NIGHT BEFORE THE PARTY, LILY CAME TO VERONICA AND SWORE HER TO SECRECY AS SHE CONFESSED: JAMES—VERONICA'S BROTHER— HAD BEEN THE ATTACKER.

I'M SO AFRAID...

VERONICA DIDN'T WANT TO BELIEVE IT... BUT SHE KNEW LILY WAS TELLING THE TRUTH.

CAN'T WE AT LEAST POSTPONE IT?

SHE PLEADED WITH HER FATHER TO CANCEL THE PARTY—WITHOUT TELLING HIM THE REAL REASON WHY—BUT HE REFUSED.

THE POOR GIRL...

AT THE PARTY, VERONICA COULDN'T HIDE HOW TROUBLED SHE WAS. AND HER BEST FRIEND JANE'S ATTEMPTS TO CONSOLE HER ONLY MADE HER MORE UPSET.

SHE'LL BE OKAY — MAYBE JAMES CAN HELP?

ARE YOU SO IN LOVE WITH HIM THAT YOU CAN'T SEE?

WAIT!

VERONICA RAN AWAY IN TEARS AS JANE CALLED AFTER HER. THEN, SUDDENLY, JAMES APPEARED.

COME INSIDE — YOU SHOULDN'T BE OUT HERE IN THIS STORM.

JAMES BROUGHT JANE INTO THE HOUSE. WHEN SHE TOLD HIM VERONICA WAS UPSET ABOUT LILY, HE SEEMED QUITE CONCERNED.

VERONICA IS STILL OUT THERE!

I'LL FIND HER...

JANE WAITED AT THE WINDOW, BUT COULD SEE ONLY DARKNESS. VERONICA DID NOT RETURN.

THE NEXT DAY, AS JANE PREPARED TO LEAVE FOR THE WEEKEND WITH HER FAMILY, SHE SPIED JAMES AND LILY FROM THE SCHOOLHOUSE WINDOW.

THEY SEEMED WORRIED ABOUT VERONICA'S DISAPPEARANCE AND THE ATTACKER ON THE LOOSE. JANE WISHED SHE DIDN'T HAVE TO LEAVE.

BUT WITH JANE AWAY, JAMES WAS ABLE TO TAKE CARE OF LOOSE ENDS...

JAMES! NO!

LILY'S HAD A TERRIBLE ACCIDENT...

...LEAVING HER NONE THE WISER WHEN SHE RETURNED.

BUT WHEN HE RETURNED ONE NIGHT AND LEARNED THAT JANE HAD DISCOVERED THE TRUTH—

THAT SHE HAD FOUND VERONICA'S OLD DIARY—

HIS SECRET LIFE AND HIS NORMAL LIFE CONVERGED.

HOW *COULD* YOU?!

THEY FOUGHT, AND JANE REALIZED HE WOULD KILL HER TO KEEP HER QUIET.

BUT JANE HAD OTHER PLANS.

SHE KILLED JAMES, BANISHING HIM TO THE GHOST REALM, WHERE HE WAS DOOMED TO STAY WHILE HE SERVED OUT HIS FATE:

ONE HUNDRED HUMAN YEARS FOR EACH HUMAN LIFE HE'D TAKEN. WITH NO WAY OUT.

UNLESS...

HE WAS ABLE TO FIND SOMEONE WHO MIGHT LET HIM BACK IN.

HE NEEDED A LOOPHOLE.

SOMEONE LIVING BETWEEN TWO WORLDS.

SOMEONE STILL CONNECTED
TO THE LIFE THAT CAME BEFORE.

SOMEONE HE MIGHT BE ABLE TO CONTROL.

SOMEONE WHO MIGHT BE WILLING
TO BELIEVE IN GHOSTS.

IF HE COULD FIND SOMEONE LIKE THAT,
HE MIGHT BE ABLE TO CONVINCE THAT PERSON
TO SET HIM FREE.

AND SO HE WAITED.

REINVENTED HIMSELF.

UNTIL I WAS BORN AGAIN INTO THE WORLD,

FRAGILE, GULLIBLE, EASILY FOOLED.

HAUNTED.

AND THEN HE FOUND ME.

I DIDN'T RECOGNIZE HIM. BUT OF COURSE, THAT WAS THE IDEA. HE CALLED HIMSELF PATRICK.

HE WATCHED OVER ME. I BELIEVED EVERYTHING HE TOLD ME. I BELIEVED WE WERE SOUL MATES, THAT WE WERE MEANT TO BE TOGETHER.

HE SAID IT WOULD ONLY BE A MATTER OF TIME BEFORE HE WAS ABLE TO COME THROUGH, TO BE ALIVE AGAIN SOMEHOW.

THAT DAY IN THE BATHROOM WHEN DAISY FOUND ME, I HAD NO IDEA WHAT WAS REALLY GOING ON.

VIVI? ARE YOU OKAY?

BUT PATRICK DID. HE REALIZED RIGHT AWAY:

THIS WAS JANE.

AND ONCE AGAIN, SHE HAD STOPPED HIM FROM GETTING WHAT HE WANTED.

HIS PLANS WOULD HAVE TO CHANGE.

SHE'S KIND OF... INTENSE, RIGHT?

VIVI? YEAH...

ONCE HE MADE THE CONNECTION, THOUGH, SOMETHING STRANGE HAPPENED.

DAISY AND DANIELLE STARTED HAVING THE DREAMS—AND HE WASN'T THE ONE SENDING THEM.

THE SAME DREAM!

NONE OF US REALIZED THEY WERE COMING FROM ME.

DAISY WAS LIKE AN ANTENNA, PICKING UP ON THIS ENERGY I DIDN'T EVEN REALIZE I WAS SENDING OUT.

BUT PATRICK DIDN'T WANT DAISY TO REMEMBER. LAST TIME, SHE'D FIGURED EVERYTHING OUT BEFORE HE'D HAD THE CHANCE TO KILL HER.

HE DIDN'T PLAN TO MAKE THAT MISTAKE AGAIN.

SO, JUST LIKE WITH ME, HE FOUND HIS WAY IN.

HE TEMPTED DAISY WITH POWER.

WHAT YOU COULD DO WITH YOUR POWER

HE TOLD DANIELLE TO KEEP SECRETS.

Okay, so here's a thing. I talked to Patrick again last night. He told me some stuff. He helped me sleep. He said he'd come back later. He said not to tell anyone we'd spoken.

HE TRIED TO SPLIT US.

WHAT IS UP WITH THE SILENT TREATMENT???

YOU DON'T KNOW WHAT YOU'RE TALKING ABOUT!

WHAT IF I DO?

AND THEN, WHEN IT WAS TIME...

...HE MADE HIS MOVE.

LATER, THEY TOLD ME HOW DAISY FOUGHT HIM,

HOW SHE SAVED US.

HOW, IN THE END, HE WAS DESTROYED.

BUT ALL I KNEW WAS...

... I WAS FREE.

FOR REAL. FOR THE FIRST TIME SINCE I DON'T KNOW WHEN.

SINCE MAYBE FOREVER.

FREE TO LIVE MY LIFE, FREE TO HAVE A FUTURE.

AND I'M READY.

FINALLY.

FINALLY, I'M NOT AFRAID.

Danielle

DANIELLE'S DIARY!

DO NOT READ THIS!!!!!!

You're still reading this, aren't you?

Well, I guess I can't really stop you.
So, go ahead.
Knock yourself out.

But you can't say I didn't warn you...

MONDAY

So . . . Daisy tried to talk to me again about the dreams and it was just so UGH.

She passed me a note and I was all, I can't do it, just give it a rest already. I'm so tired, I'm so OVER this. It's just too much. TOO MUCH.

Okay, honestly? (And I think I can be honest here, because hello, this is MY diary, and if I can't be honest here then what's the point?)

Okay, so honestly.

It's just these stupid dreams!!!

Daisy has all these freaking dream ADVENTURES. They're like practically stories playing out in her head, they're like MIND MOVIES. And it started out being for an audience of two — me and her, dreaming two sides of the same dream.

But not anymore.

I'm stuck with this one stupid dream, over and over, and it's scary. Not just, "Dude: scary," like I say in the cafeteria when I see Vivi dip her potato chips into her soda. But ACTUALLY scary. More specifically, terrifying.

I don't want to keep having this same thing over and over again, this same scary dream that goes the same way every night ending in a big blank black screen, like my movie just stopped or something.

I want to dream past the black wall, or I want to dream about something else. Anything else. My own story. Not Daisy's. Not Vivi's.

Mine.

TUESDAY

What is UP with Vivi, anyway? I'm being nice to her again WHY? I'm helping her WHY? It doesn't seem like she actually WANTS help, really. I mean, are we supposed to be helping her ghost boyfriend break out of the spirit world? What then, huh? Plus, isn't he like four hundred years old or something? (Don't judge, I suck at math.) What is everyone going to think when this old, suddenly undead dude shows up and takes her to prom or whatever? What then?

Maybe she doesn't really want him to be real. Or maybe she does, but he's not, and we're just enabling her.

Here's what I'm thinking though, as I write this in the middle of the night because I'm too afraid to sleep, Diary, I really am:

I think maybe he really IS real.

I think Daisy is just faking that she can sense him when he's around — "Ooh, it's so cold!" HA! Oldest cliche in the book! — but I think Vivi really DOES see him, and do you want to know why?

I'll tell you why. Because, Dear Diary, last night when I ALSO couldn't sleep because of the Scary Never-Ending Repetitive Dream of Terror (which I shall now refer to here on out as SNERDOT) — last night, I saw him.

Yes, yes, I know I swiped one of my mom's OTC sleep meds and am suffering from chronic sleep-deprivation and am probably hallucinating . . . Yes, I know I am totally manic and babbling right now because that's easier than being freaking TERRIFIED . . . Yes, I know I've been making fun of Vivi for months because she believes she is BFFs with

a ghost. But I'm telling you: I saw him.
AND HE TALKED TO ME.

I woke up from my horrible dream, where I was just trapped in the dark, and he was sitting on the edge of my bed, like, watching me. But not in a creepy, TWILIGHT way. Just like he was waiting for me to wake up so he could tell me something. I bolted up in bed and was like HOLY WHA??? And then he said, without his mouth even moving, like he was THINKING IT straight to my brain, "Don't panic. It's me. I'm here to stop the dreams, if you want."

Okay, so where do I start freaking out first, right??? I mean, A, yes, by all means, stop the dreams, but B, by the way, are you a freaking GHOST talking to ME on my BED in the middle of the night???? Oh, right, you said don't panic, okay, BRB, getting right on that.

I mean, seriously.

And then, basically, long story short, he used some kind of Jedi mind control thing on me and boom, asleep like a baby.

So maybe I imagined it? Maybe? But I kind of don't think so. Because for one thing, I don't know, it just felt so REAL.

And for another, I remember him saying before I finally drifted off, "Don't say anything about this to Vivi and Daisy. I'll come back tomorrow. It'll be our secret."

And hello, yes, I know about Stranger Danger and how SEKRITS R BAD, but today at school I could have said something to Daisy and Vivi, but I just didn't. I couldn't. I want him to come back.

How could I feel that way if it was just my imagination?

Tell me THAT, Diary.

WEDNESDAY

It is so like you, Diary, to be all judgy and rational and poking holes in my logic. But I'm telling you, I think this is really happening. He showed up, and I slept a little. I think that means something, don't you?

Oh, enough with your naysaying. Don't you get it? I want to have this. It's special. Vivi has something spooky-special. Daisy is electro-girl. What have I got, huh? I got nothing. So why can't I have this?

But I'm kind of scared.

Will I fall asleep tonight? If I do, will I dream? If I dream, will Patrick save me? Do I really want to be saved?

Maybe I do, Diary. Maybe I do.

Mostly though: how awesome will it be to actually freaking TALK to a GHOST? I'm going to ask him all those annoying questions people never ask about ghosty stuff. Srsly.

. . . .

It's 2 a.m. now. Again with the stupid dream.

No ghost.

Maybe I'm as crazy as Vivi.

I'm scared.

THURSDAY

I gave in and talked to Daisy about it. No, I didn't tell her the whole thing, I just . . . well, you know, I was sleep-deprived. And tired. I told her how bad the dreams are, and how freaked out I am. So I didn't lie. I just kept the part about Patrick showing up to myself.

And don't go all saying "I told you so," Diary, but it felt good to talk again. Even though I'm kind of jealous of her, I LIKE being her friend. Plus, I like talking. Silent treatment is haaaaaard.

Anyway, so then something weird happened. Vivi showed me this automatic writing thing, where you like hold a pen over paper and let your subconscious write stuff (or, yeah yeah yeah, I know, you just write stuff yourself because it's not really real) (you're such a buzzkill, Diary!) and I got a message.

From Veronica. Or, from me. From the dreams. From me in a past life. Or from the me in a past life that's some kind of spirit floating around now in my subconscious, or — OW, DIARY, THIS IS MAKING MY BRAIN HURT. But you know what I mean.

And then we all held hands and Vivi said some kind of "BEGONE, TRAPPED DREAM

SPIRIT!" stuff, and then I swear to God I fell asleep right there in Mr. Terry's room. Luckily Daisy woke me up before I started drooling.

The weird thing is, I really did feel like amazingly better. Like, immediately. So, I don't know.

FRIDAY

Okay, so here's a thing.

I talked to Patrick again last night.

He told me some stuff.

He helped me sleep.

He said he'd come back later.

He said not to tell anyone we'd spoken.

Should I feel bad? Because I know he's not talking to Vivi right now. And he should be, right, because he's her ghost boyfriend and all.

But I kind of don't.

MONDAY

So, it's been a while, Diary. I haven't really felt like writing. Let me catch you up. So, uh, Vivi's shacking up with Mr. Terry, Daisy's being visited by Patrick, also Kevin's now her full-on official boyfriend, and me? ME? How nice of you to ask, Diary. SO CONSIDERATE. I'm here, left in the dust. ALONE.

WEDNESDAY

Sorry, Diary, I forgot about you again. I've been having lots of conversations with a ghost, and — ugh, SEE how crazy that sounds? Just even writing it down??? I didn't even say it out loud and it's insane.

But it's not like I'm talking to myself,

howling at the moon, in need of a full-length designer straitjacket. He just shows up at night, and we talk.

It's been nice.

I can see why Vivi was into it, and why she's all freaked that she doesn't hear him so much anymore.

He's helping me . . . understand things. Like, things are starting to make sense. Oh, Diary, I can't describe it, it's just that talking to him makes me feel . . . better than myself. Like, me, but supercharged. Super smart. Super powerful. Super awesome. I'm not saying this is translating into, like, good grades in math or whatever. I'm just saying, I feel like HYPER energized, like I could do anything.

It's a good feeling.

And frankly? It's about time.

FRIDAY

ARGH, Diary, I take it all back. I'm confused.
I thought it was all awesome and stuff, that
he got rid of the bad dreams, but then I
started having these other dreams, and he
got all mad at me, like I was FORCING myself
to have more dreams — and they weren't
even anything REMOTELY interesting. They
were just like almost like MEMORIES — you
know, hanging out with Jane (Daisy, duh) or
running around the house with James, or
doing stuff with Lily. But he got all freaking
PMS-y on me and started shutting me out.
Seriously! I mean, WHO IS THE TEENAGED
GIRL HERE? SPOILER ALERT: NOT YOU,
GHOST.
    Anyway, so then I felt all bad and stuff, so I
apologized and then he came back — and then
it was like I don't even know. I felt like . . .

mind controlled. Seriously. Because after that?

I told about Vivi and Mr. Terry.

I didn't even plan to, I just felt, I don't know, COMPELLED, like it was Patrick making me do it. So now I'm just waiting for that bomb to drop.

I don't even know why I said anything. It was like he filled me with this energy, and then there I was, walking into the principal's office before I even realized what I was doing.

MONDAY

So, yeah, remember that bomb I mentioned? Totally dropped. Big time. Mr. Terry's suspended, Vivi's freaking. I just called Daisy to do the full-on mea culpa routine, and she just SLAMMED me. Just — I don't know. I've never heard her like that. She was total crazy Daisy. And yeah, I get it, she's mad at me. But to just totally take Vivi's side like that?

WHO has been friends with her longer? (HINT: ME)

WHO knew her secret first? (HINT: ME)

WHO didn't act like she was a total freak even though she's totally a TOTAL FREAK? (AGAIN WITH THE HINT: ME)

And yet she's all like Mission: Protect Vivi. Which has the side mission of Totally Forget Danielle.

Here's the thing.

I have a mission, too. And I wanted to tell her about it.

Patrick's here. I can feel him right next to me. All the hairs on my arms are standing up, and I feel my stomach churning. It's making my heart race, which makes me feel a little bit like how Daisy must feel all the time.

He wants something.

And I think I want to give it to him.

He just wants to talk, he says. He wants me to relax my mind, relax my thoughts, and just . . . let him take over for a while.

Just long enough to talk to Vivi, he says.

To say goodbye, properly.

He says I'm strong — strong enough to help him do this.

He's tired of being trapped where he is, and he's tired of watching Vivi suffer because of it. So he'll say goodbye. And then this will all be over. She won't be haunted. Daisy won't be having crazy past-life dreams. I won't be having nightmares.

He says this is my piece of the puzzle.

I can make it all go away.

I wanted to tell Daisy how I was going to help, but she just hung up on me.

So it looks like I'll be doing this solo.

Okay, Diary. Deep breaths.

I think I'm ready.

About the Author

Andrea J. Buchanan is a *New York Times* bestselling author whose latest book is the multimedia young adult novel *Gift*, published by Open Road Integrated Media. Her other work includes the internationally bestselling *The Daring Book for Girls* and seven other books. Before becoming a writer, Andi trained as a pianist, earning a bachelor of music degree in piano performance from the Boston Conservatory of Music and a master's degree from the San Francisco Conservatory. Her last recital was at Carnegie Hall's Weill Recital Hall. She lives with her family in Philadelphia.

Visit Andi at www.andibuchanan.com and www.openroadmedia.com.

OPEN ROAD

INTEGRATED MEDIA

Videos, Archival Documents, and New Releases

Sign up for the Open Road Media newsletter and get news delivered straight to your inbox.

FOLLOW US:
@openroadmedia and
Facebook.com/OpenRoadMedia

SIGN UP NOW at
www.openroadmedia.com/newsletters